THE HISTORIES OF
SENNACHERIB MACCAULEY

ISBN-13: 9781508938378
ISBN-10: 1508938377

THE HISTORIES OF SENNACHERIB MACCAULEY

BOOK ONE: THE RAVEN'S HOUSE

Paul Wayne Langford

This book is dedicated to Pierce, Heidi, Jennifer and Aunt Edye.

Sennacherib MacCauley would like to thank the hard work of Beth Robinson, Edye Holubec and Jennifer Langford for their support, encouragement and not letting him settle for less. This book might have been dedicated to them, but Pierce and Heidi objected.

CHAPTER 1

History is God's way of reminding you what doesn't work. As for what does work, that's for you to discover–

—FROM SENNACHERIB MACCAULEY'S INTRODUCTION TO *THE HISTORY OF THE UNIFICATION*

TIBS EXCUSED HIMSELF from the table. He flicked his head back flinging his long, fire-red hair out of his eyes. Smaller than most eleven year olds, or for that matter nine year olds, the dishes clattered as he moved them to the water.

Nathan parted his beard so he could see his stomach, trying to weed out the crumbs from the hair, "Still seeing imps, boy?" He teased Tibs.

"Stop it." Tibs didn't answer the question. I don't think he trusted Nathan enough to tell the truth. It was better not to answer.

Nathan kicked his velvet purple robes back with his feet while he swiped at the boy, "Rrrrrr." Tibs easily escaped his grasp not even jostling the dishes.

"I'm not five anymore." Tibs young eyes flashed a superior glint at having deftly avoided the wizard's grip. He turned and took a step but his boot laces were now tied together, "Not fair!" he screamed as Nathan laughed. Tibs struggled with first his right, then left foot before he started to fall.

His father, Sir Jesse, caught the dishes with the expertise only a seasoned warrior and dedicated juggler could have, as if he had practiced this a thousand times before. With his other hand he stopped his son from falling, hardly flexing his muscular arms.

"You're not funny!" Tibs chided the wizard.

"I am too funny!" Nathan protested, "Let's ask your father. Sir Jesse am I funny?"

"Does smell count?" Sir Jesse queried.

"Certainly." Nathan assured him.

"Then yes, you are very funny." Sir Jesse chuckled. "Now stop the games," with Nathan, Sir Jesse could turn from chiding to scolding in a second, he was almost family, "I didn't have to tell you we were having venison, Nathan. If you're going to play tricks, don't do them when Tibs's is carrying the good china."

"Good china?" Nathan tried to look innocent. "I only eat here because your plates and silverware all made of wood."

"You tied my laces together!" Tibbs accused Nathan.

"How could have I done that?" Nathan put on his pouting face.

"You're not supposed to use magic like that!" Tibs's face reddened to almost the same color as his hair. He gripped the laces and started untangling the knot.

"How would you know how I'm supposed to use my magic, and I thought you liked to see me do tricks." Nathan teased the boy.

"Not on me!" Tibs brushed himself off.

He's almost too old to be any fun, Nathan thought to himself.

"You couldn't win in a fair fight." Tibs challenged.

"Who wants to fight? And if I did want to fight, why would I fight fair? Then I'd lose." Nathan pulled out a toothpick and started digging dinner out from between his teeth.

"No one else wants him over for dinner. Why do you put up with him?" Tibs said sourly, still unable to get the shoelaces untied.

"I've known Nathan longer than I have you, Tibs." Sir Jesse answered softly.

Tibbs kicked his father feet in protest.

Nathan bent over and touched the knot lightly with his fingers and it came unraveled. He smiled, "Truce?" he inquired.

"No." Tibs brushed the dirt from his clothes. The kitchen floor was hardly less dirty than dirt. "He thinks he's funny, but he's not."

"He thinks he's funny but he's SNOT!" Nathan pulled his busy white eyebrows and cackled a laugh, his nose making him look like some mad, wild bird.

Despite himself, Tibs laughed.

"You see, I am funny!" Nathan snorted.

"That doesn't prove anything." Tibs tried to sulk again, but that seemed difficult with Nathan in the room.

Sir Jesse washed the plates with grace. He enjoyed tossing the cups in the air and spinning the plates, but it didn't show on his face. His chiseled features showed the signs of age, like marble that has cracks, even his wrinkles seemed stony. It gave him more authority, but his eyes betrayed his enjoyment.

"Your boy needs a haircut," Nathan returned to his three foot long beard and pulling the crumbs from the meal out of it.

"Long hair is vanity." Sir Jesse cut his hair close to his scalp. "Even on the face." He threw the wizard a glance.

"I like my hair long." Tibs voted.

"Then why don't you cut the boy's hair?" Nathan blustered. Sir Jesse stopped everything and stared at the dirty water in the bucket. The silence made Nathan regret asking. He knew why, of course. *Tibs's mother. Tibs looks just like his mother.*

"Let's have a game then!" Nathan announced, changing the subject as he turned over three oaken drinking cups.

"I just cleaned those," Sir Jesse protested.

Nathan reached up and pulled a red wooden ball from behind Tibs's ear. Tibs came nearer to the kitchen table to watch.

Nathan put the ball under a cup and moved them around and around. "Where is the ball?"

Tibs snorted and pointed to the middle cup. Nathan picked it up. Of course, there it was. He slipped the ball back underneath.

"That's a stupid game," Tibs quickly judged.

"Many people use this game to deceive people, to make people think they have magic." Nathan moved the cups around and around again. He touched Tibs nose and said, "Pick a cup."

"It's too easy, you hardly moved the cups."

"Then humor me," Nathan smiled sinisterly.

Tibs pointed at the middle cup, but no ball under it. "You cheated!"

"Cheated?" Nathan laughed. "I didn't even use magic, my mangy munchkin."

"Yes, you did!" Tibs protested. His hand poised to flip the remaining cups when Nathan put his hands over both.

"You have to guess." Nathan raised his right eyebrow, challenging the boy.

Tibs picked the right cup, no ball. Then before Nathan could move he flipped over the remaining cup, no ball under any of them.

"I was right, you used magic!"

Nathan held up his hand revealing the ball. "Tibs, my boy, anyone can learn to do this. No magic involved." Nathan put the cups back on the table, upside-down.

Sir Jesse dried his battle-scarred hands on a towel. "A game of cups? This is what you've been leading up to all night."

Nathan moved the cups even faster on the table. "People need to know the danger that's coming."

"No one is coming." Sir Jesse, scoffed.

"Misdirection is more powerful than you imagine." Nathan kept the cups moving.

"It's the same on the battle field. If the enemy is afraid or overly-confident, you have the advantage."

Nathan tapped his forehead. "Precisely! Fool the mind, and then it's too late."

"Without your magic you couldn't fool me!" Tibs turned the cups back over.

"You haven't seen any magic yet, young Tibs, that's my point," Nathan tried to throw the red ball from one hand to the other, but he threw it too hard and it escaped him. It bounced on the table and into Sir Jesse's scarred hand before they even saw the hand move.

Nathan looked into Tibs's eyes. "You want to see real magic?"

Tibs looked at his father. His father shrugged.

Sir Jesse handed Nathan the ball. The wizard absentmindedly grabbed the stone hanging on a chain under his shirt. He became still as granite. Tibs could feel something change. He turned over the right cup, red ball. Nathan motioned for the boy to continue. Tibs turned the center cup over revealing a second ball. Finally, he turned over the last cup and found a third ball. Tibs grabbed the three balls attempted to juggle them, which meant, obviously, they were all on the floor in a sneeze.

"You see, magic!" Tibs said triumphantly, "Without that magic what could you do?"

"I have to agree with the boy. How was that different from what you did before?" Tibs father asked Nathan.

"How?" Nathan prodded, "Are you teaching this boy anything, Jesse?"

Sir Jesse raised one eyebrow at Nathan.

Nathan nervously turned the cups back upside-down. "Let's try this." He concentrated. Tibs tried to take a step toward the table, but Nathan stuck out his arm and propelled him backward, away from the cups.

Tibs's father put his hands on Tibs's shoulders.

Nathan theatrically waved his right hand. The cup on the left rose into the air. Overflowing from under it was a deadly snake.

Nathan waved both hands, and the other two cups flew into the air. Under the middle a very colorful frog croaked, and under the last one a deadly spider poised tensely, observing.

The snake regarded the frog. The frog eyed the spider. The spider didn't seem to see anything at all. The frog shot his tongue out and the spider vanished. Before that frog could even taste his succulent supper, the snake had struck and the frog disexisted, swallowed by the snake.

"What's this game?" Sir Jesse thrust Tibs behind him. The snake now turned its head toward the three males. The snake coiled, raising its head above the table. It faced the knight.

Tibs could hear the tail rattle. He had never seen such a snake before. He knew he should be afraid, but the beautifully polished scales, revealing a pattern of brightly colored squares, outlined in black coal, shined in such a way he couldn't be afraid. Against the smooth wood of their kitchen table, the beauty startled Tibs. Sir Jesse saw only the glint of the snake's green eyes. The two combatants measured each other.

Tibs's father dared to take a couple of steps backward, groping behind the pair, looking for his sword that hung on the wall by the kitchen door. The rattling became louder. The snake rose even higher, preparing to strike. Its three-fisted head had now risen to the same height as Tibs's father's eyes. *How much strength must it have to raise its head that high?* Tibs didn't know if his father could reach the sword, take it from its scabbard, and defend himself before the snake struck.

CHAPTER 2

Most wars are not decided by kings and armies, but by cooks —

—FROM SENNACHERIB MACCAULEY'S PERSONAL JOURNALS

THE FROG HAD swallowed the spider. The snake had swallowed the frog. The snake opened its mouth, to bite the three in the kitchen. It couldn't have been that hungry; it had just swallowed an amphibian. Maybe it was having a bad day. And why not? It was sunning itself somewhere in the desert and suddenly found itself under a wooden cup in a strange place surrounded by people, one of whom hadn't had a bath in a month.

Its tongue slipped through its lips as if to say, "You look big, but tasty." It looked Sir Jesse in the eyes. Most men wouldn't do that. It felt no fear in the warrior's gaze.

The snake suddenly stopped hissing, closed its eyes, and shook its head as if to shake off water after a shower. It blinked, twice. It winked each eye. Then it opened its mouth wide, coughed, and fell over. The head fell on the table with a sharp "smack." Then the whole snake body uncoiled and slipped to the gray stone floor, like a ribbon ball unraveling, falling with another satisfying slap.

Tibs didn't often see his father speechless. Sir Jesse reached behind himself and took his sword from the wall, unsheathing it in the same movement. Holding it with one hand where most men would have needed two, he pointed the sword at the snake. "Take no chances," he hissed at the snake, another one of his many mottos.

Nathan, unafraid, marched right up to the reptile, and picked it up by its head.

"What happened?" Tibs father pointed the sword at the little man.

"What happened?" Nathan snickered and slapped a knee with one hand and the other knee with the snake's head. "It's still happening my unobservant cavalier!" Nathan dropped the snake.

Tibs gasped.

The spider crawled out of the snake's mouth, alive.

"I'm sorry, little fella, can't have you hanging about around here," Nathan said as he stepped on the spider.

Nathan looked to Tibs and then Sir Jesse. They were speechless, so he took the lead. "The frog ate the spider, or tried, and the spider bit him on the tongue. The venomous spider killed the frog, but before the frog was quite dead, the snake ate the frog. Since the frog was poisonous, the snake died."

"But the snake was, was..." Tibs father poked at the dead thing with his sword.

"Yes, it was venomous too, but you see that didn't matter. The frog was bigger than the spider, but died by a small bite. The snake was bigger still than both, but died from poison in the frog's skin."

"I put my faith in my sword." Tibs's father swung his blade at Nathan.

"Careful with that thing!" Nathan stepped back, obviously afraid of the blade. "Throw the snake out, my boy," Nathan went to the hearth to pick at the venison hock still sitting on the plate.

"Isn't it still dangerous?" Tibs stepped meekly toward the dead snake.

"A wooden snake?" Nathan scoffed.

Tibs looked down. The snake had changed, having become a brightly painted piece of wood. "Now that's magic!" Tibs picked up the toy, the joints moving this way and that, making it feel like a stiff rope or a loose stick.

Nathan stuffed a burnt piece of fat into his mouth. "Do you understand the lesson?"

Sir Jesse snorted. "Lesson? You threatened us with a snake!" Quickly, he flicked his sword and touched Nathan's hand with it. Miniature lightning bolts scattered all over the kitchen.

"What are you doing! I'm a wizard! You know I can't touch metal!" Nathan rubbed his hand, a black burn mark on it, and most of the back of his palm turned red. "Do you know how long it will take to heal that?"

"I thought maybe both of us should learn something tonight." The knight purposely turned his back on Nathan and sheathed his sword.

"No one received grievous wounds like this," Nathan blew gently on his burned fingers. "And you missed the danger." Nathan stopped, surprised. "Wait a minute. You! You, Sir Jesse, victor of a thousand battles, warrior seasoned by pain, struggle and conquest, missed the danger. A nice moment for me."

"Don't presume to teach me. I don't cower in the woods hiding from all the other wizards in the world."

Nathan looked hurt.

Sir Jesse swallowed hard. "I apologize." Sir Jesse pointed at the meat as if to cement the apology. "More?"

"Is that what you think I'm doing? Hiding? Maybe it's true." Nathan pouted.

"What was your point?"

"My point, my point? Oh, my point." Nathan stood up, clasping his hands behind his back. "While you measured the snake, who was measuring the frog, who was measuring the spider, I stood behind you."

Tibs had rarely seen Sir Jesse surprised. His father took a moment to think. He looked behind himself and back at the table. "You were the danger."

Nathan continued, "The snake, frog and spider are certainly dangerous. Perhaps one has to address them first before assessing the real danger, but the most dangerous one is not these—it is the one who controls them. Who conjures them. That is what is coming. That's why I hide in the woods as you call it. At best, I'm the spider, but I've known those who stand behind the warriors, and when they act, I don't think there will be any warriors left."

Tibs made the wooden snake attack the roast only half listening, and then wandered to the kitchen door looking out behind the manor where they lived.

That's when he saw it.

His body became still, his arms fell limp to his sides, the snake, still in his hand, scraped the floor. *This isn't possible.* His ideas of possible and impossible sometimes ran against good sense, but not this time.

A house. *Should I say something? Will they believe me?* They never believed when he saw imps or leprechauns.

The house. The house seemed to have grown into this shape, or perhaps it was weaved with logs and branches. If it had been in a forest, it might have been invisible. Trunks twisted around one another to make the walls and porch, a thatched roof seemed kissed by flames, black and brittle. A carved raven hung over the front porch, threatening and protective at the same time. The elaborately carved boards hammered over the door. *Is someone trying to keep something out or something in?*

"Dad, ah, house. House." Tibs pointed into the yard.

Nathan came and stood behind the boy. "What are you on about, my sproutling?"

"Tibs, I'm not in the mood for any of your games." Jesse walked up behind his son, slapping him on the head playfully.

Tibs stepped outside. "There's a house right there." *How could they not see it?*

"You see a house?" Nathan stepped out into the yard.

Sir Jesse and Nathan didn't see a house. What they saw did startle them. Sir Jesse's great warhorse, Fibber, bucked and kicked. "Fibber, what's gotten into you?" he shouted at the horse.

The sun went down. The sound of a dozen empty barrels hitting a barn floor all at once filled the air. A gust of wind knocked over Nathan and Tibs, blasting the kitchen, overturning the chairs and table, and knocking the roast to the floor, dog food now.

Nathan stood up. Sir Jesse's arm held his sword as he assessed the danger.

Nathan began to panic. "House? Tibs, where is it? WHERE IS IT!"

Tibs sat up, the wind nearly all gone from his lungs from the impact. "G-g-gone," he sputtered, trying to regain his breath.

"What was that?" Sir Jesse barked at the burly man.

Nathan groped the air where the house stood. "Something big. Something magic, I can feel it." Power poured through his skin. "Uh-oh," Nathan managed to blurt out as his body stiffened. His beard spread out like a fan and he spun in place, tooting like a trumpet. He rose in the air about six inches and there was another explosion and tiny paper pink flowers fluttered all around the wizard. He fell to the ground as Tibs and Sir Jesse sprinted to him.

Sir Jesse picked up his head and the odd man sneezed. "What happened?" Nathan inquired.

"I'm not sure you want to know," Sir Jesse showed him a handful of paper geraniums.

"That was only *leftover* power." Nathan looked at his fingers. They were changing colors.

Tibs couldn't stop it, he laughed.

"Hilarious," Nathan seethed at the boy. "This can't be a good sign. Something powerful." He turned toward Tibs. "You saw something?"

"The house." Perplexed, Tibs stood. "It was a house with, ah, a porch like, trees, growing, house! Didn't you see it?"

Nathan looked back to the night, into the courtyard. "We have to find out what that was."

"I said a house, you couldn't have missed it." Tibs stepped out toward where the house appeared.

"Is it there now?" Sir Jesse dropped the old man's head looking around.

"No, of course not, are you saying you didn't see it?" The adults didn't answer Tibs, so he added, "It's gone, with the noise."

Nathan stared around the yard as the shadows gave way to darkness. He struggled to stand, slipping on the flowers. Tibs laughed again, "Don't just stand there, give me a hand!" Tibs gave him his hand and Nathan pulled, both of them falling into the pile of flowers which were now blowing away in the breeze.

Sir Jesse's sword pointed to the place the impact had started. His muscles twitched, longing to act, but nothing presented itself for attack. He kept ready. "Nathan, if this is one of your tricks—"

"It's not me!" Nathan protested. "I would never, I mean, the flowers, maybe, but this might draw attention, this..." He lost his words. Then Nathan turned towards Tibs. Nathan's blank face betrayed no hint of his feelings. This scared Tibs more than anything else Nathan had ever done, including what was known as "The Skunking of the Great Hall."

Sir Jesse ran to the barn to get something to help him calm his prized horse, who now ran about in circles kicking and biting the air.

"You saw it." Nathan grabbed Tibs by the shoulders and looked into his eyes and around his head and even took his hand and smelled it.

"You didn't?" Tibs tried to deflect the wizard.

"No." Nathan frowned. "But then, I can't see imps, or leprechauns and the like."

"You think I see that stuff?" Tibs bit his lip nervously. Adults never let up, he said he saw them once at nine years old and they never forget.

"I know you see them," Nathan snorted.

"There are no such things as—" Tibs began, but Nathan interrupted him.

"Every wizard knows they're real, it's just that no one can see them, unless you're five and under. Anyone older stops seeing them. I've only ever met one exception to the rule," Nathan scowled at Tibs.

"It's not my fault!" Tibs protested.

"Of course it's your fault. I have no one else to blame but you, so it's got to be your fault. But why is it your fault? That's the real question." Nathan staggered to his feet, leaning heavily on Tibs as he did so.

"Wait a minute!" Tibs protested, "You knew they were real and you didn't say anything to me!" Tibs struggled not to strike Nathan. "Everyone for years calling me twitter-pated and addle-brained and you knew I told the truth the whole time!"

"I had hoped you'd grow out of it, Tibs," Nathan said as if that explained everything.

"Why on earth would I want to do that?"

Nathan stopped his exploration and turned toward Tibs again. "Don't you remember the stories, Tibs? People who see the magical creatures come to horrible endings. I like you. I don't want you bewitched or trans-formed or murdered. Now, tell me everything about the house."

"Tell yourself!" Tibs stomped into the kitchen, clenching his fists.

Nathan only half listened to the stomping. He could still felt the dark magic in the air where the house had been. He didn't want to open himself up to it again. *This will be a problem*, he thought.

—6

Nathan had disappeared, of course, because testing day had arrived in Brig'adel. Toraline turned eleven since last year, so had the twins and Sy. The librarians came once a year to every village in the eleven kingdoms to test, taking any children who had the power. They blighted any villages that didn't parade all their children, but that didn't stop some parents from hiding theirs. And it didn't stop Tibs from trying to hide Toraline.

"They'll find me," Toraline and Tibs sat behind a herd of sheep. She pulled the flowers braided into her long hair to her nose. She wore them not to honor the wizards, of course, but because as the blacksmith's daugh-ter she felt she always smelled of smoke.

"If you had let me dye your hair white, they'd never find you in these sheep." Tibs risked a glance into the square.

"Nathan would have told us if I had magic, right?" She spoke softly.

"Wouldn't you know?" Tibs poked his head above the sheep again, if she really had magic, she'd have done some already, or so he thought. He didn't understand it, and asking questions could only led to teaching, and who would want that?

"We'd know," She tried to convince herself. "*When they touch the metal comb to my hand,*" She began.

"*White sparks fly to alert there is magic in the land,*" Tibs finished. Every child knew the rhyme.

"Lord Telford has the whole guard out, he's taking no chances with Sylas." Sylas' nobility might be in question as he was a hostage son, and not a real son of Lord Telford. The librarians normally didn't take nobles, but Telford didn't want to gamble with the son of the most influential Cush Lord in the world.

"If they take me away, would you miss me?" Toraline didn't look Tibs in the eye.

"Miss you?" Tibs pounded his chest for emphasis, meaning he wouldn't let her go without a fight.

She sighed. Tibs didn't know if she sighed for the test or the lack of a bigger champion.

"They'll take you away over my dead body," Tibs added a bit late.

"She's here!" Saunders and Zips, palace guards, reached down and plucked Toraline from her place in the herd of sheep.

Tibs grabbed her feet. "You're not taking her!" He pulled as hard as he could to stop them.

Zips held Toraline in the air and looked down, seeing Tibs dangle below her helplessly. "What about the boy?"

"You couldn't give him away." Saunders laughed.

Zips shook him off and they dragged Toraline to the ceremony. Tibs fell dully into the mud. The sheep protested. The guards practically ran through the crowd carrying Toraline side-ways and then upside-down, before setting her right-side-up next to Sy and the twins.

Tibs struggled to his feet in time to see two bald men ride into town on horses. They wore the purple velvet robes of the magi, with collars in grey fur. The horses equally arrayed in robes that fell to their feet, trimmed in white, the foursome seemed to fear nothing in this world. They stopped and surveyed the crowd. "Quite a display of might for a testing ceremony," one librarian jeered.

"Get on with it." Telford's round body merged with the huge war-horse underneath him. His armor gleamed, framed by his red cloak, his shield bearing the family coat of arms announcing his nobility. To his right Sir Jesse sat on his horse, Fibber, in his full armor, a silver column of strength.

The two wizards dismounted, "This isn't very hospitable of you, my Lord. Most villages wouldn't risk angering the Congrey with swords and arrows and spears. But you Telford don't seem to have that much wisdom."

"Lord Telford to you!" Sir Jesse barked drawing his sword and pointing at the wizards.

Telford contemptuously looked away from the pair.

"Who is first?" One of them took out from his sleeve a wooden box with runes carved in it. Tibs tried to get closer, but the whole village had turned out for testing day, and most of the animals for some reason. Tibs battled the sheep, trying to get closer. He knew he'd be standing there next year and he wanted to see what could happen.

The twins stepped up together.

"Ah, the sons of the Telford! No wonder you have men in abundance. If it was just the blacksmith's daughter you wouldn't even be here." The wizards sneered.

"Lord Telford isn't like the petty nobility you're used to. He knows each child by name, and would come out for every testing," Sir Jesse boasted. The crowd cheered.

"Get on with it, test the twins, Sy and Toraline." Telford waved his hand.

"Not like other lords? That we can see." They opened the box. Inside a comb with four metal tines nestled in velvet. The handle was carved wood, it had to be, the librarians couldn't touch the tines. One silver needle, one iron needle, one golden needle and mysterious fourth that glistened in the sun. The taller of the two wizards took out the comb, it sparked in his hand. He grabbed the wooden handle better, shaking his hand in pain. One spark and Toraline would be theirs.

The shorter wizard grabbed one arm of each twin and held them still in front of the tall librarian. The wizard's gaze taunted Lord Telford as he jabbed each twin quickly and deeply. They bled but did not flinch.

The soldiers however stepped forward, some cried out.

Lord Telford held up his arm up and his soldiers controlled themselves.

"You get to keep your twins." The wizards contemptuously moved on to Sylas, his long blond hair whipping his face and shoulders. The comb started sparking even as it came close to him. "This one is ours!"

Telford urged his horse closer to the pair. "He's a hostage son. A noble, untouchable."

"Who's son is he? Wait! The Cushite prince." He waived his hand. "Noble born, Noble bound. You are free, magus, rule well. But remember that one day you might wish you had come with us." They both bowed to Sylas. Tibs had never seen wizards bow to anyone. Dismissed, the three boys disappeared into the crowd.

The librarians approached Toraline. She stood straight and tall. How could she help it? She was tall. She presented her hand, which trembled a bit. They grabbed her muscled arm. The wizards gazed at her for a moment. She looked away.

Tibs bent down and fingered the knife he hid in his boot. He readied himself for action. No one would take Toraline on his watch.

The wizards pressed the needles to her arm, gently. No sparks. "All these guards for a girl of no import. A waste of your time, Telford, and ours." They remounted their horses and rode up to Telford. "Too bad the one with the magic isn't yours."

At Sir Jesse's signal the guards pointed their pikes at the pair.

"That one has green, use him while you can." They laughed and slowly walked their horses out of the square.

Telford waived his hands and the town dispersed. Sir Jesse removed his helmet and called out, "Tibs!" but Tibs ignored him dragging Toraline out of the square.

"I was ready to take them both out," Tibs tossed his knife into the air meaning to catch it again, but he missed and it stuck in the ground next to his foot.

"Would you be careful with that thing!" Toraline pulled it out of the ground and slipped it into Tibbs boot. "I don't want your father taking it away again, you moped for weeks."

"I did not," Tibs stuck out his lower lip, moping slightly. "I can hear him calling, let's get out of here before they give us chores."

Using the crowd for cover, they slipped out of the square and out of sight.

Making their way toward the woods, Tibs saw Gabe. Gabe lurked. Gabe never felt comfortable in a crowd, he hung out at the edges, always on the verge of slipping away. At the end of the street, Gabe spied Mrs. Swipple too late. She saw Gabe, spat on the ground and made some motions with her hands. Gabe took off toward the woods.

"Good riddance, jinx," the old woman spat again and vanished into her house.

"Swipple's an Old Crone." Tibs kicked the dirt.

"Tibs!" Toraline didn't exactly disagree, but one didn't say such things out loud.

"She's as close to a crone as you'll ever meet." Tibs declared. "She goes on about Gabe, I, I hate it. Spitting like that. Silliness. I bet her spit kills things, not, ah, it does nothing about protecting herself."

"Gabe set his coat on fire," Toraline spun, enjoying a rare moment of unplanned time, petals from the flowers in her hair littering the street like snow.

"The MacGregor makes him walk through the woods." Tibs spun next to her.

"It caught on fire in the rain." Toraline teased.

"What?" Tibs looked at her with one eye, he hadn't been listening.

"Without tinderbox or match." Toraline skipped down the street.

"What? The coat again? Whose side are you on?" *Better change the subject*, Tibs thought. "Glad they didn't find any magic in you?" Tibs asked.

"I wasn't worried," Toraline laughed.

"Right." Tibs took his turn at scoffing.

"I heard about this girl from Rame taken away from her family and they didn't even let her tie up her hair, like the family would hide her."

"We would have hidden you." Tibs reminded her.

"I shouldn't have been nervous at all, I work with metal all the time and never spark," She twirled again and started walking backward down the street so she could see Tibs, who fell behind because of her enormous strides with her long legs. "Do you think wizards eat?"

"Nathan eats more than our horse, Fibber." Tibs made the classic mistake of actually trying to engage Toraline in conversation.

"I've often thought that wizards could conjure food into their stomachs, why bother to chew? Would they have to cut it really small before they did that? Or do you think they just mash it up? I mean even an apple would just sit there…"

They turned the corner of the muddy street, treacherous from a rain in the night. Tibs saw four figures silhouetted against the sky as the road flowed into the south along the woods. Gabe, still trying to hide. And he'd know the other three anywhere, Sylas and the twins fresh from testing. It took him a moment to understand what he saw. Three boys threw stones. They flew through the air and stopped at the Gabe's shadow. Sylas looked angelic framed by the expanse of blue behind him. His light brown hair, almost blond, and a smile as disarming as a troop of crack soldiers meant he rarely paid for his misdeeds. The twins, tall but still growing looked gaunt and thin in silhouette.

Bam! Sylas threw another rock and hit Gabe square in the back. Gabe stopped moving.

Why isn't he at least running? Does he think playing dead will help them with these nobles? Tibs thought. His hands found fists. His brain found direction. He'd been suspicious of Sylas ever since his father left him here a year ago. Sylas' evil had to be stopped. He sprinted toward the trio.

"Tibs!" Toraline followed, what else could she do? "Stop!" Did she understand everything that went through Tibs mind? She didn't have to. The fists, his face and sprinting without his father chasing him told her enough.

Tibs did the unthinkable. He listened to her. That wouldn't have been a problem, except Toraline didn't think he would. She toppled over Tibs, sending them both into the mud.

The terrible trio stopped throwing rocks long enough to laugh at the mud-covered pair. When Toraline pushed herself to her feet, they stopped laughing at her. She could have put them all in the mud, and she could have done it in seconds. They directed all their mirth at Tibs. That might have been fair. Tibs had gotten the worst of the fall. The first fall buried his face in the mud. Then Toraline used him to get herself to a standing position, knocking the wind out of the boy and pushing his face further into the mud. Tibs' buried body prevented him from standing gracefully. As he peeled himself from the street, the mud making a marvelous "popping" sound as he heaved himself to his knees, they all began to laugh at him, including Toraline.

Laughter. Tibs could only see Sylas laughing.

Sylas. Sylas took liberties no son of a knight should take. Sylas used his good looks to fool people, which made him a liar of sorts. And now he attacked the children of Telford's fief. *This cannot stand.* Tibs, covered in mud, his face burning red, simmered with so much anger, the muck started to dry, attempted to stand.

Gabe disappeared in the turmoil.

"You shouldn't be throwing things at Gabe!" Tibs sputtered through the dirt and mud. "You have to protect him!"

"Look who's trying to teach the nobles!" Sylas laughed. "Mud baby."

"You know the code of the knight!" he screamed at Sylas. Sylas came and towered over Tibs, for a moment. The slick road gave way under Sylas, and he had to step back to remain tall. Toraline came and stood behind her friend. Her strength matched their combined manpower and they knew it.

"A knight fights his own battles," Sylas dismissed Tibs turning around to return to the protection of the castle. He had to pull his feet up as they were sinking every time he stepped. Sylas meant to exit powerfully, but he more or less had to stagger away.

"I fight my own battles!" Tibs couldn't seem to peel his legs from the mud. He forced himself to his knees again, and his lower legs sank deeper into the road.

"I'm sure you do." Sylas laughed and the twins followed suit. "And lose them too."

Tibs shifted one leg forward, but his body didn't move forward, it sort of stayed in place. He moved his other leg, but that just drew his first leg back to where it started. He crawled in place, while buried in the mud and fell on his face again. By the time he came to the end of the mud, the twins and Sylas were gone.

Toraline put her hand on his shoulder, "There's nothing you can do, he's a hostage-son. If you attack him it's like declaring war on the Cush."

"I don't care, I hate the Cush." He scowled.

"They didn't kill your mother," she tried to stroke him, but he flung off her hand.

"What do you know about it? What does anyone know about it!" He sat in the mud. "This isn't fair!"

"Life isn't fair!" Toraline sat next to him, she couldn't get much dirtier.

"You, shouldn't, no, ah, don't talk like my father!" Tibs stared after the boys, percolating, so angry he couldn't think.

"They're nobles, they can do what they want."

Toraline's practicality bothered Tibs. "No. They don't get away with this."

"So what do you want, revenge for Gabe? Isn't revenge just as bad as what they were doing."

"Not revenge, justice." Settling on his course of action, he began to think of a plan. "And they'll never know it was me."

CHAPTER 3

———— ෨ ————

It's been said that wars are not fought in a day. They are fought in two days, one to start and one to finish, and the days between don't count because that's just a bit of maneuvering between the two—

—from Sennacherib MacCauley's *Famous Wars*, Vol. III.

USING MOST OF his ten-year-old brain, Tibs decided to lay a trap. The Lord's Festival came some ten days after testing day. Lord Telford said he liked to throw a party for the village when the first berries could be picked in the spring, but many suspected he threw the feast to relieve the tension of the testing. He provided the meat, and the village provided the pies. Lord Telford's width betrayed his love of pie.

Sylas and the twins never took the road to get to the village, Tibs observed, but cut across a portion of the woods. The road meandered around a hill, and the wood grew over it. A strong child could save time by making the effort to climb the hill. The Lord's Festival with its games, food, and potential for mischief, drew the children from all over the countryside. They all took the shortest possible way, no matter the effort.

Tibs woke early in the morning when the darkness still lingered. Chores. Get those out of the way before he set his punishment in motion. He sprinted out of his bed. He had dressed the night before to save time. He galloped down the stairs through the old great hall, into the kitchen, grabbing the egg basket and handfuls of grain. This early in the morning, the room glowed orange, cold but homey. He got outside and the chickens weren't even awake yet. That wouldn't do. He couldn't gather the eggs till the hens were out of their nests. He kicked the coop a couple of times and woke up the chickens and the rooster who crowed his displeasure. Tibs brought down the door and the rooster poked his speckled red-and-white head out their home, croaking and complaining.

Tibs stuck out his tongue. "See how you like it!" He hissed at the rooster who staggered down the little ramp out of the coop, followed by the chickens, and threw grain on the ground. They started pecking immediately. Food changes most creatures' moods and they were jovial in a few seconds. Tibs gathered the eggs, set the egg basket in the kitchen and ran to the stables. He filled the feedbags for the horses and set about cleaning their stalls. He quickly ran back to the house, grabbed some bread and cheese, and an old apple, eating it as he ran back to the stables to take off the feedbags and let the horses out into the fields. Normal horses, of course, could have just eaten the grass, but because these were warhorses, they were given a good breakfast first. *Nothing tires out a horse more than a day of eating*, Sir Jesse had told Tibs, and so they needed a good breakfast before grazing.

The path from the bridge to the village through the woods being a shortcut had no markings. Children memorized the route. An old oak towered above the hill like a tower, lording over the whole valley like a king. After reaching it from the bridge, one ran diagonally down the hill toward the bend in the road and into the village. Tibs knew that Sylas and the twins would take the shortcut. All he had to do as set the trap.

I need a simple trap, Tibs thought to himself. *Tie a string between two trees and cover it with leaves.* He knew they had to come down the hill. At the top of the hill, he met his first disappointment. Not enough leaves. A winter of decay and the spring rains would mean the trio would see the leaves had been moved and they'd be suspicious. *It's got to look natural*, he poked around the trees off the path. *Burying it? No*, he decided. *They'd just step over it. It has to be high to trip them and low so they won't see it.*

22

Then Tibs remembered something his father had said. *People don't see the obvious.* He didn't need to hide the string. He found two good trees growing opposite each at the top of the path. He tied the string around them both about ankle high. The string's color matched the dirt and could hardly be seen.

Time to get back home. He had to be in the village when everything happened, or they would suspect him.

He sprinted down the path through the village to the town square. He smiled as he approached the well for a drink of water. Looking around him, another problem occurred to him. The sun's eyebrows peeked over in the east. The quiet of the deserted street didn't smack of The Lord's Festival. Everyone still slept. The festival wouldn't start for another six hours. What would he do until then? *Practice!*

The Lord's Festival had a series of games for children and adults: races, ax throwing, log tossing and more. There were no prizes, but the winners could boast about it till the Fall Harvest Festival where envious rivals would surely take them down. Now that Tibs had two digits to his age, he felt sure he would be able to boast till fall. He had set his mind on ax throwing and so he returned to the manor to work with his father's lightest throwing ax.

Walking into the kitchen, Tibs found his father. "Why are you up so soon?" His father asked him. Tibs, using all his powers as a ten-year-old, ignored his father and walked straight to the fire in the hearth, delightfully warm on this spring morning. His father cleaned his favorite broad sword while taking bites of his breakfast. The blade glinted in the firelight and picked up some reflections from the sun.

Tibs turned around to warm his nether regions and felt his father staring at him. "What?" Tibs asked.

His father looked, unblinking, and said nothing.

"What?!" Tibs repeated. His father couldn't know about anything he had done. He'd got up too early. "What?" He tried to look for an ax, but he couldn't concentrate. Sir Jesse stood and put his fists, knuckle side down, on the table. He menaced his son, still saying nothing. "What! I did my chores." Tibs stamped his foot in protest. "You're always yelling at me to do them before breakfast, so I did." His father cocked his eyebrow. "You can't punish me for doing what you ask me to do, can you?" His father stood and crossed his immense arms over his chest. "I haven't done anything, and you can't prove I did!" Tibs covered his mouth, talking too much.

"Ah-ha!" His father came round the table after Tibs. "What is it you haven't done?"

"Nothing!" Tibs exclaimed.

"Nothing? You haven't done nothing, so you're admitting you have done something."

"What? NO!" Tibs painted himself into a corner. "I wanted to practice for The Lord's Festival." He picked up a long handled ax from the wall. It fell to the ground because of its weight. Tibs tried to lift the heavy iron head into the air and put the handle over his shoulder so he could saunter out of the kitchen with some dignity, but it took three tries to get it on his shoulder and once there, he felt he should have just dragged the thing outside. "I'm going to practice ax throwing if that's okay with you. That's what I'm doing."

"I'm watching you," his father warned. Sir Jesse reviewed the facts. One, Tibs woke before him. Two, Tibs had done all his chores without being asked to do them. Three, Tibs had gone out and returned and four, Tibs had accomplished all this before his father ate breakfast. Nothing is more suspicious than a boy who does his work. Sir Jesse would keep an eye on Tibs all day to figure out what mischief he planned.

Tibs had the idea no one would pin his crime on him, since he would have an alibi. Still, his father watching him made him nervous, not for what he had done on the path, but anything he might do at the festival.

However, he couldn't worry about any of that. The time had come for ax throwing practice. *I'm going to win this year, nothing can beat me,* he thought to himself. *And no one can prove what I've done.* His father out of earshot, he risked laughing to himself. *I'll win at the games and I'll have justice. On the same day. Those squeak pigs will eat my swill, and no one will catch me. One string and revenge, I mean, justice is mine.*

Tibs dragged the ax to the old stump where his father practiced his ax throwing. He had wanted his father's lightest ax. He spit on both palms and picked up the one he had chosen using all his strength to get it over his head. There, the ax promptly dragged him backward. Lying on his back in the dirt after falling, he realized he could hardly lift this ax. *Too late to go back and look for another, not while my father is still in the kitchen.* His father's withering gaze had almost broken him the first time, he'd never survive a second stare. He stood back up. He swung the ax low to the ground and threw it toward the stump. It spun twice and crashed to the ground four feet from his hands. The closest they might let him get to the target for his age group was twelve feet. That meant his ax fell eight feet short of the target. Except that's not right either. It fell eight feet short in length, and four feet in height, the target was in the air after all. The best he could do was cut some of the grass on the path to the target. Suddenly the day which had looked so bright and welcoming, began to feel cloudy.

By noon the whole village smelled of meat and pies. Small children ran the streets like miniature tornadoes, kicking up dust and dirt. Lord Telford rode up on his massive horse and announced that the games could begin.

The adults began to toss logs. The children had a foot-race. Tibs lost. The adults threw their axes. The children did their obstacle course. Tibs lost. The adults had knot-tying contests. The children displayed their sewing for the judges. Tibs lost.

Then Sylas and the twins staggered into the festival. They had taken the morning to dress in their finest clothes. They had also declared that they didn't care about the games; those were for children. They knew the teenagers would take most of the pride, why fight for the unattainable? Tibs always fought no matter what.

Now, one might imagine the worst: a bruise or two, perhaps some mud on their clothes and dusty dirt everywhere from the path. Except they didn't fall on the path. They fell off the path, down the steepest part of the hill, through the trees, through the bramble and into the river. Their beautiful clothes were ripped. Their hair infested with bugs and twigs, like bird's nests only messier. And to top it off, mud covered them from toe to skull.

Lord Telford shouted, "Were you attacked?" He couldn't hear what Sylas yelled, but he saw the string in his hand. People surrounded the trio of boys, asking questions about what had happened, and Tibs could hear some people telling each other the story:

"They fell down the hill!"

"Someone sabotaged the path!"

"They were almost killed!"

"Who could have done such a thing?"

Tibs snickered. That would teach them that they weren't untouchable. This village had someone who would protect the weak and young.

Lord Telford called over some people to help the trio get cleaned up. They weren't going to let this incident affect the festivities. The boys were dirty and scraped, but hardy. They would not let this saboteur ruin The Lord's Festival. People cheered their bravery. People patted them on the back. The guilty party would be caught and punished for this heinous deed, some vowed.

Tibs scowled. Punish the person who did this to them? Didn't they know these boys deserved this? And now they were praising the trio. How had things gotten so mixed up?

"Tibs!" Nathan put his arm around the boy and pulled him away from the crowd. "What's with the sour face?"

Tibs looked at Nathan. He couldn't know, could he? He didn't really understand what powers wizards had, only that they had powers. Nathan couldn't read minds, could he? "I was just wishing I could win more contests." He told the truth, but not all the truth.

"People who get their wishes don't always want them."

"Yes they do, they're wishes!" Tibs objected.

"Let me tell you a tale." Nathan's story went something like this.

A grateful old couple received three children in their old age. People said they were much too old to have children, yet there were the girls. One too many to hold in both hands, and that was half the fun. The grateful parents named them Tresta, Fresta, and Nesta. They knew the girls had magic in them from the moment they could talk, but not strong magic. They couldn't move mountains, or grow mighty oaks or even stop one soldier from attacking an innocent. Small magic they had, but as little as they had, they had too much. Tresta saw the past, anyone's past. When she held a hand, that person could remember things they'd forgotten. They lived memories as if they were happening right in that moment again and reveal the heart's fondest wish. Nesta could see the present. If you asked her a question about the present, she could answer. Hunters asked where to find deer, and she told them in which meadows they were hiding. Fisherman asked her where the fish hid, and she directed them to the right part of the river. And lords would ask her where their enemies lurked, and she told them.

And then there's Fresta who lived in the future. The moment the future became the present, she forgot it as if it never happened. She couldn't answer questions properly because when you asked her a question, in that moment, it became part of the past and the question and the answer were gone from her head. It made it very difficult to have conversations with her. As they grew older, they grew closer, because only when united did they have something like a complete memory. And they understood one another where no one else could. Even though talking to them was difficult many came asking for their advice. Most people ignored the powers of the two, and spent their time wooing the one who could remember the future. One day a rich man came to ask about his future. Fresta spoke without warning him what she saw only might happen, not that it would happen. No future is set in stone until we live it. What she said was this:

*A great deal of money in your hands,
spread deep and wide throughout the lands.
Money is not your destiny,
a king is what I see you to be.*

When he heard what she said his heart filled with ambition. He used his money to buy an army. He worked to make himself king. But he didn't know the country he wanted to rule so he spread it through three kingdoms. Surely providence would give him one or the other or the other other. He intrigued and spent all his money. When the kings found out about his plans to put himself on one of their thrones, they put a bounty on his head, and the rich man had to hide. He found himself living on the streets, hunted like a fox. Soon, his riches were gone, his home burned, and he lived begging to keep himself alive. In the gutters and streets, in the alleys and fields, he made friends. All of them homeless people like himself. After some time the beggars made him their king. So it came true. He became king of the beggars.

So, you must never look to a witch or wizard for advice about the future. The future will come whether you want it to or not and knowing it may bring about your own destruction. Nor should you wish your wishes true, if they do, they may destroy you. What about the sisters? They disappeared one day and though people hunt for them from time to time, they have never been found. Perhaps it is just as well.

Tibs felt Toraline's hand on his shoulder. "Three-legged race?" She smiled. He tried to smile back and nodded. Better to go on with the games; it would look less guilty.

Nathan continued to watch the boy as the pair went to join in the games.

They gathered with the other children, including Sylas and the twins, and pairs were picked. Toraline insisted that Tibs be her partner. She outran every child in the village. *Maybe I have a chance,* he thought. Sylas paired with one of the twins, Tibs couldn't tell which. Toraline strapped her leg to Tibs's and turned to him. "Do you want to win?"

"What?"

She mouthed her questions slowly as if to a infant, "Do...you...want... to...win?"

He nodded. Then he heard "GO!" from one of the adults and the race started. He knew he looked ridiculous. The tallest girl and the shortest boy tied together? He questioned her sanity. Then she bent over, picked him by his waist, and took off down the field.

While the other runners tried to get a good rhythm in their running, Toraline only had to be fast and keep both hands around Tibs. For all anyone could tell, she carried a sack of water. She cleared the end of the field feet ahead of the next pair, two sixteen-year-olds. She dropped Tibs on his side and began to jump up and down. All the adults came over to clap her on the back, and cheer for her. Bragging rights for the next six months!

They took no notice of Tibs. He doubled up and then managed to untie the string, crawling out of the crowd.

As he stood, he found Sylas and the twins towering over him. "Congratulations on your win," they laughed.

"Must have worked hard to learn how to be carried like that," Sy sneered.

Tibs now saw the downside of winning. Her victory would last six months, but his would never be forgotten. Carried across the finish line. How humiliating. And just when he thought it couldn't get worse, Sylas leaned in and whispered into his ear, "I know you did it."

The three stepped back and "congratulated" him again and then walked off.

How could he have known? Tibs thought.

Nathan didn't need to hear Sy to know what he said. It confirmed his suspicions. When the trio arrived, Nathan scanned the crowd. Most everyone showed anger or shock, everyone that is, except one person. Tibs. Tibs crossed his arms over his chest and smiled, all the while looking at Sylas.

If Sylas took after his father, he would take his revenge in private. *Something would have to be done about this*, Nathan thought.

_6_

Three days passed. The sunlight crept over the horizon and into Tibs's room. Something felt wrong. Something moved on his head! He reached up and felt his hair. He brought down his hand. Maggots crawled over his fingers and down his palm, *They must be all over my head!*

Another two days passed. Sylas sat at lunch and took a big swig of apple cider. He swallowed, but it didn't feel right. Something stuck in his teeth from the drink! He pried it out with his fingernails and found a grub. He looked into the cup to find that the cider spiked with crawling insects. He wanted to be angry, but first he had to be sick. He ran out of the feasting hall.

Coming away from the swimming hole, Tibs reached for his clothes. They had moved. He knew they couldn't do that without help. He did find his boots, but filled with rocks and small sticks and a bit of mud. *Mud! Argh.* Naked, he had to slink back to his house. He kept to the bushes and leafy plants as he skirted the village to get to the manor from the river. *Luck's on my side.* He thought to himself seeing a pile of green leaves in sprinting distance between him in the house. In it he took refuge before making his last mad dash to the protection of his house and his clothes. He didn't discover the cut leaves were poison ivy until he had taken refuge in them.

Sylas and the twins may never have known why the war started. However, they spent all their free time focused on Tibs and had forgotten Gabe completely, so in that sense, Tibs's goal to keep them from throwing rocks at Gabe had been achieved. A knight in defense of the innocent would count himself victorious with poison ivy blotches and his target rescued. However, because of the personal nature of the rashes, Tibs felt he needed to step up his game to win. For that, he needed help. He couldn't go to his father. Upon learning about the poison ivy, his father had laughed. And as an adult, he might bring perspective to the whole matter. Tibs didn't want perspective. He chose instead to confess to Toraline.

He found her working in the smithy. The heat assaulted him as he entered, and Toraline's skin, covered in fine soot, glistened with her sweat as she worked the bellows. "Glad you're here!" She coughed a bit. "Fire always gets hotter when you're around."

Tibs smiled weakly. "You do all the work, all I do is watch."

She smiled weakly and pushed the hair back from her eyes. She pushed down on the struts that made the bellows breathe into the burning coals. It sparked to new life and he could feel the heat. She didn't notice the heat, except to know if the bellows had enough to do its job. Tibs came close to the fire, it's dancing and heat made him nervous in a way he couldn't explain. His hands shook sometimes when he came near. *Was that fear?* He wasn't sure. He didn't like it. He didn't want people to see any weaknesses. He tried to stop it, but they shook even if he put them under his armpits. Still, Toraline's friendship made it worth coming to the smithy to test himself. She took no notice of him. She never mentioned his hands. She sometimes never even spoke to him until she finished her task, whatever it happened to be. She turned to tools, to make sure they were clean, sharp, and ready. Tibs thought about how to bring up Sylas. He should not have worried.

"What's wrong with you?" She pointed at the red and white blotches on his arms and legs.

Nathan had given him ointment for the itching, but cloth on the rash made him itch more, so he wore as little as possible. "What did you do?" She pounded a metal stay, to be used later for a barrel.

"Me?" He started stoking his anger. "Sylas did this. He stole my clothes and put poison ivy all over the place."

She wanted to laugh, he could tell by her face, but then something entered her head that killed the mirth.

Ah, Tibs thought, *Perhaps she'll see things my way!*

But instead she said, "What did you do?" with an emphasis on the "do."

"Don't look at me," he began, but she cut him off.

"You did something, I can tell."

"You remember what they were doing to Gabe," he retorted.

"You did do something." She saw guilt in his eyes. "I can see it, I can, oh!" She put her hand over his mouth in shock. "The Lord's Festival! You're the one who tried to kill Sylas and the twins!"

"No one tried to kill them!" He allowed himself a small smile but put a frown over it quickly. "And there is no way they could know I did it."

"But you did do it, and they know it and I know it, and anyone who looks at you will know it." She crossed her arms. "Tibs, you can't—" but this time he stopped her.

"Don't tell me what I can't do when it's already done. There's no proof that I did it. There's no way they could know, so when they put maggots in my hair, what happened next is on them, not me."

"You haven't!"

"Stop it! The point is I need help now. I can't let them get away with this without doing something!"

She shook her head. "You have to leave this alone. Your father's going to find out—"

He'd interrupted with an idea for the next punishment, but she'd counter not just with a refusal, but also with common sense. "Where are we going to find the time to build a wooden rabbit in the woods?"

He thought the right idea might win her over to his side, but then she'd counter with, "How do you expect to pull a mature tree over? You'd have trouble pulling down a sapling," and she would continue with her lecture.

Even the perfect ideas met scorn. "If you want a skunk that badly, you'll have to catch one yourself." He now regretted telling her at all. After an hour, he lapsed into silence. She didn't seem to notice. She continued to work. What could he do without her strength and size? Tibs needed a miracle to take the war to the next level.

"My father's calling me," he lied.

"Maybe I should tell him," she threatened.

"Nooo, you can't do that!" Tibs whined.

"I better."

"How long have we known each other?" Tibs pleaded.

"I don't know, forever?"

"You don't know?" He smiled for her.

Toraline glanced at him, "Stop it." He continued smiling, "STOP IT. I'm working." He did nothing but smile. "All right! I suppose I can't tell him, but I want to! You have to stop, Tibs, you can't start a war between us and the Cush."

"It's not the Cush, it's Sylas, and he's, they, oh, never mind." He stomped out of the smithy, down the street and through the woods on his way to the manor. He ducked when people were in sight, he didn't want them laughing at his rashes and the blotchy white ointment. The woods would help him think. They would help him focus. Alone he could plan. Alone he could cultivate his anger and sense of righteous indignation.

Alone, he didn't have to pretend he couldn't see the magical creatures. Pidwell buzzed up to his head and threw an acorn at him. Pidwell was smaller than most imps, and that was saying something. Imps sort of have human bodies with four wings, slightly larger than a dragonfly. Pidwell was bright pink, he would have said red, but pink described him better, with dull transparent blue wings. He fluttered into Tibs's view. "What's wrong mortal boy?"

"I'm not in the mood, Pidwell." He swung his hand at the puckish creature.

It must be stated categorically that people don't believe in imps. No one sees them or any magical creatures after the age of five or six. This is universally true.

It goes without saying, but if it wasn't said, you wouldn't know, Tibs never stopped seeing them, or fairies or leprechauns or other magical creatures.

Pidwell threw another acorn at him, hitting him on his crown. "Stop it!" He struck out at Pidwell.

"Maybe I can help." Imps were not known for helping, they liked to inflict suffering, like horseflies.

"You help me?" Then it occurred to Tibs. Imps liked to drive people crazy. Tibs wanted Sylas crazy. Therefore, maybe imps would help him drive Sylas crazy. It didn't occur to him that Pidwell might use this as an opportunity to drive everyone crazy. "You can help me!" Tibs spilled his concerns about his war with Sylas.

Pidwell smiled, a warning sign in impish language. "Ah, cherub child, you have come to the right imp." He rubbed his hands. "No one exacts revenge like we do."

"I don't want him dead." Tibs continued to walk through the woods.

Pidwell laughed. "Dead, no, but revenged, yes!" He buzzed around Tibs's head telling the boy of his simple, elegant, smelly plan. Tibs then did what in his right mind he would not have done. He trusted the pugnacious pixie.

Days later, they approached the castle bridge. The nobility used to live in the manor where Sir Jesse and Tibs lived, but about two hundred years ago they moved. Now they lived in the castle over the river. It started as a bridge, and then a bigger bridge, and they put in a guard house, and a house for guards, and then another house, and it grew into a palace. The castle squatted over the river, resembling a huge crab with hundreds of eyes. The red stones and clay made a striking contrast to the green woods that surrounded it.

Tibs reached the castle at twilight, just as the sun set, in a cloud of excited imps. No one could see the imps but Tibs. He moved silently over the rough terrain. They filled the air with noise and were swooping up and down, side to side. He kept telling them to be quiet, but no one could hear them, and they knew it. Pidwell showed him the crack in the foundation of the bridge.

Tibs had to make his way twenty feet under the bridge to get to this spot. The massive bridge spanned hundreds of yards, not an engineering marvel, more of an accident. It started small, and over the centuries the townsfolk made it wider and more massive. Climbing under the bridge it gradually grew darker and colder. Standing above the water clinging to the rocks coated Tibs with a layer of shiny, moist slime. The water rushed just below him, swift, white, and noisy, masking any noise he might make.

The imps laughed as he made his way under the bridge, feeling for the crack that Pidwell bragged about. His fingers slide around on the slick stones, and then he felt the crack. The rock foundation of the bridge used clay to fill gaps between stones. It worked for short periods of time, but eventually, water would wash the clay away, and it would have to be repaired. Tibs fit perfectly through this gap. He'd have to remember to tell his father about the entrance; they'd want to patch it up. He'd have to wait a few weeks after the rumor of this incident passed, of course.

He pushed his body into the crack but got stuck on the rough rock. He pulled himself out and removed some clay to make the opening wider, just a bit, making the whole thing more noticeable. His body slipped through the crack easily, but his head stuck. He shifted his neck to one side, turned his nose downward and then began to panic. Who would ever find him here? A hundred years would pass before they found his bones. Then he pulled his chin down and his head popped through.

Slowly, Tibs made his way through the bowels of the castle. The drains stank, the walls sweating a storm as he waded up. He didn't want to know what made that smell. The dim light brightened as he moved up through the lower levels. Casks of mead, ale, and beer lined the walls as he moved down another corridor. He realized the smell no longer came from the floor—it emanated from him. How could he make it all the way to the top of walls smelling like a pack of wild dogs who came out of an outhouse? "Pidwell!" he hissed.

The imp buzzed around his face and tapped him on the nose. "Stop that!" Tibs said angrily. "How am I supposed to sneak anywhere smelling like this?"

"I don't notice any difference," the imp tittered.

Tibs balled up his fist to take a swipe at the pest when Pidwell waved his wand and covered Tibs in some sort of liquid. The smell dissipated. "What did you do?" Tibs's shock at the fairy's immediate help is understandable. Pidwell's usual behavior would include taunts and tricks before helping him, if he even did help. Still, Tibs smelled better and they both had a prank to do.

"You could say thank you." Pidwell raced down the corridor.

The lower levels were used mostly for storage: food and supplies for the soldiers and emergencies. Tibs slipped up a staircase, down a hall, then another staircase. At the end of the hallway, Tibs looked out into the courtyard. *How can I get to the top of the walls without being seen?* He crouched behind the door for a moment, leaning against a battered and worn wicker basket. He heard someone coming down the hallway, so he jumped inside the basket. The person opened the door, crushing him momentarily, and then went on their way, not even giving him a glance. He peeked out and smiled.

Taking the basket, he slipped into the traffic of the courtyard, staying along the walls. When someone came, he simply put the basket over his head and crouched down. Small basket, small Tibs, perfect disguise. No one looked twice at him. The fresh air smelled especially good coming up out of the bowels of the castle, even when covered in wicker.

On the way up the stairs to the top of the castle walls, he barely had time to hide in the basket. A guard came down and passed him by as if he weren't even there.

The wide castle walls had room for hundreds of archers standing four or five deep. Lord Telford wanted no armies to even think of attacking. Looking outward at the hilly forests that surrounded the village, Tibs momentarily felt awe. The beauty of the countryside overwhelmed him. Then he heard the noise.

"Chicken feet! Get your Chicken feet!"

"Knives and axes sharpened!"

"Carrots!"

Adding them to the noise of live poultry and sheep, he could hardly hear himself breathe.

"There they are!" Pidwell pointed at the trio gathered at the base of the wall. He could see them snickering together, eating something with their bare hands. Above the three on the wall swarmed hundreds of imps. The guards of course saw no imps, only gnats. Tibs and Pidwell made their way around the wall till they stood above their prey. The imps Pidwell brought buzzed excitedly, waving for him to begin. They pointed at the three buckets, sitting there just as Pidwell promised. The smell coming out of them put the sewers to shame. He mixed swamp water with oil, and some disgusting plants Pidwell discovered for him in the forest. The mixture smelled worse than anything he had ever smelled.

Tibs picked up one of the buckets. He didn't think about how many rules he had already broken. He didn't think about the danger he had put himself in just by being there surrounded by a bunch of jittery archers and spearmen. Another day he might have listened to the grumpy river, or the trees bending in the wind, as if to distract his attention from the boys below.

On another day, he might have noticed the flashes of light in the clouds above his head. They were malignant, ready to menace the whole valley, but he took no notice of them. He measured the distance in his head the muck had to drop, and where the boys stood and how fast he could pour three buckets. Pidwell whistled and his friends picked up the two other buckets. Problem solved. He grabbed the one that would drench Sy.

Below, the river turned from bubbling anger to being on the verge of losing its temper.

He said to himself, *Justice*, not revenge. He nodded to the imps and poured the unctuous mixture on Sy's head, while they poured theirs on the twins. It drooled out of the buckets and hit the three with a pop and a gurgle.

The three boys screamed so loud Tibs almost joined them. He looked down. The mixture inched down their bodies like molasses. It steamed. Pidwell had heated it magically before it reached them. It oozed down their backs. They reached up to pull it away from their hair and faces, and that only succeeded in spreading it to their hands and arms.

Tibs now found the flaw in his plans. He stood on the castle walls surrounded by spearmen and archers after essentially attacking three defenseless nobles. Normally, someone who did that could expect a dozen arrows sticking out of their chest. He had to escape, quickly. The crack in the foundation of the bridge felt a million miles away. He heard Toraline's voice in his head. "That's all well and good, but how are you going to get down from the castle walls when they're full of guards and bowmen, and a courtyard full of knights and the gate with its doors and portcullises—" He could feel her haunting him. He might have outrun Sylas and the twins in their current state, but the guards? He noticed two knights near their horses. They moved toward the trio to investigate. *Doomed.*

Then it began to rain. Not a light, gentle rain nourishing dandelions and tulips, but a torrential downfall. Tibs could hear the moans of the guards and the clanking of their weapons and footsteps.

Then the guards understood. Someone had attacked the terrible trio. The first responders cried out, "Attack! We are being attacked!"

The lazy guards perked up, started yelling, and ran around before one of them pointed to the walls and said, "From up there!" In the rain, refracting the light in a most peculiar way, they didn't see a diminutive boy but a hulking dark figure threatening the whole village. Pikes pointed at Tibs. He could make out random words in the rain.

"Capture him!"

"...Kill...!"

"...Torture...!"

Tibs knew death stalked him.

Pidwell beckoned, pointing over the wall. Without blinking, Tibs jumped. Tibs had enough time to think this thought: *Is my brain unhinged?*— Then, splat, he found himself in a barrel of water. His head stuck out of the top for half a second when the barrel burst, sending wooden slats in every direction. The metal stays that surrounded the barrel spun off in two directions like spinning arrows.

The guards screamed.

Someone yelled, "I'm hit!"

Others shouted, "Spears!"

All were accusing the dark figure on the castle wall. One man bellowed, "The castle's being attacked! By a regiment of barbarians!"

The fall hurt. Tibs couldn't rub his wounds—he had to get out of there. Pidwell glowed by a door in the courtyard. Tibs sprinted across the courtyard and slipped through it. The corridor led to a stairway. Tibs tumbled down it. Outside, he could hear the rain falling still faster. The floor underneath his wet feet grew wetter. The lower floor of this particular castle used every entrance as an exit for the water when it rained hard.

Tibs threw himself down a stone staircase and came to the drain. He had no time to admire the carvings that lined the walls, telling the story of the Telford Family, or admire the work of the stone masons and their pattered floors. Pidwell disappeared inside ahead of him. Tibs slipped off the lattice cover and jumped. He fell a few feet, slipped on the stone work and found himself falling down a drainage tunnel. He had hoped to replace the lattice, but he couldn't reach it now. They would know which way he went. More bad luck. The violent water poured from the sky through the corridors sweeping him lower and lower. He wanted to go out the same way he came up, but all the drains looked the same. He slipped too fast and tried to slow himself by scratching at the walls with his fingernails and feet. He didn't have to worry, because two seconds later, he lodged his body in a crevice, stuck. He didn't want to think about what blocked the huge drain, it would be disgusting he knew. *Great*, he thought. *If they don't see the open grate, all they'll find is my rotting body here.* The rushing water made it very difficult to move at all. He fought, he pushed, he tried to stand, but he couldn't change his position. Then the water began to rise. His body became a damn, the water pooling around his waist because more came down into the drain than went through around him. *Is drowning painful?* He supposed he might find out.

"Pidwell!" he coughed, his mouth filling with water. He heard Pidwell laugh. He had forgotten the number one rule with imps. They liked to see people in trouble. The myth of the little demon standing on a person's shoulder encouraging them to do evil and laughing when it turned out wrong probably came because of imps. One last chance to free himself, he thought, better start pushing.

Tibs held his breath, submerged his head and pushed. Then something changed. The water almost crested his chin when the debris shifted, and down he slid through the drain.

For a moment the darkness bothered him, he'd never say frightened.

Then castle spat him out. He slapped the riverbank like raw salmon shooting the rapids.

He took a moment to get his bearings. He had choices open to him. He could give himself up and confess. He could stand his ground and fight. Both of these choices would end with him in the dungeon, at least for a night, and then his father would think of a worse punishment. He could jump into the river, but with the rain and the rocks, he would probably drown. That left running. Not surprisingly, he ran.

He took two steps, trying to get up some speed, when a wave from the river grabbed him, tossing him into the flow. He grabbed a rock and pulled himself out of the river. Tibs allowed himself a smile for cheating death. Pulling himself up to a sitting position, he saw Pidwell, laughing.

"You could have warned me about the storm!" Tibs spat at Pidwell.

"Like I arranged a storm! And without it, you'd still be up in the castle!" Pidwell giggled.

Tibs stood up, much more carefully this time, and tried to sneak along the wall under the bridge. The storm attacked him. The vengeful river tore at his arms and legs. The wind punched his body against the stones of the bridge. Tibs gasped for breath. Pidwell's magic kept him free from harm. He fluttered about as if this were some sort of entertainment.

Suddenly, flowers burst all around him, an explosion of life. And he heard a voice. "I think I got him!" He recognized Sylas's voice. *He's only just been given his wand! How could he have learned spells this quickly? Is that normal?*

The twins cried, "He's making for the river!"

They were right. He ran along the river, but now that he heard them, he changed direction. He looped inland, trying not to slip on the slick grass.

"Why not stand and fight!" Pidwell's wings buzzed in his ears. He batted at the imp and then looked for a rock to hide behind.

"I'm done with you!" Tibs sputtered. The rain came down hard enough to get into his mouth every time he opened it.

Pidwell laughed. "Wait till the blond wizard turns you into sunflowers."

A boulder lay just ahead. Tibs slipped behind it and took a second to scout his route. He needed to go by the darkest path. At the moment, he could almost walk across the field without being seen from any direction, but still, *no sense in behaving brainlessly*, he thought. *Pick a route.*

"You're going to get caught!" Pidwell buzzed ahead of Tibs. He foolishly followed the imp. Tibs hadn't taken twenty strides when another rock burst into flowers. Tibs sneezed: allergies.

"Down there, I heard him sneeze!" Sy yelled gleefully to the twins, Farin and Florin.

They had speed. Tibs had to give them that. They had to go through the gates and come under the bridge from inside the castle, in the rain, and they had done it. Plus, they had to do something about the ooze he had poured on their bodies. Tibs dodged the flowers, running toward the cover of darkness in the forest.

Precisely at this moment, the night turned into day. A spare bit of lightning cracked over them, striking a tree to Tibs's left. It caught on fire, for a moment blazing with strength and vigor, but then diminishing in the rain. Thunder crackled over him, almost knocking him over. The light lasted long enough for Tibs to see Sy flick his wand in his direction.

A delightful smell enveloped him, green, alive, but trapping him nonetheless. His skin tingled, and the rain only made it that much more wonderful. He fell.

He looked down at his leg, and tendrils from some plant were growing around it, anchoring him to ground. The vines went from moving to swarming in a few seconds. Even as he tried to pull them off his leg, they began to grow around his hands. If he didn't need to flee so badly, he would have marveled at the sight. Now both legs were trapped. He tried to wiggle out of his boots and pants. The plants gripped his body too tightly.

Pidwell whispered into his ear, "Come on, you have a plan for everything, let's see you get out of this!" Tibs grabbed for the imp's tiny legs, but Pidwell whisked off into the forest, laughing.

This time, he thought. *I'm really in for it.*

CHAPTER 4

Magic has been called a crutch by some people. A really effective crutch by others. The truth is that magic itself is just a tool, and can be used well or badly. In the wrong hands, it can be no more than an annoyance to its neighbors. In the right hands, it can be used to bring people together and change villages, towns and cities for the better, or worse—

—FROM SENNACHERIB MACCAULEY'S PERSONAL JOURNALS

TIBS THOUGHT, *I better just give up,* when he felt a second pair of hands tearing the plants out of the ground by the roots. Toraline had come. *How did she know where I was?*

The plants withered under her callused fingers and she pulled his legs free in a few seconds. At the time he marveled at her strength. Later he would realize his mistake.

"I heard that someone tried to kill Sylas and thought of you." She smiled for a moment. "Did you think about an escape plan? And attacking from the walls, with guards and pikemen and the horses..." She slapped on the back of the head as if to knock some sense into it. He felt so grateful, he didn't care.

She pulled him to his feet. Vines crawled all around them, avoiding Toraline for some reason. She took off toward the wood, and he followed in her tracks. *Perhaps working with so much metal made her immune to this spell,* Tibs thought. It didn't matter—freedom beckoned.

"You could have at least not chosen the day of the worst rainstorm of the year—"

He interrupted her, "You heard someone had attacked Sylas? Who told you that?"

She jerked her head back over his shoulder. Old Gus tottered behind her. He played with some string tied around his waist like a child, and though he looked like the oldest man in the village, he was. A mysterious figure, most people pitied him, giving him food and helping stay out of the rain. His tattered clothes reflected his lost mind. "Gus?" Tibs pondered. "How did you know where I was?"

"Because I heard this is where you were the first time." Gus smiled. He did like to help.

That's the best I'll get out of him. Tibs had no time to question the old man, an impossible task in the best of times.

"Let's move." Toraline urged.

The pair made a last dash for the woods and found themselves in the bramble.

Tibs dared to look back. Old Gus danced in the rain. He laughed and opened his mouth to the fresh water falling from the sky. Then he stopped laughing and noticed his left leg, caught in the vines. He pulled it, but it wouldn't come out.

Tibs stopped. *I should go back and help him.*

Toraline put a hand on his shoulder. "He came and fished me out of the house and dragged me here. And what will they do with him?" She asked

"Nothing." How could anyone punish him? The plants grew up Gus's legs anchoring him in place. He didn't seem to care.

No one would blame him for this attack. He could never have pulled it off.

Where are the terrible trio? thought Tibs. If the castle guards had thrown the spell that slowed him down, he would have been captured. However, the trio of boys on their trail saw Tibs entangled in the plants. They took their time. They yelled that they were coming and were now laughing that their tormentor would soon be theirs to torture. They reveled in the anticipation.

Toraline pulled Tibs toward the woods, and they sprinted into the forest.

They looked behind them. Sy screamed, "What is this!" The trio had discovered they had captured Old Gus. Tibs started laughing.

Toraline started in on him again. "I can't believe it. Have you no sense? In the castle of all places? At least you could have kept to the woods, where you might have some slim chance to get away, and now you're just sitting here laughing—"

"Shhh!" he hissed. "Do you want them to hear us?"

She fell silent and then laughed. "You must have some sort of death wish." They exchanged smiles.

"How could I to know he'd mastered the stick already?" They turned and walked deeper into the woods. The stick. He referred to the wand that focused Sy's magical abilities. Sorcerers could use many things to focus their magic, certain rocks, crystals, and jewels, but beginners used wood.

"What do you know about it? As much as me!" Toraline teased as they made their way through the woods.

"I don't want to be a sorcerer or wizard or any of it," Tibs sneered.

"I know, I know, a knight, like your father and his father before him." Toraline had heard it before.

"Who wants to live a life where someone else has to cut up their meat?" Tibs laughed.

"Nathan just eats it off the bone."

"I will not be a magus." Tibs said emphatically.

"Like you have a choice. It comes on you, Tibs, no one knows why. Why can't you just do both?"

"You know as well as I wizards can't touch anything metal, and what does a knight use but metal?" The facts couldn't be argued.

"Maybe they wear the metal because of the wizards, have you thought about that?" She asked.

He hadn't.

"What did you think Sylas would be doing once he got his wand?" Toraline taunted. "Picking his nose with it?" Tibs lungs strained to get in more air as she ran faster and his mind ran slower, or he would have chimed in with a "yes." Toraline turned, concerned. "We don't have time to rest. We have to be in bed by the time they get to the village, or they'll know for sure that it was you. And then the punishments will begin." She talked all the way home. The way she could run and talk at the same time awed him.

He snuck up to his room, and slipped into this bed. The sparse room reflected his father's philosophy: *A knight travels light.* The trunk sat at the foot of bed, the only other object in the room. In it he concealed all his possessions. They filled perhaps half the trunk. *Maybe I'll escape punishment,* he thought. He closed his eyes and fell asleep.

Tibs woke in his bed, none the worse for the scare. He stretched and smiled. *In and out of the castle without being caught, that's an accomplishment. And no proof of my crimes.* Tibs laughed to himself. He looked out the window. The sunlight streamed lazily into his room gently warming the bed as the morning brightened.

Sun?

Sun streaming in?

Tibs sat up, panicked. Day? His father would kill him for not being in the fields helping the farmers. *Good knights help the farmers, good knights help the farmers,* Tibs could hear his father's voice in his head. Why hadn't anyone screamed at him to wake up? *A large village can afford knights who do not work, our village is small, if we don't help, everyone starves.* He pushed aside the horsehair blanket and got out of bed, his father's voice still terrorizing him. He pulled on his boots and sprinted down the back stairs toward the kitchen. They must all be in the fields by now. His leather boots slapped the stairs as he sprinted into the kitchen. He had planned to grab a bit of meat or cheese and run out the door to the fields, but what he saw in the kitchen made him stand stark still. His father waited. *Doomed,* Tibs thought again.

CHAPTER 5

It's not always about what troops a king has, but what his enemies think he has, that turns the tide in war—

—FROM SENNACHERIB MACCAULEY'S *CONTINENTAL DIPLOMACY IN THE YEARS OF THE KHAN*

HIS FATHER JUGGLED oranges. Sir Jesse liked to tell people he broke his nose juggling maces, which are sticks with chains attached to them, and the chains have metal balls peppered with spikes. Juggling them might break a nose, or a head and certainly a tibia. Tibs thought his father could juggle anything, but he remembered his father breaking his nose, not with a mace but while getting a bowl off the top shelf of a cupboard in the kitchen. He slipped off the stool he stood on, flinging the bowl into the air, and then the bowl came down right on his nose. Blood dripped everywhere. Tibs might have been terrified by the whole incident if his father could have stopped laughing. Even through the blood, his father had perspective, *always laugh at yourself.* Sir Jesse said through his laughter, "One of the best knights in all the eleven kingdoms brought down by a mixing bowl."

Still, juggling wasn't a good sign.

As a knight in service to Lord Telford, Sir Jesse had to keep sharp, mentally and physically. Juggling helped his combat skills and made him one of the most prized fighters in the eleven lands. That's what Tibs knew. At the moment, Tibs could tell that his father juggled to amuse himself.

Sir Jesse juggled as an alternative to killing someone. His rough hands worked automatically. The fruit didn't spin in the air; at the top of the arc they almost seem to stand still. His father's eyes didn't focus on anything. Sir Jesse trusted his hands and arms to do right.

Tibs stood still, waiting. For a few moments they stood like this in the kitchen. Then Tibs's stomach grumbled.

"Hungry?" his father asked. His father didn't stop, but he used a rag on his shoulder to wipe sweat from his sodden eyebrows. He did not drop an orange.

Tibs nodded meekly. "I was going to go down to the field."

"You won't be going to the fields today. You'll be going to Wilcox's farm and moving manure."

Tibs's first inclination to say, "What?" and complain, he stifled. Instead he nodded.

"Very good, you remembered 'a knight controls his temper.'" His father caught his oranges and put them on the table. "Sit down here, Tibs." Tibs sat on the kitchen chair. His feet still dangled in the air, and he hated it.

His father paused and looked at the boy, weighing what to say next. "What were you doing at the castle?"

"Castle?" Tibs pretended ignorance, which came easily to him, since often he had no idea what his father meant when he spoke.

"Are you going to play a game with me?"

Tibs met his father's gaze. His father, he knew, had nothing on him. No one saw him. No one heard him. They had a suspect in custody, Old Gus. Lying came easily, and maybe that was why he did something quite remarkable. He didn't take the easy road, but the hard one. He told the truth. "No." But then he added, in his defense, "I wasn't seen, I wasn't caught, I slipped up to the walls and was out before anyone even knew." Tibs reasoned a military-style plan carried out perfectly might sway his father to be a little forgiving.

"Don't you know that the guards could have filled you with arrows any step of the way, and if the place had been warded..." His father slapped the top of his head in exasperation. No leniency here.

Tibs winced. He didn't consider that the castle might have been protected by magic.

His father continued, "I have a son that breaks into heavily guarded castles to pull childish pranks. You are almost of age, you know, you have to stop this." He stood up and looked out into the yard. A few chickens scraped for food in the dirt behind the kitchen. "If you go on like this, someone will die. You know that." Tibs looked at his feet. His shoe leather looked thin, almost time to make a new pair. The broken seam on his left big toe would could be repaired, maybe he could get another two months from these, but no more. After he had thought about his shoes, he realized his father continued to talk. "Sylas didn't kill your mother."

Why did everyone bring her up? "This isn't about her." Tibs's face turned red. Anger filled his whole body. *She had nothing to do with any of this. This is something between me and Sylas.* Oh, and Gabe he added self-righteously.

The fact that his father had brought up his mother's death at this moment made him think the Cush, Sylas's people, really did have something to do with her death.

His father continued, "Sy is a hostage-son. Does that mean anything to you? No, because if it did, you'd treat Sylas with respect because of his father, the Lord of the Cush. Lord Telford is trying to cut down on hostilities and all you're doing is making it so when Sy goes back home to his father when he's eighteen, he'll hate us even more." His father turned and faced Tibs squarely, in such a way that Tibs had no choice to but to meet his eyes. "And you would do well to remember that Lord Telford's eldest is in Sylas's father's hands. Edward played with you, didn't he? When you were small, or, smaller anyway. How do you want one of your own treated over there? With the same kind of contempt?"

Tibs shook his head.

"Today you will clean the stables, move all the manure to the compost heap, and then aerate the whole pile."

"Dad!" Tibs stood.

"Don't." His father's face exuded sternness. Nothing less than a huge hammer would change his mind at this point. Tibs backed down.

Sometimes even granite has a crack in it, so small, if struck in the right way, a small tap with a tiny stick can make it burst open. Trying a new tack, Tibs said, "No, no, what I mean is that everyone will know I did it if they see me punished like this." His father's eyebrows creased. He could see the crack. Tibs tapped a second time. "There are no direct witnesses. I didn't leave anything behind. No one could know I had anything to do with this. I used the castle's buckets, and no guards saw me enter or leave the castle." He could tell from his father's look his case had merit. "You have a few of the boys saying it was me because they saw someone trapped in the fields, but they didn't find me—they found Old Gus."

His father used silence as a weapon. Tibs felt his father would wait a century for an answer to a question. Neither son nor father could look at each other. Then when it felt to Tibs that he'd started growing into the ground his father whispered, "How did you get on top of the castle walls?" His eyes were on Tibs's boots. Tibs starting swinging them proudly. Sir Jesse poured a bit more verbal syrup. "The guards are saying an assassin sent from the Black Heart herself tried to kill those boys. He appeared on the walls, jumped to the courtyard, set off an explosion, and disappeared into the drains." Tibs crossed his arms. *Assassin? Yeah, I'm an assassin.*

He tested a smile. It felt good.

His father kicked the chair to get his son's attention. "Then I investigated and found that a small boy fell into a barrel, causing it to break into pieces, and looks as though he might have been swept into the drains like a piece of trash by the rain. Naturally, that made me think of you." Tibs stopped smiling. He had almost forgotten about his father's intelligence. "What do you suggest?" His father folded his arms this time and looked down at his son.

"What were you going to give me? Three days of pushing manure?" he probed. How much trouble did his father think he caused? His father nodded. Angry, but not furious. Probably because no one could pin this on him. "I'll do four days, but I only serve them half a day at a time, twice a week for four weeks." It would look like he had done little things to deserve punishment—instead of something huge.

"You climbed the wall by yourself?" His father turned his back. Tibs knew Sir Jesse smiled as he said that.

"No, there's a hole under the bridge that gets into the drains and up into the castle. It should probably be fixed," he added meekly.

"You will move the manure to the compost pile this morning. We will talk about you fulfilling your whole obligation as we move through planting season. When you finish, come right out to the fields." His father stood up to leave the house.

"Wait!" Tibs yelled. "I'll smell."

"That you will." His father smiled at Tibs for the first time that morning and then walked through the house to the front courtyard, adding, "Worse than that stinkwater."

"Hold, hold on!" Tibs stood up and leaned on the kitchen table. His elbows still bent. His height prevented him from really leaning, but he could push himself up and dangle his feet, which he thought made him seem taller. It didn't.

His father looked at his son expectantly.

"Can I, can I have breakfast first?"

Sir Jesse looked coolly at his boy. "Be quick about it, or I'll add on another week."

Tibs didn't need to be told twice. He ripped a piece of bread from the loaf, not even bothering to cut it, and looked for some cheese, pulling open the cupboard. The door swung and then fell, the bottom hinge broken. Tibs had forgotten. *Someone will have to fix that*, he thought.

His father didn't look back to see what Tibs did. He knew Tibs would obey. Four days. Tibs thought he'd gotten off rather lightly. His mouth full of bread, his left hand full of cheese, and his right hand pulling an apple from a bowl on the table on his way to the barn, then he heard something that made him stop.

Lord Telford bellowed, "Jesse! Get over here!" If they had had glass in their windows, it would have rattled.

"Those boys came from this village!" Lord Telford snarled. Telford purple face matched his girth, making him look like a plum. "Sylas says it was your son. Saw him plain as day."

"Plain as day, at night? You said the culprit was beset by Sy's magic, and he's in custody."

"Those idiot guards, they arrested Old Gus," Telford sneered.

"Not your man?" Sir Jesse could sound innocent when he wanted to.

The men didn't have to discuss it. Old Gus wasn't their man. He was never their man. He didn't seem to have the brains to carry out a lunch, even if already packed into a basket. Telford knew his men weren't the best and brightest, but they had not only arrested Old Gus—they had attempted to interrogate him.

Telford had walked down the hall some eight hours before, still pulling on his cape showing the signs of his office and rank. An hour had passed since Tibs showered Sy and the twins in stinkwater. Old Gus sat in a chair in the torchlight with guards questioning him. "What's your name?"

"Oh, start with the hard questions first!" Old Gus replied.

The other guard chimed in, "Old Gus!"

Old Gus never missed a beat. "Glad to meet you."

The first guard interrupted, "No, *your* name is Old Gus."

"It is? It's just like this feller's."

"No, my name isn't Old Gus," the second guard yelled.

"It seems to me you two have to get some facts straight." Old Gus never lost his temper; *as even as a church step*, people said.

That's when Telford entered the room. The lord's look silenced the room. Old Gus smiled and stood as Telford entered.

Old Gus smiled and said, pointing at the second guard, "Old Gus here tried to ask me some questions."

The night hadn't gotten any better. Telford's sons and Sy were out in the rain, searching the forest for the culprit. He had to send his guards out into the night to drag them back and then lecture them about how dangerous the woods were at night. He inspected the scene of the crime even before his sons had told him what they thought had happened. Another lost night of sleep, and increased frustration, and Telford wanted to punish someone. So he had come to Sir Jesse.

Now, Tibs couldn't make out every word Lord Telford spoke. Even though Telford threatened trouble, Sir Jesse didn't even sweat. Still, Tibs didn't want his father punished for something he did. He went through the house to the window looking into the courtyard. Tibs prepared himself to walk into the courtyard and confess everything when he caught his father's eye. Sir Jesse must have been looking for him. Sir Jesse silently warned him back with one of his silent hand signals. Like a good soldier, Tibs faded back into the shadows.

Telford stood a foot shorter than the older knight. "Old Gus had nothing to do with this, you know that!" Telford scratched his head and pointed at Tibs's father, firmly saying, "You're saying your son had nothing to do with this?"

"Do I look like I know?" Another avoidance.

"You need to bring him under your control, break him. He'll only cause us more trouble." Telford spat in his anger.

"I will not bring him up like I was brought up, nor like Cynthia, Cin, Cindy." Sir Jesse looked Telford right in the eyes. Telford sat in his saddle on his show horse with Sir Jesse on foot and Telford shrank. "He doesn't need breaking, he needs direction. That he has, he will be your best knight just as I have been, even better, I'll bet."

Telford stroked his mustache, flicking the ends nervously, thinking. "That boy is trouble. He always has been, ever since your daughter died."

Daughter? Had Tibs heard right? He had a sister who died? She must have been older, since his mother died when he was very, very young. He would have to ask around town about this.

Tibs didn't see what happened next, but a second later Telford actually stuttered. "The h-h-heat of the m-m-moment." Then the lord composed himself. Sir Jesse made Telford stutter.

What does that mean? Tibs pondered. He knew other nobles admired his father, but to make Lord Telford back down to Jesse, a lowly knight?

Telford continued, "You know what it means to have Sylas with us, especially since we learned he has power. Green power! You know how difficult it's been not to see my son for three years. Tibs will ruin everything we've worked for."

"No, my lord, he won't."

"I've only one other son, none of the others has power, we can't expect help from magic. None of the other children even have bloodlines that carry magic. And, I know you like him, but you can't argue, Nathan is a buffoon, disappearing when the librarians appear, it's ridiculous. What will we do if, if, if ..." Lord Telford walked in a circle, agitated and worried. Tibs had never seen his lord anything but angry. How could he be afraid? He commanded all those men. He had that castle. Who could challenge his power? Everyone in the village feared the lord.

"You sound like the Black Heart is coming for you." Tibs's father laughed. "I'll keep you alive as I kept your father, and maybe live to save your sons."

The rotund lord seemed to have made some sort of decision. He nodded. Telford pulled the reins and pulled himself up on his horse. In the saddle, he could be mistaken for nothing but a lord, but Telford had changed in Tibs's eyes. Nobility didn't mean invincibility. His lord knew fear just like anyone else. Tibs hadn't conceived that possibility. He thought for a moment. He didn't like the idea that his lord could be scared. What could frighten such a powerful man?

Maybe pushing manure for a couple hours would get the bad taste out of his mouth.

⁓

A few days later Tibs found the Raven's House for the second time. The dark clouds and intermittent rain had finally given way to a bright sunny day. Tibs had a day without extra chores, and he wanted to use it up. He and Toraline were planning on raiding Farmer MacGregor's garden for some carrots. *An even more daring exploit because of the bright sun overhead,* they thought. Of course, noon meant MacGregor napped, but his dogs didn't. He trained them to bite carrot snatchers.

"You gonna give me any carrots?" Toraline laughed at Tibs, pulling some of her hair through her mouth. She hadn't put her hair in a braid today. Tibs thought she looked almost grown up.

"No," Tibs said with irritation. Carrots were the traditional gift from a sweetheart. *Why did she have to be such a girl?* He had gotten up early to go to the river to wash the smell off his body and out of his clothes. He smelled it so much, he couldn't tell if he had really gotten rid of it, it felt like it followed him. *Please don't let me get used to the smell!*

The road seemed more like a creek, the mud thick from the rain during the night. They walked toward the farm with the forest on their right. Their feet sloshing through the muck, the only sound for miles, except for the song of a robin. For a moment Toraline and Tibs stopped. They gazed at the farms and looked toward the woods. The sun warmed their skin. When had a day seemed more perfect? They looked at each other and laughed. They knew they had the same thought. Toraline ran ahead. She had no trouble dancing through mud; she moved so fast, her feet never sank.

Tibs tried to follow. He took his first step, and his foot sank almost to his knee. He needed to sit in the mud to pull out his leg. Clean clothes? Not anymore. He tried to make his way to the grass beside the road, his only hope of catching up to his friend. She didn't help him. She knew that would have made him mad, especially after The Lord's Festival. She had grown used to waiting for him. It didn't bother her. It didn't bother him either, as long as she waited.

Toraline had just jumped over the coarse fence that led to the back of MacGregor's farm when they saw Nathan. They planned to attack the carrots from the woods, not the road—an easier escape route.

Nathan laughed seeing the two. "Flowers!" He pulled flowers from Toraline's nose.

"I wouldn't touch those," Tibs warned.

She grabbed them and stretched her arms around his waist, being very tall with long arms, she made it three quarters of the way around.

"Don't tell me, don't tell me." He looked intently into her eyes. "You're after, after..." He paused and pinched his nose, his hair fluttered and he burped, and then he barked, "Carrots!"

How does he do that? Tibs wondered. *He always knows what we want or what we are about to do, as though he could read our minds.*

"I can read your minds," Nathan said.

"I know for a fact you can't!" Tibs challenged. "What am I thinking now?"

"I only read minds when there's something interesting going on," He looked down his nose into Tibs eyes. "No, nothing there today." Nathan read body language.

Toraline laughed, and Nathan joined in.

"Shush!" Tibs waved his hands at the pair, "The MacGregor will hear you."

"Shushing me? SHUSHING ME!" Nathan bellowed like a bull whose tail had just been pulled. MacGregor's dogs started barking. Then the neighbor dogs started barking. The cow in the public land started pawing the street and snorting. In the distance they could hear cursing from a man thrown from his horse. Then Nathan added, quietly, "Of course, I'll shush." He laughed a big belly laugh and then simmered down like a tea-pot losing heat.

"Thanks so much." The words dripped from Tibs lips like slush from a roof.

"I was looking for you, Tibs." Nathan's stern face brought the boy to a halt.

"Me? Why?" Tibs had plans for the day, and carrots were only the beginning. He didn't want Nathan ruining them.

"You're to learn to read." Nathan serious look made them realize no joke lurked in his words.

"What!" Tibs objected. "Knights don't need to read!"

"What kind of nonsense is that?" Nathan corrected. "Everyone should learn to read, it's just fun. And a knight needs to read even more."

"Knights protect, not read." Tibs argued.

"Sir Jesse protects with every weapon in his arsenal, that's true, but he uses weapons only as a last resort. Usually he uses his wisdom, his wits, his education, his strength, his compassion and more before he even thinks of drawing a sword."

"He drew his sword on those wizards on testing day."

"That's probably right, but they have a history, the wizards and your father. It's not his first go around with the Congrey."

"I'm supposed to start learning to fight," Tibs complained.

"At eleven?" Nathan snorted.

"Soon!" Tibs raised his arm, bending it and raising his fist. His muscles had yet to develop. From the look of his arm, some might have wondered how he had the strength to lift his hand.

"I suppose you could try to learn to fight, but you will also learn to read. Five of you. Toraline, of course, you Tibs, the twins, Farin and Florin, and Sylas. Oh, and young Gabe."

"That's seven," Toraline said.

"Six," Tibs corrected.

"Well, six bodies and five brains between them." Nathan smiled and touched Toraline on the nose. "And I'm counting on the fact that you, my lovely girl, have two brains." He turned to leave.

Tibs protested, "Read! I won't do it!"

That stopped Nathan short. "No?" He turned back and glared at the boy. "No?"

The old man stopped laughing. Nathan clasped them each on the shoulder, and the two were forced to look him in the eyes. They could not bring themselves to turn away.

He began whispering. "You feel safe here in Brig'adel, that's good, we want you safe, but it isn't all safe. Beyond the forest there's a gathering tide. Waves that shake and change the world, You need to be prepared to meet them so you aren't swept away." Nathan looked to the forest and beyond, down the road, down, perhaps, even to the sea. "I see the eleven lands, I see their protectors, their detractors, their destruction coming …Without knowledge and wisdom we have no hope, without another generation to stand and fight the good fight against evil, this land, all lands are lost…" Nathan shook his head and then, with his right hand, he grabbed the bridge of his nose, as if to pinch the image from his mind.

Nathan turned to the children. "Anyway, my cottage in the woods tomorrow, just after your chores." He started to walk back toward the town. "And The MacGregor is awake. I'd go somewhere else."

"There's no way he could be expecting us!" Tibs protested.

"No?" Nathan reached into his pocket and pulled out a carrot. He took a large bite and walked away.

What! Tibs thought. *Nathan beat us to the carrots?*

Toraline and Tibs turned toward the farm. They could see MacGregor in his carrot patch, stomping his feet and raging with anger. His three dogs ran around his feet, sniffing, looking for the culprit. He had his pitchfork. *Not a good time to try to steal his carrots,* thought Tibs.

"My father says The MacGregor sharpens that fork," Toraline informed Tibs. They gulped, thinking about being on the receiving end of that thing.

Toraline turned back to Nathan. He had disappeared. They looked toward the fields, down the road toward the manor, but no trace of him anywhere.

How does he do that? Tibs wondered.

She pushed her long hair out of her eyes and looked down the road toward the farm.

Tibs looked at The MacGregor. "We could never get them now." Then he saw it, as if it had always been there. "Unless we use that house as cover." He sniffed the air and began to make his way toward it.

"What house?" Toraline's eyes darted down the road where Tibs stumbled trying to avoid the mud.

"The house!" He had seen the house before, he knew it. Stepping in the wrong place, he found himself knee deep in mud. "HEY!" he screamed. Toraline pulled him up and set him on the grass.

"You're not going to sucker me into this game." She sniffed. The air smelled strange somehow. She smelled pine, but she couldn't see any pines around.

Tibs danced along the clumps of grass, avoiding the mud, and made his way to the house. He touched the porch.

Toraline, meandering behind him, screamed, which made Tibs turn, and as he did so, he stopped touching the house. Which made Toraline scream again.

"Why are you screaming?" Tibs hissed. His mind still had a few carrots in it, and he didn't want MacGregor to look in this direction.

"The house." Toraline whispered. "It, Nooo, and then, bam! Yes, I ah, Tibs, it's gone."

Tibs looked up. Dark brown, almost black thatch on the roof. The porch looked woven instead of cut and nailed together, gnarled branches grown into a house. There were boards over the windows. "You don't see the house?"

She now stood beside him. "No." She reached out and touched the porch and then pulled her hand back as if it had been burned. "I see it when you or I touch it."

Disappearing house. He wondered if the boards were over the doors and windows to keep things out or keep things in. There were runes carved on the boards, which he now recognized as writing. Then he saw the carved raven over the porch. "It's the house!"

"I know it's a house, where did it come from?" She came up behind him for a closer look.

"This is the house that appeared near Fibber's field." *How had it gotten here?* "I think it moved itself." Tibs thought about stepping back.

"Do you think it's dangerous?" Toraline couldn't let go of the house now, or it would disappear on her.

"Yes, yes I do."

CHAPTER 6

It is to be remembered, that as bow gives way to the yew bow, and swords gets bigger and stronger, that the greatest weapon isn't something you control with your hand, it is something you control with your mind. It is knowledge. Wars are lost and won not with the number of men and the might of weapons, but with new thoughts, ideas and above all, the faithfulness of those who fight—

—FROM SENNACHERIB MACCAULEY'S HISTORIES OF THE ELEVEN KINGDOMS

"SHOULD WE GET, really get, on it?" Toraline questioned Tibs as he poked the porch from the ground.

The bark still coated the logs, like the house lived. "Hello! Yes! Look at the boards, that's writing."

"What does it say?" She asked, then quickly added, "Oh, I forgot, you're a knight and a knight doesn't read."

"Shut up." He squinted at the writing. He took a step onto the first stair up to the porch.

"Don't!" She pulled at his shirt.

"It's a porch, how can it be dangerous? I'm only looking through the windows." He took another step up and stopped, hesitating at the last step.

"The windows are boarded up, you squirrel hunter!" Toraline knew she had to work on her insults, but later.

"It's old, can't you feel it?" He took the final step.

Toraline took the first step behind him, she couldn't help herself. She didn't want to get closer, but she wanted to be near if Tibs got in trouble, which, truth to be told, was most of the time. She realized the pine she had smelled came from the house. The branches were weaved from pine trees. There were no needles on it, but the strong scent enticed them.

Who would make something like this, who could live in something like this? "The home of the Black Heart?" Tibs snickered.

"Don't joke about the Black Heart. She eats children." Toraline pulled on his shirt again, to get him to move backward off the porch, but Tibs tore his shirt out of her hand and tried to walk boldly toward the door, except his hand shook. He hid it from Toraline.

"Scared of a baby time tale? The Black Heart is going to eat me!" Teasing her made him feel less scared about being on the porch.

"Don't." Against her will she stepped on the porch itself, trying to stay close to Tibs. "My father says she's real."

"Like fairies and leprechauns." Tibs realized his examples were terrible, since he had seen both fairies and leprechauns. *Too late to take it back.*

"If something was going to happen, it would have when I stepped up here, right?" He tried to sound convincing.

"How am I supposed to know?" She turned toward practicality. "I know horseshoes, not magical, invisible houses!"

"Why would a magical house come here? We're not a big, important town." Tibs wanted to touch the boards, but kept his hands back. His hands tingled when he brought them near the planks covering the windows and doors. "Why can I see it and you can't."

"I can see it now."

"That's a big help." Tibs scowled, no he wished he could read. "Can you read any of this?"

"Read? Me?" She kicked him in the shin.

"It's invisible and it moves."

"And it's creepy and probably haunted and evil!" Toraline wanted to keep going but she saw Tibs reaching up to touch the boards. She pulled his arm back. "Don't touch it!"

The weather-beaten boards had more than words, they had carvings too. The porch had a relief of a raven over it, as if guarding it. These carvings had birds all over them, mouths open, wings poised for, *For what?* Tibs thought. *Flight, attack?* The wind-worn boards had seen many summers and winters.

Toraline's fingers dug into his arm. "Do you think anyone even lives here?" Arranged haphazardly, the nails stuck out, as if whoever nailed them into place didn't care how they looked. The carvings flowed from one board to the next as if they were all one piece. In the center, right on the door, surrounded by words, another raven, exquisitely carved into the planks. You could count the feathers on the bird.

She reached over the door, for the carving of the raven to touch the bird.

"Don't," Tibs warned.

"You were about to do it!" She reached towards the carving.

Tibs couldn't stand it, so he reached out and touched the doorknob.

They heard a crack in the sky, as if lightning struck a tree, twice. The rickety wood beneath their feet moved. The house tilted, leaping upward. The children spun into the air, tossed like bales of hay from a hay-loft by a very strong farmer, and the bright day turned to darkness.

CHAPTER 7

*Boys or girls, men or women, have no idea what they are
until they are tested. Tests don't come from books.
They come from life, from events. When trouble comes,
you discover what you are.
I've found that's the moment most people discover they don't
like themselves. The trick is to prepare as hard as you can so
when the tests come, You will still like yourself afterwards—*

—SPOKEN BY TIBERIUS THE FIRST, WHILE TEACHING A
GROUP OF NEOPHYTES TO BECOME KNIGHTS

WHEN TIBS OPENED his eyes, he saw something that made him sick: Pidwell's face and nose, distorted and wavering like a candle flame in his brain. The imp looked into his left eye, but only his left eye. Since nothing looked into Tibs's right eye, Tibs felt the world tipping sideways. Pidwell firmly grasped Tibs left eyelid. If you have ever felt tiny little hands actually pulling your eyelids open like curtains, you know it's rather disconcerting. Tibs screamed and batted the fairy away.

Pidwell cried out. Tibs looked over at the crumpled imp, laying on the grass. He hadn't meant to hit Pidwell so hard. Pidwell lay on the ground, surrounded by long grass. He rolled over to his stomach, imps always roll over to their stomach, because they have wings on their back. The imp pushed up with his arms, but obviously he hadn't the strength to move. He fell to the grass.

Tibs's heart skipped a beat. He reached for the wood creature.

Pidwell convulsed on the ground.

As Tibs reached out in concern to the little thing, he suddenly felt pain running through his hand, an arrow lodged in his palm. Pidwell's convulsions were a ploy so the little imp could load an arrow in his bow.

"I'll—!" Tibs cried out, slapping at the ground where the imp lay, but Pidwell flew away before the hand could connect.

"HEHEHEHE!" Pidwell could hardly contain his glee, flying away.

Tibs looked down at this hand and saw the arrow. Imps laced their arrows with mosquito venom, so Tibs knew that in a few minutes he'd want to scratch his hand like crazy.

He pinched it with his fingers, but the darkness made it hard to see, almost impossible.

Darkness? He looked around. Toraline lay on the grass beside him, unconscious.

It's late. Tibs's first thought, that he had missed dinner, then he realized his curfew had passed. "Toraline!" Tibs kicked her in the ribs, hard. She cried out, sat up, and punched him in the stomach knocking the wind out of him.

"What happened?" She stood slowly, shaking her hair away from her face, looking up at the sky.

"It's night!" Tibs wanted to scream at her. It came out more like, "Ahra, nuffti-ah," as his breath escaped into the night leaving his lungs empty.

Toraline sat up. "It's night! Why didn't you say something?"

Tibs shrugged, fell to the ground and managed to find his breath again. "I tried."

She rubbed her head. "How long have we been out?"

"Draco is over my house." Draco is a constellation of stars that comes out in summer. He moves around the horizon as if walking around the edge of the world. But he only comes out when it's late at night and disappears before morning.

"We gotta get home." Toraline was practical as usual.

Toraline helped Tibs get to his feet and set him to running home. "We've got to find that house again," Tibs panted.

Toraline cried. "What do I tell my father?"

"Just tell him you were with me!" Tibs cried.

"Are you kidding, this late at night?"

"It's the truth, but not the whole truth. Do you want to tell him the whole truth?"

"No, no of course not." She reasoned.

It might have been better if they told their parents, but they couldn't have known that then. Tibs tried to sort his thoughts as they ran home. *The house is gone. It's a magic house, an invisible house that moves from place to place. Dangerous. What are the chances of us finding it again? Almost none. I have to find it.*

Tibs knew Toraline's father wouldn't believe the truth even if they told him. His practicality would overrule anything they said. Magic houses? Runes and carved boards? Those things didn't happen in Brig'adel. Worse still, they might believe them and order them not to look for the house.

"Should we tell Nathan?" Toraline asked, apparently thinking along the same lines as Tibs.

"He hides in the woods when the Congrey comes. What good will he be with this?" Tibs wanted to keep this between Toraline and himself. "Just tell your father we lost track of time."

"Lost track of six hours, that will go well." Toraline scolded Tibs.

"It's not my fault, you were going to touch the raven." Tibs defended himself.

"But you touched the doorknob."

"Won't be doing that again."

⸙

Their day began with torture: extra chores, parents questioning them on their behavior, over and over, until they would have agreed to any story just to stop the questioning. But that wasn't the end of it. After the chores and breakfast, they were sent to school.

When Nathan told them about the school, Tibs burned because he wanted to fight, not study. Since they had found the house, everything had changed. Tibs wanted to read the words on the boards over the house. He had to be ready the next time he saw that house. And he had to keep it secret from everyone but Toraline. Tibs met up with Toraline as they walked the road outside of town.

"He made me sweep out the house and clean the clothes," she complained. "I had to scrub the floors, the actual floors! Including the root cellar!"

Tibs responded in the only way that made sense. He laughed. He laughed until her foot connected his backside. Then it didn't seem as funny. "Don't feel so bad about it, chores have never killed me yet." Tibs snickered rubbing his gluteus maximus, that is, his rump.

"I've been working the bellows since I could walk and he has me scrub the floors," she snorted. "Who does he think is going to be the next blacksmith?" It wasn't unheard of that a girl should become a blacksmith when her father had no sons. "I already do most of the heavy work since he hurt his leg." She reminded Tibs, "No one else knows how to work the equipment but me."

A porch ran all the way around Nathan's cottage. The walls, made of brown clay and logs had but two windows in the front, both of which stood shuttered to the daylight. It seemed impossible to see inside, but no matter, there couldn't be more than one room in it, and that room surely couldn't have more than a fireplace, table and bed. The greenish roof made it hard to make out against the meadow and forest.

They knocked and heard what sounded like a suit of armor falling down two flights of stairs. Tibs reached for the doorknob to help whoever was there when they heard, "Just a minute," then groaning and more clanging.

Toraline pressed her ear against the door when after the crash and a long scream they heard silence. Finally, footsteps staggered toward the door. Nathan struggled with the door as it opened a crack striking him on the nose.

"Ow!" Nathan squinted at the children, rubbing his nose. He had only his tunic on. It barely reached his knees, and the children wished it reached the floor. His wild hair matched his bent beard, as did his hairy legs. "You're early," Nathan growled. Behind him they saw a bedroom, the floor littered in clothes, and an unmade bed.

"No we're not." Tibs tried to walk into the house as if he owned it. Nathan put his hand on Tibs's chest and pushed him backward.

"Oh, no. No, no, no." Nathan looked Tibs directly in the eyes and he stepped onto the porch to join them there, closing the door behind him. "You're, you're, Ah-HA! You have something on your mind, you almost never have something on your mind."

Suspicious, Nathan examined the children from their toes to the heads. "Something's changed. Tibs, your head is usually, unusually empty, but now is full, and Toraline almost always has ten things brooding in the back of her skull, but now there is only one thought flitting in there. I can see it in your eyes, as clear as water. Tibs burning with thoughts and Toraline's mind is calm and practically empty, except for a single thing."

They didn't deny it, their eyes confirmed everything he said. How did he do that? Well, truth is, that when children are rattled, they're easy to read, and Nathan had been reading their minds all his life, not in the sense that he knew their thoughts, but he knew them, from birth.

Nathan waved his hands over his body. They couldn't see how he did it, but one moment he stood like a man homeless for thirty years, and after his hands twirled over his body, he seemed almost regal in neatness. His beard was suddenly combed, his hair tamed around his ears and even his eyebrows trimmed and calm. He took Toraline's chin in his hand and stared at her. She found she couldn't look away. "You know what Tibs' is thinking about," he challenged her.

She did what any girl would do with Nathan approaching. She gulped and stepped backward. The magician stepped toward her, grabbing her arm and pulling her close.

Nathan appeared to grow taller. He looked down into her eyes. "What is Tibs thinking?"

Tibs could see it in his eyes, the one thought that had filled her head for the past twenty four hours bubbling, trying to escape, like steam from a kettle. "NO!" Tibs tried to put his hand over her mouth too late.

66

"We saw a house that disappeared yesterday," she blurted out. Relief spread through her whole body.

Nathan touched her head. "I can get the truth out of you another way!" he threatened.

"It is about a house, an invisible house!" she protested.

"Few have lived through my interrogations, but if you continue fight, I'll, you'll, we'll..." He paused and looked over to Tibs, and then back at the girl. "Wait a minute. It IS about a house?"

"It's just an old house." Tibs tried to make the whole thing seem small, even though it felt huge.

"Disappearing houses? Where have I, wait, disappearing house! Like the one the other day?" Nathan opened the door to his house and walked inside. The room had changed from a messy bedroom to a large, clean reading room with a big table in the center, comfortable chairs surrounding it, and the walls were lined with books, scrolls, and pictures.

"Maybe," Tibs tried to sound nonchalant. "What happened to the room?"

"The exact same house?" Nathan's surprise increased. "I've been looking into that. The magic involved in making a house disappear is staggering! It's relatively easy to get it to disappear from one direction, or a few angles, but from everywhere? That takes power, that takes cunning, that takes..." Nathan sputtered to a stop, trying to look at his feet. "Do I have shoes on?" he asked. They shook their heads. "I thought I missed something."

"You didn't miss anything, did you?" Tibs looked at Nathan's eyes.

Nathan stared at Tibs for a second, or perhaps half that, and winked, before turning back into his house.

Toraline missed all that in the presence of the scrolls. She couldn't help herself. She walked up to one of the shelves and pulled down a scroll. She unwound it. "I'll bet the library in The Congrey doesn't have so many scrolls."

"Don't be daft, girl," Nathan snarled. "The Congrey has a thousand times more than this." He went to one wall and pulled down a few scrolls, dropping one. "Don't just sit there, stand, stand, stand." He disappeared under the table to get the scroll he'd dropped.

"We are standing," Toraline said.

"I mean, sit, sit, sit." Nathan pushed scrolls toward them. "Read these and see what we can find."

Tibs, never shy in this kind of situation, blurted, "We don't know how to read."

"That's right, I forgot." Nathan scrutinized them. "What a bother. I suppose I'll have to teach you."

"Have you ever heard of a disappearing house?" Toraline prodded the old man.

"Have I ever heard? Why I've heard it all! I've heard everything! I've heard of a dragon sparing a town because a stable boy taught it to sneeze. I've heard about the king who gave half his kingdom to a boy who told him what his dream meant. I've heard about a star that came down to earth to experience cold. That didn't turn out well, I can tell you. I've heard everything!" Nathan's face turned red in anger. "To dare insinuate that I've never heard..." He muttered something to himself and then looked up at the sky.

He came to a full stop. He scratched his head.

Then he turned around and looked right at Toraline, admitting, "No, I don't think that I've never heard, that is, ah, no. I've never heard of such a thing, not a house disappearing. A horse once. Men have tried to...But I can imagine a house disappearing! And that's almost the same thing."

"What we want to know—" Tibs started to say, but Nathan cut him off.

"Where did you see it?" Nathan shot at Tibs.

"You walked right around it coming back from MacGregor's farm."

Nathan stroked his beard. "I should have felt its magic. I must have been very distracted."

"By food," Toraline added.

Nathan sighed. "Nothing distracts me from magic. The spell must have been very powerful. Even more than I thought." He slapped his knees. "Why can't anything ever be easy? Just once in my life, easy would be welcome." He waved his hands, and the table cleared of books. They flew into the shelves and across the room so fast that Toraline and Tibs had to duck to keep from getting hit. "We have a job to do."

Tibs sat and leaned toward Nathan. "To find that house!"

"No." Nathan shook his head.

"Aren't you interested in the house?" Tibs confronted the old man.

"Yes! But in order to find it you have to learn to read. Here's your first word." He pulled out a blackboard from his sleeve. He waved his hand and he had chalk. He drew on the blackboard with the chalk. Tibs and Toraline were awed, they'd never seen such a thing before, in fact, they thought Nathan was doing more magic. I suppose it is a type of magic, even today.

Still, this bit of tomfoolery wouldn't distract Tibs from his goal. "How does this help us find the house?"

Nathan laughed. "The house is invisible, it moves from place to place. We can't wait around for it to knock on our door, so, our only hope is finding the house in the scrolls." He pointed at the library that surrounded him. "When we find it in the scrolls, it will make it easier to find it in the world."

"You think someone took the time to write about it?" Tibs could hardly believe that.

"If it's filled with as much magic as I think it is, I'm certain someone must have written about it." He looked down his considerable nose at both of them. "Lesson number one," Nathan began. "House." Nathan wrote the word on the board.

Tibs and Toraline had no idea how the squiggles represented a house. Nathan pointed at the blackboard inquiringly. "Letters? You've seen letters? Hasn't anyone taught you these?" They shook their heads, afraid to speak.

"Well, now it's too late." Nathan erased the letters from the blackboard.

"Too late?" Tibs stood up.

"The others are here," Nathan laughed.

"Others?" Then they remembered. The School.

How would they keep this all a secret from the others? It might be easy not to tell Sy and the twins, but what of Gabe? That boy had the way of a bumbling mole. During a dance, Gabe had been showing the town how he had learned some new steps. He began to knock down the food table, but the dance ended when the whole barn collapsed. One felt so sorry for the boy that they had to keep him as a friend and tell him secrets. He always kept them.

Knocking on the door filled the room. "They are here." Nathan grabbed the scrolls and flung them into the air. They went back to their places as if guided by hands. Nathan went to the door and pulled it open. There stood the twins, Florin and Farin, and Sy. Three of the same feather, his father would have said, "Tall, strong, and noble."

Sy sneered as he entered, "I still can't see why you can't come to the castle to teach us."

"It's a secret school. We could hardly keep it a secret if I came up there in full view of the whole village."

The trio stopped in their tracks, the taller Sy glaring into the room. "You didn't say we'd be learning with the animals."

"That's the best you can do?" Tibs said. "I might have tried, 'Brush the fleas away and let's start really scratching.'"

"Or, 'Now that the servants have cleaned up, send them home and we can learn,'" Toraline added.

Nathan stretched out his arms. "Welcome to my little school! Everyone take a seat around the table and we will begin." He pulled the twins and Sy inside. Behind them on the porch, stood a very timid Gabe. Nathan always had a big smile for Gabe. "How is Gabe today?"

Gabe looked down at his shoes, as usual, hardly daring to meet anyone's eyes.

Tibs glared at Sy, daring him to start something. He would find a way to finish it. But the nobles did nothing. Sy didn't even look at Tibs. Of course, to Tibs the "way" Sy didn't look at him made him angry. Sy sat and flicked his head backward. His hair settled on both sides of his head, over his ears, in perfect symmetry. The twins' hair never obeyed them as

Sy's did. They tried to imitate Sy's style, but their dark brown locks could hardly be tamed and they looked a mess.

The lights went out. They sat in total darkness for a moment, and then a lone light shined on Nathan. He began to speak. "At this table there will be peace." Nathan looked around at the children. "Whatever problems you have out there, when you come to my house, they end. Do you understand?" He looked down the children. Each in turn, Sy, Farin, Toraline, Tibs, Gabe, and Florin, looked down at the table and nodded.

"I have to warn you as I warned your parents." Nathan began. "School is a dangerous undertaking. Not for the faint of heart, or lily livered, you can choose your own organ." He cleared his throat. "For three centuries there have been no schools outside the Congrey."

Tibs applauded. Perhaps you might have too, but Nathan meant this as a terrible thing.

"The Congrey wizards have closed every school down on the island and want to do the same on the continent. They want their university to be the only source of knowledge everywhere. If they catch us teaching you to read they would certainly kill me, and they might take you back to their library where you might not never be seen again."

"I would have learned to read." Sy said with confidence.

"Yes, as a noble, you'd learn, but they'd watch you." Nathan's voice took on a deep tone, like an actor reciting lines. "You need to know there is something more powerful than magic, or swords or kings and knights and wizards. It is knowledge. The people who change the world all have it, all use it. Those who seek to keep the world the same, or to oppress the comon folk, all forbid it. The people who have the knowledge control the seas and skies, the land and animals and all the people. All knowledge begins with..." Nathan looked around the room as if waiting for an answer.

Gabe raised his hand. "Reading?"

"You see why I like you, Gabe?" Nathan smiled. With that, they began to learn to read.

Some days later, Tibs had just finished his chores, which today meant helping plant the last of the late summer wheat, and he headed over to Nathan's house. The twins and Sy were almost always there early, getting in extra practice in reading and writing. This, of course, made Tibs furious. He couldn't stand the thought of those three ahead of him on anything. Today, he sprinted along the road trying to get there first.

Oddly, a farmer sprinted past him going the other way, toward the village.

He thought. *What would make a farmer run? Escaped pig? Daughter eloping? Market day?*

He turned around and looked toward the village. *SMOKE.* That could only mean one thing: Fire in the village. It could wipe out the whole town.

Tibs reversed course, running back into town. Everyone had to help, noble and commoner alike. They'd need every hand.

The fire came from the center of town. *The smithy!* He started running faster. Toraline!

Now, of course fires are in smithies. Smithies needed fire and a good set of bellows to melt rock to extract iron and gold from raw rock. Then fire is used to make nails, horseshoes, knives, weapons, and even fancy bric-a-brac.

Tibs saw not a fire in the smithy, but the smithy on fire. The thatched roof shrieked fire. The walls moaned as the flames rushed upward.

Tibs saw Toraline. She stood in a line from the well to the smithy, passing full buckets toward her home and empty buckets toward the well to get more water. Without a word, Tibs got in line. He took a bucket and passed it to the next person, who in turn passed it to the next person. A few of the strong men threw the little buckets of water at the raging fire. It didn't even make it sputter, but they had to do something to protect the other buildings. More and more people were running from the fields to help with the fire. An empty bucket came back the other way. They needed more buckets.

That's when Tibs noticed an old man screaming instead of helping with the fire. He looked around and found Gabe, staring at his own feet, looking guilty.

"Outta here!" The man actually picked up a rock and threw it at the boy. Angus MacGregor, the carrot farmer. Tibs grabbed another bucket and swung it to Toraline's mother, who happened to be next in line.

Gabe looked terrible. He looked as if he had been assaulted by a soot monster.

MacGregor picked up another rock and yelled, "If I see you come into town again, I won't miss!"

It didn't take a genius to figure out what had happened. Somehow Gabe had caused the smithy to burn down. Tibs's body tensed like steel. *This is not right.*

"Get outta here!" MacGregor threw another rock. This one hit Gabe in the chest. MacGregor picked up another one, bigger this time. Gabe didn't move, or speak. He just stared at his feet. Tibs could see tears running down his cheeks making a muddy river through the soot that covered the boy's face.

This will not stand, Tibs thought.

Tibs grabbed another bucket and left the line still holding it.

"Tibs!" Toraline's mother reached for the bucket for a moment as Tibs stomped off in the direction of the MacGregor. But the gap in the fire line closed and she grabbed the next bucket swinging it toward the next person in line. She had no time to interfere—a fire needed putting out.

Oddly enough, Tibs had the same thought as he approached the pair. MacGregor stood with another rock in his hand. His bald head shined with sweat in the sunlight and fireworks. You could tell he wore a hat all the time by the line that circled his head. His crown didn't see sunlight very often. MacGregor pulled his arm back to throw another rock, only this time he aimed at Gabe's head. Tibs came in front of him and threw the water right into his face.

MacGregor stood there, rage pulsing through his whole body. He started hyperventilating, breathing in and out, faster and faster. He couldn't say anything. He swayed in shock for a moment. He dropped the rock.

"Gabe is one of us!" Tibs said. Tibs turned around toward the other boy. "Get in the line and start passing buckets," he ordered handing Gabe the empty bucket.

Gabe didn't have to be asked twice, two blinks of an eye and he took a bucket from Toraline, but he kept all his attention on Tibs.

"You are a menace!" MacGregor cried at Tibs. He picked up the rock again.

"Me?" Tibs challenged. "You're throwing rocks at a boy! With all this destruction, couldn't you find something better to do than pick on him?" You might think a boy of Tibs' age couldn't say this, but he had heard his father say things like this hundreds of times, almost always directed at him. His father had prepared him for a day like this.

"You threw that water right in my face!" the farmer sputtered.

"Seemed to me there were two fires that needed to be put out." Tibs turned his back on The MacGregor and walked back to the fire line.

"Get back here." MacGregor grabbed Tibs's shoulder. "You don't treat your elders like that!"

Tibs looked him straight in the eyes. "Gabe is one of us! Love it or hate it, he's one of us!" Tibs pulled his shoulder out of MacGregor's hand. It hurt. It hurt a lot. That pain registered somewhere in his head, but he pushed it aside. "No one treats one of us like that while I'm around. They don't treat Gabe like that, they don't treat you like that!" Tibs didn't walk away. He stared MacGregor right in the eyes. MacGregor clenched and unclenched his fists till his fingers started shaking in anger. "Are you going to throw that rock at me? Or are you going to do something about the fire?" Tibs never blinked, daring the old man to club him with the rock. Tibs realized Farmer MacGregor struggled in his mind, the old man wanted to throw the rock. Tibs could see it in his eyes. It occurred to him that he might get hurt.

MacGregor looked down at his hand, and stopped shaking. The veins in his neck stopped throbbing. MacGregor dropped the rock. He backed up a step or two. He looked at the ground. Tibs couldn't tell if he had shame in his heart or not. All he knew was that the old man ran over to the smithy and started pulling burning logs out of the building.

Tibs stood there for a moment and noticed his hands shook. He grabbed is right hand with his left to make it stop, but it wouldn't. Then he felt his father's hand on his shoulder and relief spread through his body. He turned and hugged his dad. For a moment, the two were one. His father stroked his head and asked, "You gonna help put that fire out or not?"

Tibs looked up at his father, and his father winked. Approval. Tibs nodded.

"You saved Gabe. Time to save the smithy," his father whispered.

Tibs ran to the bucket line and started passing buckets.

This didn't prevent anyone from talking. They talked about one thing: how did it all happen?

Not even Gabe knew, though he was there. The best possible guess is this: Gabe loved to watch the smith working and today the smith pounded out shoes for some of the Lord Telford's horses. The smith asked the boy to hand him a small hammer sitting on a wooden table. Somehow, in his reaching for the hammer, he knocked the table over. The table knocked over a stack of half finished swords, which flipped over three wheels being readied for a wagon. One of these flipped and rolled. Toraline's father left the fire to stop one wheel barreling toward a cooling breastplate, which would have dented if hit by the wheel, another wheel sped outside, and the third went through the fire. Coals tumbled onto the floor, igniting spare straw. It moved from the floor to the walls to the roof before the smith could act. The only thing the smith saved from the fire was Gabe, still in shock as the fire took on a life of its own.

It could have happened to anyone, but it happened to Gabe.

The whole thing might have passed over, except for one thing: Gabe's gratitude.

The next day Tibs tried to get to Nathan's cottage early to talk about the house.

"Tibs, shall we go in together?" Gabe asked. How long had he waited there to greet Tibs, Tibs didn't know. He didn't like it.

After a long day in the classroom, Tibs tried to sneak into the woods for a prank on Sylas. He ran out the door and into the woods. He skirted the thickets and went up the hill. He spiraled down the hill toward the river road and doubled back toward the castle. He wanted to get ahead of Sy so he could set off a hive of bees he found. He crawled the last few feet toward the road when he heard a soft voice behind him.

"Tibs, what are you doing?" Gabe asked.

He had to let the twins and Sylas go by unstung.

"I'll never help anyone again," he muttered so that Gabe couldn't hear.

They walked back to the village and Sir Jesse caught up with them there. "Don't you have chores?" Sir Jesse didn't ever ask twice. Tibs knew he better get a jump on them. Sir Jesse like to punish Tibs for not doing chores with more chores.

As Sir Jesse walked toward the castle, probably to meet with Lord Telford, Gabe walked beside Tibs as he made his way back to the manor.

"You want me to help you with that?" Gabe asked.

Do I want help? Do I want to do half the work? Do I want twice as much time to do my stuff? "I could use a little help." Tibs smiled. *This could be pretty good.*

Not only did Gabe do half the work, he actually did most of it. And the next day he did all Tibs's chores. Tibs discovered he had a personal servant, one who didn't complain or talk back or need pay, and he liked it.

Sometimes Gabe didn't do things right. Tibs redid it cheerfully and taught his friend how to do things better. Part of Tibs's chores included taking care of his father's armor. After Gabe had done Tibs's chores, they would go to the field near MacGregor's farm, where the house appeared. Tibs wanted to feel the air where it stood. He wanted to make sure it wasn't there. And then he would think—*Was it ever here?*

He didn't tell Gabe what he looked for, and Gabe never asked.

Then they would go to the school. Sometimes when Nathan spent time teaching the others something, Tibs would go through random scrolls looking for the word "house." He surprised himself when he began to understand the words on the page. And every week they added new words.

"Never say the words out loud," Nathan warned them.

"Why?" Sylas's questioning had become legendary.

Farin chimed in first, "Because they might have magic spells on them and you'd turn us into newts." The children laughed.

Nathan corrected them, "No, no, no." He coughed, "Saying the words gives no power, magic works on the power contained within the person not in words on a page. No, don't do that because it really annoys me when you do it, especially when everyone does it at the same time."

In less than twenty seconds, all the children read aloud the words on their pages. Nathan complained and raged, but secretly the children learned faster.

Then came the day when Tibs' father assigned him to aerate the manure. "It's your turn!"

"Dad!" Tibs protested. "Why do I have to do it?" His arms flopped at his sides, so depressed they could not move.

"Every child has to do it, we have to prepare it so it can be spread on the fields in the fall so we have crops not just for next year, but the year after and the year after that. Manure feeds the lands, just as the carrots and oats and things feed you."

"No, no! That's not what I mean!" Tibs protested. "I already know all that, but I did it two weeks ago, Toraline hasn't even had her turn at turning it yet and I have to do it again? It isn't fair!"

"I'm having you do it twice, for fairness's sake."

"What? How does that work?"

"You're my son, and I assign who gets the job. People might accuse me of showing you favoritism by the day I give you, or the time of year you have to do it. You know there's more manure in August than June, so in order for people to know that I don't show any favoritism I make you do it twice and so I keep my integrity."

"I don't care about your integrity." Tibs sulked. "And it smells."

"Smells like money to me," Sir Jesse poked his son in the ribs.

"Money, ha!"

"More manure, more crops, more crops, we can sell some and that means!" He pointed at Tibs.

"More money..." Tibs scowled. "You are so strange."

Tibs approached the mountain with great dread. He dragged a shovel and a pitchfork. One to turn the piles and the other to poke holes in them.

And then Gabe appeared.

This won't be so bad after all. Tibs smiled to himself.

Tibs took a nap under an old oak tree. The fact he took a nap meant he knew his actions were wrong. If his actions were pure, he would have paraded himself through the town, or gone to investigate the house, or walked to Nathan's cottage. As it was, he let Gabe do the work, but he stayed beside the pile so as to not draw attention to himself.

Tibs thought—*I'm just saying near in case Gabe starts a fire or something*—Gabe did set things alight on occasion, so he had a point.

As Tibs dozed, he thought about what it would be like to have a lot of servants instead of just one. One could take care of the manure. Another would do his work in the fields. A third yet would take care of the chickens and cows around the manor house. He'd have one to read to him and another to mend his clothes, and all his time would be spent on making himself the most fearsome warrior the world had ever known. He would have time to ride, and joust, and practice the sword.

While his thoughts wandered pleasantly through the battles he would win for his lord and the honors that would be bestowed on him because of his strength and skill, another part of his brain began to ask for attention. This part of his brain said something like, *There's something wrong here.*

The main part of his brain would reply, *Nothing wrong with being the greatest knight the world has ever seen!*

The small part would say, *It's awfully quiet out here.*

His main brain would come back with, *Who can hear anything over the battle's sound as I wield my ax and ride my horse.*

This little tiny part of brain chipped louder, *The birds have stopped singing, the crickets have stopped chirping and Gabe has stopped working.*

Gabe stopped working? That woke him of his revelry. Maybe the manure had exploded!

He wished for a joyful fire.

His father stood over him instead.

Tibs had been found out.

CHAPTER 8

In all the annals of time, there are no annals about watches or
clocks or sundials—

—FROM SENNACHERIB MACCAULEY'S *ANNALS ABOUT
ANNALS*

HIS FATHER LOOKED at him. Just looked. Tibs snuck a look over at Gabe,
who stood with the pitchfork drooping and mouth slacking. Not the most
encouraging pose.

Tibs groped for words that would make this all seem normal and
good. His father didn't give him a chance. He did the worst possible thing
he could to Tibs under the circumstances.

He said nothing. He shook his head. Then he walked away.

Tibs glanced over at Gabe as his father disappeared from view. Gabe
smelled, as the rude people say, ripe. He not only smelled; He managed to
coat his body with manure. Gabe smiled weakly. They both knew trouble
galloped toward them. They also knew that for some apparent reason the
trouble hadn't started. This made them both more worried than if Tibs's
father had just killed them in his anger.

Tibs got up and started moving manure. Under the circumstances it
seemed the right thing to do. Gabe had already done most of the work, so it
didn't take long. They finished, time for lessons at Nathan's. Tibs thought
about going and finding his father. Gabe started toward the cottage and
Tibs looked back toward the manor house. This time of day usually had his

father drilling troops. One day Sir Jesse had them fending off attacks from marauders from the sea, the next week from an attack by another kingdom by knights on horseback. The life of a soldier, even then, is one of intense boredom, repetition with moments of intense excitement, fear and desperation. Sir Jesse made sure his few troops were ready for their moments.

"Are you c-c-coming?" Gabe asked meekly.

Tibs stood there for a moment, torn. Maybe he should go back home and take what punishment awaited him. What good would it do to put it off? At Nathan's, he would only think about the impending doom. How much learning could he do under such circumstances? Fear outweighed duty, and he turned and walked to Nathan's for his lessons.

As they stepped onto the porch, Nathan appeared in the door. "Oh, no, oh, no." He held up a hand to stop the pair. The rest of the children sat around the study table. "Gabe, I'm afraid I can't have you inside." Gabe had done his best to scrape himself clean, but the smell traveled with him. Tibs thought about taking Gabe to the river to wash off, but they didn't have time. Nathan had punishments for those who were late.

"You can study out here"— Nathan pointed to a chair on the porch. Tibs could have sworn the chair wasn't there a moment ago. "Tomorrow you will come early and clean my chair." Nathan turned around and went back inside.

Tibs looked at Gabe and the chair. He glanced inside at the others. Monsters and children all set to learn from Nathan. The twin monsters laughed. He couldn't see them, but he knew their laughter. He could see Sy smirking in that way Tibs hated. Tibs wanted to go inside. The smell overpowered. But instead, he called through the door, "I'll be studying out here too." And he sat on the steps and jerked his thumb at the chair, telling Gabe to sit and get ready for study. Tibs sat on the steps and made the best of it.

After studying a bit, Tibs allowed himself a smile. He knew that Nathan would tell his father that he had stayed outside with Gabe. This kind of behavior his father loved to celebrate. Maybe in failing one test, he could pass another.

In all honesty, he didn't stay outside out of friendship with Gabe. He stayed outside to show the others he had superior morals. That's not humility, that's pride, and no one would reward him for that.

The day inched by. Imagine a colony of ants carrying away a watermelon piece by piece: A work of speed. The most annoying part, the flies loved Gabe. They dived at him. They spiraled around him. Out of a spirit of fair play, they also bit Tibs.

Nathan let them go a few hours later. Gabe went straight to the river. Tibs took the woods. He didn't want to go home. Where else could he go? Toraline had work rebuilding the smithy, so he walked alone.

As kicked his way through the woods hardly lifting his feet, anger blossomed. Why should his father punish him? Gabe made his own choices, could he help it if it benefited him? If anyone should be punished, it should be Gabe. He had said, "No" at first, but Gabe insisted. He didn't create this mess. Gabe did.

That's what I'll do. Tibs thought. *I'll look my father in the eye and tell him I did nothing wrong. It's Gabe's fault.*

Then he remembered his father's look as he stood over him by the pile.

It will never work. Yes, he knew his father would never believe him, but that's not why. It wouldn't work because he didn't even believe it himself. As the sun crept around to the other side of the world, he surprisingly found himself at home. He wandered slowly through the house, his feet echoing in the emptiness to the kitchen. No one home. Dinner waited for him, but not his father. He ate it, alone. After dinner, he stood outside the kitchen, beside the fields where his father kept his prized horses. No father. Night crawled over the day, and darkness came. Time for sleep, but Tibs didn't want to slumber, his dreams would keep him awake. He went upstairs and slipped into bed. He waited, his eyes unclosed, unrested. He tossed and turned, and still he did not hear his father in the house. His fear melted into worry like a candle becoming a lump of wax. Had his father been killed? He'd never known his father to be late in punishing him. Late coming home, yes, but never when he needed a "teaching moment." Worry exhausted Tibs, and sleep took him from behind like a thief.

He awoke. The day had started, but it did not feel new. It felt like "worse." He did his morning chores. No sign of his father. Or of Gabe. He had planned with Toraline to sneak over to the training fields where the older boys learned to fight and copy whatever they did. On a normal summer day, that's where his father toiled. He didn't want to go now. His father either wouldn't be there, in which case, Tibs might be an orphan and that would be terrible, or his father would be there and decide to punish him in front of the whole village, which might be worse.

Where did he want his execution to take place, in the privacy of his home or the public field in front of the whole village?

Alone in the kitchen, he ate his breakfast. The food had no taste.

Then he heard his father enter. He turned slowly. His father didn't look mad. Tibs tried a smile. His father smiled back. *Not too scary.* His father walked outside, and Tibs followed, expectantly, like a prisoner knowing execution is coming, but not knowing how it will be done.

His father walked toward the stables, and Tibs followed. Beside the stables were two hatchets and stacks and stacks of wood that needed chopping into firewood.

"Firewood, in July!" Tibs protested. His father gave him a look. Tibs looked at his shoes. His anger disappeared under that gaze. He dared to protest, quietly, "This will take days…"

His father turned around and looked at Tibs. "No, it will take one day, Tibs. You must have this finished before you come into the house for dinner. I know you can do this, because you've been so efficient with all your work this week."

"Dad!" Tibs started to protest. It would take two grown men at least a day to chop all this wood. For him, it would take two days at least, maybe three. Maybe four! His brain protested, *no living boy could chop that much wood without dying.* He turned toward his father, ready with a quick protest, but when his father glanced at him, the protest died in his throat.

"When you finish, come to me immediately. But not one minute before." His father turned his back and walked to the fields for training. Tibs could see the flags flying, which made him kick his foot. Flags meant horse and rider training. Tibs knocked himself so effectively, his feet wound up over his head, and he fell to the ground.

Brushing off the dirt, Tibs picked up the small ax. Its battered head newly sharpened. The handle worn smooth from thousands and thousands of strokes. He rubbed the handle for a moment. Then he bent over and picked up a gnarled log. The stacks and stacks of logs had all been cut into one-foot lengths. His father must have worked hard to set up this chore. When did he have time to do this on top of everything else? He thought about this for a moment. His father had done all this extra work to find a suitable punishment for Tibs? That didn't make any sense.

Then other thoughts crept into Tibs's mind. Why couldn't he be like other fathers who just beat their children and then had a mug of beer at the inn right outside the castle? But his father didn't drink, except when ordered to by his lord, a point of pride for him. Tibs suddenly had a thought. If his father were a tree, he would be an oak. If he were a stone, he would be granite. If he were a bird, he'd be an eagle. If he were an animal...Tibs had to think about this. He'd been taught a lot about animals. He worked too hard to be a bear, or a lion. Badger didn't seem respectful somehow. Then he understood. His father would be a war-horse. Everything his father did protected and helped others. Somehow his father thought this punishment would protect and help Tibs. *My father must be mental*, he told himself.

Tibs examined the logs. Forty at the bottom, ten high. *How much is that? A thousand? Two thousand? More?* He couldn't be bothered to do the math. How can a boy calculate a wall of pain? Tibs had to cut all this wood, or he wouldn't eat another meal. Suddenly, his stomach growled. *I just had breakfast*, he grumbled to himself. It's one of those mysteries of life. When someone talks about not eating for a few days, everyone who hears that suddenly wants a nice big meal.

He picked up a log and set it the old stump used to chop wood. He broke up the log into four pieces, two clean chops just as his father had taught him. Then he bent over and set up another log.

That's when Gabe walked up.

"I've been looking for you, Tibs." Gabe said. "What are you doing?"

"What does it look like I'm doing?" Tibs anger took aim at Gabe. *If he hadn't done what he had done, I would never had done what I had done and then none of this would need to be doing.*

Gabe didn't notice Tibs scowl or the sharp tone of his voice. He smiled. "Let me do this for you!" He reached over to take the ax from Tibs.

Tibs stopped him. "No, Gabe, no. The only way I'm ever going to get all this done is if you help me—"

"Right!" Gabe interrupted. Seeing the second ax, he bent over to pick it up.

"Stop, stop, STOP!" Tibs knew the gargantuan task could only be done through teamwork. He also knew that letting Gabe help would be wrong. As soon as Gabe had offered to help, with all that good natured joy he walked around with, Tibs knew the fault came from inside him. He had to bear this alone.

"I'm happy to help!" That made it harder for Tibs to do the right thing.

"This is my punishment, Gabe. You can't take this on for me." Tibs took the ax from Gabe's hand and threw it at a tree. To his surprise it stuck there. "Woah," they said in unison.

If he had thrown axes like that on The Lord's Day, he would have won a medal.

"My father left all this stuff here so that if I wanted, you could help, but if I did that, I'd be making the same mistake over again. As my father always says, I intend to make new mistakes, not repeat the old ones."

"I-I-I won't take n-n-no for an answer," Gabe started nervously stammering. He went over to the tree and pulled on the ax. He couldn't pull it out.

"NO!" Tibs yelled. "Don't help me!"

Gabe bit his lower lip and looked to the ground. For a moment, Tibs could see right into Gabe's heart. He had always been pushed aside, cast out, ridiculed. For a few weeks, Gabe had been needed. For a few weeks, he could pretend Tibs was his friend.

"Look..." Tibs searched for the right words. Gabe tried to interrupt him, but Tibs barreled right on. "I've never had a friend like you, Gabe," he said truthfully. "I'm going to tell you something you must never repeat to anyone. I need to be more like you."

Gabe stopped stammering. He stopped doing everything. No one in his life had ever said anything even remotely like that to him.

"You give to your friends without holding anything back." Tibs surprised himself with his own words, even more because even as he said them, he believed them. "You smile when people yell at you. Nothing seems to bother you. You are a man in a boy's body."

"That not true," Gabe began, but Tibs stopped him.

"You are a true friend, and I've been taking advantage of you." Gabe stopped talking again. Tibs continued, "I don't deserve you as a friend, but what I will do is try to be a better friend, and that begins right now. You may not help me." He took a breath, because he really wanted the help, he really needed the help, he knew he couldn't have it. "You're my friend, Gabe," Tibs assured him. "You don't have to do anything for me to be that. It's just what you are." And with that Tibs picked up a little log, set it on the tree stump and started making little logs with the ax.

Gabe looked at the wood. He looked at Tibs. "I got you into this mess. Let me at least help a little."

"No."

"What if I just keep you company?" Tibs thought for a moment and then nodded. So Gabe sat down and watched Tibs work. He sat with Tibs till supper. Neither he nor Tibs ate lunch.

It had been a nice day. The sun shone brightly, but not hotly. A breeze came off the river filling the air with moisture, which kept the hard-working boy cool. Night began creeping up the horizon as the sun meandered down, dimming as it disappeared.

Tibs didn't notice the nice day. He didn't notice Gabe finally going home. His hands hurt. His right thumb bleed from a burst blister. He found some cloth, wrapped his hand and kept working. Toraline wouldn't have blisters, but she worked with hammers in the smithy, so she had calluses.

Every time he chopped, pain shot up his arm. *That's the point*, he could hear his father say. Dinner passed him by. So did the sunset. Now he had sores, blisters, splinters, and scraps. He picked up a log and set it on the stump. It took most of his strength to lift it up. His hands shook. His first stroke missed. *Most of them miss now.* He tried again. This one hit, but he didn't hit it hard enough to stick into the log. He finally had it in pieces on his sixth try.

He didn't remember falling asleep. He could hear the crickets. *Outside.* He knew that. He felt pain. His head rested on a log. The pain HURT, but not enough to wake him up. He felt a hand on his shoulder. He brushed it off. *Sleep, I must have sleep.*

ASLEEP?

He opened his eyes and saw his father. Panicked, he started apologizing, but his father shushed him and said, "Finished."

"Not even close," Tibs muttered, trying to figure out if more sleep would be a better option. He managed to open his eyes. To his surprise, the logs were cut. One unchopped log lay on the stump. His pillow. The rest waited for winter. "What happened?" He said that out loud. He didn't know what had happened. Had he chopped in his sleep? He had been chopping in his dream; he knew that.

"I know you didn't let Gabe help." Tibs's father picked up his son, the advantage of being a runt; your father could still carry you home. His father probably had strength to lift any of the men in town, but not with the care he now showed his son.

"You'd never be able to carry Lord Telford," he muttered to his father, laughing to himself.

"You'd be surprised," Sir Jesse sighed.

In his father's arms, Tibs felt light and warm.

His father started walking to the house, and then began the lecture. "What you did for Gabe in standing up to MacGregor was a noble deed, worthy of your mother's memory," his father began. "You are so like her, and our blood runs strong through you. I was so proud. What you did to Gabe afterward, that took away any of the honor you might have earned from the first deed. We are free men, Tibs. Gabe is a free man. We fight for our land, our families. We fight so we can plant and feast and sometimes starve. We don't make others our slaves, even if they are willing. You'll run into all sorts of men in this world, men who enslave others, sometimes through force, sometimes through devotion, and you have to be ready to resist the easy path in order to take the right path."

They were already at house. His father walked up the stone stairs to the upper floor and his room. "Gabe just wants to be one of the boys. Don't take advantage of that. That's not the kind of men we are. That's not the kind of man I want you to be."

Tibs was asleep when his father put him in the bed. His father laughed. "Probably my best speech as a father, and you slept through it." Tibs hadn't, really. From his dreams, his memories, this moment was to be one of his best. He would need it when he grew older.

Who had finished the chopping?

Tibs's father never admitted to finishing it, nor did his friends. Another mystery to be solved.

The days of summer passed, sometimes slowly, often fast, and keeping them was like trying to hold water in your fist—it always managed to escape. Tibs studied hard and looked for signs of the vanishing house. He wished he had better observed the field where the house appeared. Did the wheat bend? Did the leaves bounce off the house? There must have been some sign of the house. All he knew for certain was that he would see the house again. He could feel it in his bones. That's what his father would say. He didn't know what that meant for certain, but he knew he would see the house again.

Then came a rare week. Tibs had no extra chores, and few regular ones. The food grew, the days lengthened, and he had time to do what he liked. An untimely chill drove the flies into hiding, yet the cold didn't turn the children away from the trees, which had to be climbed, nor the grass, which had to be trampled. A glorious summer day which only came along once in a lifetime.

Tibs could only look out at the day. He studied in Nathan's classroom. Only the fact that he didn't know how gloriously wonderful the day outside became gave him comfort. Since Nathan's classroom had no windows, he pretended the weather pounded the walls and the trees making everyone miserable.

"I could use a little more sunlight here," Tibs would hint to Nathan. Maybe he would let them out early.

Nathan would snap his fingers. "Of course!" And five candles would appear on the table in front of Tibs. Nathan thought this funny. Tibs didn't.

Sylas stared at Tibs.

The two boys' eyes met, and Sylas said silently, mouthing loudly, "Dead. You. Dead, dead. Soon." Then they both glanced at Nathan. This wasn't new. He'd been saying that for days. They waged their war as hard as ever as Tibs discovered a recipe for itching powder using a weed that grew all over the forest. He found it while reading. Who knew reading could help in waging a secret war? I am not at liberty to reveal where the powder went, but it is enough to understand that that one incident gave Sylas incentive to take the war to another level.

Nathan poured over a scroll and then burst out laughing. "His shoes just kept..." He slowly looked around the table at the children. "You had to be there." Nathan stood up, hitting Sylas and Tibs on the heads. "Don't protest," Nathan said loudly when they were about to complain. "You know what you did."

Nathan cleared his throat and began to teach. "Brig'adel is a minor city in a minor fief in a minor kingdom on a minor island filled with conflict and clueless people. And believe me when I say I wish I was one of them."

History? You're interrupting my research with history? Tibs sighed, perhaps too loudly.

"Boring you already, Tibs? Please don't get bored for another three minutes. Our little city has only two roads of any significance, the one that runs along the river from the mountains to the seas, and the one that runs through and over the river. It's muddy in the rain and frozen in the winter and I've never seen any dust, but lots of dirt. Who can tell me why Brig'adel is important?"

Gabe raised his hand and Nathan pointed to the young boy. "The bridge is the only way c-c-across the river."

"Of course, Lord Telford charges people to cross the river and that gives him some income."

Nathan paused just long enough for Tibs to express his feelings. "Why do we have to know this?"

"So people take less advantage of your ignorance," Nathan stressed.

"If Sylas is going to protect his ignorance, he'll need a larger castle." It just came out of Tibs's mouth before he could stop it. The twins glared. Nathan looked down his nose at Tibs.

"That kind of talk isn't helpful, master Tibs." Nathan sighed. "You'll stay after class for an hour." That made Sylas and the twins laugh. "I see you three are bucking to join him."

"No, no, not us," Sylas said as he shushed his companions.

"Knowledge is power. More power than the bridge."

"You mean the castle," Tibs challenged Nathan.

"If you like. The castle and the bridge are one and the same. They've been building that bridge for four centuries. It's the largest one in the eleven kingdoms."

"Why are they called the kingdoms when there is no king?" Toraline asked.

Nathan clapped. "What an excellent question! We have no king because we don't want. We've had them in the past, and the kingdoms fight between themselves each claiming to rule the others, but no one wants to be nice to the others long enough to really have a king. A king comes with some burdens. They have to have an army, they have to have castles and a navy. All that costs money and food and many of us would have to sacrifice some comfort to have a king. I suppose when the kingdoms really need a king, one will find us. Until then we will fight with each other."

Sylas didn't use any sound as he mouthed to Tibs, "You, murdered, by me."

Tibs cocked his head as if he hadn't heard right and repeated, "You, a numbered monkey?"

Sylas shook his head and repeated.

"A slender room key?"

Sylas pounded his fist into his palm and pointed at Tibs, as if this would solve the communication problem.

"How does grinding flour help with you being a monkey?"

Nathan continued to drill the children on history all afternoon. Sylas and Tibs heard hardly a word.

Nathan stressed history's importance. If history is important, the pair would have no chance for survival.

The school day ended, and Tibs got up to leave with the others. "Oh, no, you're staying here," Nathan reminded him. Without any good nature at all, Tibs moaned pathetically and sat in his chair, slumping down as far as he could. This gave Sylas the opportunity to snap him on the head on his way out. The twins laughed, and so did Toraline. Tibs glared at her for joining the enemy, but she only shrugged, adding, "It's funny."

"Now then, what are we to do with you?" Nathan smiled at the boy. "Your father has made a point that you are to treat Sylas with respect befitting his station."

"You mean donkey?" Tibs sneered. Tibs had moved from monkey to donkey sometime during the lecture.

"No, no, no." Nathan shook his head. "This won't do." He stopped smiling and stroked his beard. Suddenly his beard started moving, Nathan looked frightened. He reached into the beard and pulled out a live bird, which he took to the window and let go. Then he turned back to Tibs as if nothing had happened. "Sylas will be a lord, one day. Lord Telford wants Sylas's father's good will, and how will that happen if he hates us all because of you?" Nathan didn't look at Tibs as he lectured him. He searched through his scrolls.

"Why do you pretend, Nathan? I know you can wave your hand and get any scroll you want!" Tibs had been observing the old man in close quarters for quite a while.

"Not true, my magic has restrictions as all magic does," Nathan gave a half smile. "My magic has been called one of the least useful kinds of magic ever bestowed upon anyone."

"What kind is it?" *This could be interesting*, Tibs thought.

Nathan waved his hand. A scroll came through the air and smacked the old man right in the head. Tibs laughed. Nathan caught the scroll but did not join in the laugher. Then he caught Tibs's eyes and started laughing after all. "Still, a bee cannot become a lady-bug, even if it has spots." Nathan looked at the scroll. "This isn't even the one I want."

"Which one do you want?"

"If only I knew." Nathan threw the scroll in the air and it traveled right back to its place. "I'm one of the few wizards the Congrey has banned from their university. I accidently created a plague of stink bugs. Among other things. They have no sense of humor." He took another scroll and rolled it across the table to Tibs.

Tibs pulled the scroll close and unrolled it. *Not made of paper.* It felt leathery, just a little brittle. "Old?" He asked?

Nathan nodded.

He scanned the page automatically, looking for the word "house." He could understand about half of the first sentence. It seemed strange, but in the third paragraph, he saw the word. "Is this it?" Tibs asked excitedly.

"Well, that depends on what you think it is," Nathan said vaguely.

"I swear I'm going to kill you if you don't just come out and tell me!" Tibs tried his best to read the words written in the scroll.

"Tibs," Nathan's smile left his face, "research doesn't often hand you what you're looking for. Sometimes it takes several scrolls, histories, and other things that give you clues, and then when you put them together they give you an answer. I can't be sure, but this may be one of the pieces of the puzzle—that is, it may be about the house you saw." Nathan pointed at the scroll. "It describes here a house appearing one day in the middle of Dorland and disappearing about sixteen hours later. It could only be seen when someone stood on the front porch. They sent for a witch in area to tell them what it was, but it vanished before she could get there." That was almost the same thing that had happened to Tibs. Nathan didn't stop. "I think the house appears in different places on different days. Moving the house isn't a great feat of magic, but moving it so often, and keeping it invisible takes real power. More than a dozen wizards, two dozen even. And then there's the scroll."

"What about it?" Tibs touched it again. It almost felt like skin.

"It's old, beyond old. Five hundred years, at least. I think the house moves through time as well as space. Did the house seem that?"

Tibs shook his head.

"I'll take that as a 'no.' The magic for that, I would have said it was impossible before I saw this." Nathan clapped his hands. "All this points to a group of magi working together. No one person could have that much power."

"What about the Black Heart?" Tibs said it as a joke. He tried to laugh, but Nathan didn't laugh. He looked serious.

"I have wondered." Then he stuck out his tongue and ruffled Tibs's hair.

"What good is this, then, if it talks about a house that may or may not be the one I saw? How can that help us?"

"First, it tells us we're not crazy. Well, you're not crazy, and you're not lying. It also means that others are looking for the house." Nathan stopped for a moment, thinking.

Tibs understood. "We have to find it before they do."

"I think, my boy, that I may have to make a trip to the Congrey." He tapped his nose.

"You said they'd never let you in," Tibs did remember some things people told him, despite what his father told everyone.

"And you'll have to come with me," Nathan said.

A trip? Tibs had never even left his village before. "My father would never let me go."

Nathan said sadly. "We need their library. As soon as we tell them what we're doing, they'll want to take the house for themselves." He stretched his back. "We can't have that. They have too much magic already. There must be a way." With that Nathan took the scroll from Tibs and propelled the student out of his house, slamming the door behind him.

And what did Tibs think after this conversation, in which he learned about magic, about politics, about world-shaking changes? He thought about how the old fool of a teacher hadn't kept him after school as long as he threatened and hadn't punished him at all. Tibs took off through the woods as fast as he could before Nathan could remember the punishment.

Pidwell fixed all that joy.

A vine rose up and tangled his legs. He fell flat on his face and heard the little imp laughing. "If I ever catch you, you, you, you..." Tibs hit himself on the head for not coming up with a great insult.

Pidwell laughed and spun away through the woods.

Tibs stopped. No thorn arrows. No taunts or comments. Pidwell just flying off into the tree without saying anything? Frightening. From experience, Tibs felt something more would be coming, and he proceeded a little more cautiously.

Tibs studied the woods, looking for something out of place. He could hear the leaves rustling as the breeze flew through the woods. The branches swayed back and forth in rhythm with the earth. The birds flew around as if on a normal day. At the base of an oak he saw a small face. In the distance he could hear the river sputtering. A deer sprinted through the bush in the distance.

Wait. A small face? He looked back at the oak. The bearded man gasped, jerking his face behind the tree. Wee folk. First the imps, and now the wee folk watching him. He turned away from where he saw the face and started whistling. He walked a few paces this way and that, not going in particular direction, before he leapt toward the base of a big tree, the leprechaun firmly in his hands.

"Well, what do you want you big lummox?" The bearded face turned red with anger.

"What do I want? Why are you watching me?" Tibs said.

"Why in the all the woods of the world would I be watching a great big git like you?" Surprise filled the leprechaun's face. "All that's going to happen is a little boy getting a thumping from an army of wee folk."

The little man pushed and pulled, trying to get out of Tibs's hands, but Tibs kept his grip.

"Hands off! Depart! Heave off!" The little green man twisted but finally gave up.

"Why are you watching me?" Tibs asked.

"I've orders, I've orders!" the leprechaun finally said.

"From who?"

"The king, if you must be knowing, like I would take orders from any other." He looked sheepishly into Tibs's eyes.

"The king of the leprechauns? Why would the king take any interest in me?"

"Because you're eleven, if you must be knowing." He said as if that explained everything.

"What does that have to do with anything?" Tibs said.

The little man wheezed and coughed and sputtered as if Tibs should have known exactly what was going on. "Eleven, and you still spy Pidwell and the imps."

"And you," Tibs added.

"Worse and more so!" The leprechaun battered him with his fists.

"I've always seen you," Tibs explained.

"Fooling me won't help you. You know all your friends stopped seeing us years ago, but you keep seeing on like it was the most natural thing in the world and not really knowing it is evil, evil, evil!" With that he tried to escape again, but Tibs was too quick.

"No you don't." Tibs would not let him get away.

"Yes, yes, yes." The leprechaun struggled, this way and that, before he finally gave up again. "Yes, I don't." And he folded his arms once again. Then he looked at Tibs out of the corner of one of his eyes. "You did be seeing me, for true and no malarkey?" he said.

Tibs nodded.

His shoulders sagged with sadness. "We're protected from the big folks by our magic, but if you see us, maybe the magic is wearing off, and what will we do then?" His eyes started tearing up. "Where will we go where you humans can see us? Who will protect us?"

Tibs put the man down and sat at the base of the oak. "I hadn't thought of that."

The despondent leprechaun forgot to run away and sat down beside the boy. "You hadn't? You mean you're not a-doing it on purpose?"

"Purpose? How could I do it on purpose? I'm eleven!" Tibs sat down and pulled up a piece of grass, sticking it into his mouth.

"There's a hole in your argument as big as the world, but I'll accept it for the moment." The leprechaun stood up and brushed himself off. "As soon as I stop thinking about it, I'll see it." He nodded to the boy, as if that said it all. Then the leprechaun, master of camouflage, turned around and scurried through the wood, disappearing into the underbrush.

Tibs got up and started walking toward home, making for the road. They had been waiting for him. Not the imps, nor the wee folk, but Sy and the twins. Three horses thundered down the road, and in a moment Tibs found himself trussed in a blanket and tied it up. Then they dragged him through the dirt. Their great revenge had come.

CHAPTER 9

Sometimes great days are terrible days in disguise. You see, it's often through trouble and despair that people resolve to change something, and one little change in one person can change the whole world—

—FROM SENNACHERIB MACCAULEY'S *HISTORIES OF THE ELEVEN KINGDOMS*

HE COULDN'T SEE, wrapped in the blanket, his body dragged through the forest. He could feel himself bouncing off tree roots and rocks and hitting tree trunks as they moved in some direction or another. He lost count of his bruises in less than two minutes.

The dragging stopped.

He could hear the boys dismount from their horses, laughing. They pulled him out of the blanket. He blinked in the sun.

They wore masks, a wolf and two lions, but he knew them. They grabbed his arms and dragged him into a sort of hole dug in the forest. It smelled, and steamed. In he went. At first he thought they might be tarring and feathering him, but tar didn't smell like this. Black tar burned, this didn't, and it looked brown. Tar could kill people on its own. It blocked the pores in the skin, and people died of suffocation.

The twins didn't let go of his arms. He tried to pull them in, but they each had at least thirty pounds of body weight on him. They hardly budged and his struggles only made them laugh harder. The other boy,

Sy, or the one he assumed was Sy, forced his head under the surface of the muck. He barely had time to get a breath. Sy just held him there. His lungs started burning. His chest heaved, but he concentrated on keeping his mouth and nose closed. He convulsed and began to panic, thrashing so hard that the twins let go. He got his head above the muck, his whole body covered with slime. His ears rung as they pulled him out and covered him with feathers. Not tar and feathering, but close.

He pushed himself up onto his arms and started laughing.

"What's so funny?" one of them asked.

Tibs pulled the stuff away from his nose and eyes. He didn't dare open his eyes yet. Still laughing, he said, "You're dressing me as a chicken, and you're wearing masks! You're the ones who are afraid."

One of them slapped his face, hard. A chunk of the muck flew off his face making it easier to breathe.

Then they mounted their horses and disappeared.

The mud dried quickly. He tried to brush it off, but that only moved the feathers from one part of body to another. He forced himself to his feet. He weighed an additional forty pounds, at least. He dragged one foot forward. He couldn't lift his leg. Then he dragged the other leg. He dared open his eyes. Nathan's cabin must be nearby, but his best help would come if he walked home. Fewer people would see him that way.

He saw Pidwell hovering. "Some help you were." He spat at the imp.

"What could I do?" Pidwell laughed and spun off into the forest.

Tibs dragged another leg forward. Behind a tree he saw the face of a leprechaun. The same one he'd caught watching before.

"And you, you could have done something," he yelled at the wee little man.

The man, surprisingly, came out from behind the tree. "And what could I have done, I'm begging to know?"

"Anything!" Tibs sighed, dragging another leg forward. He couldn't bend his knees anymore. He'd be stuck like a statue if he didn't hurry.

"We don't rightly interfere into the affairs of big folk." The leprechaun apologized.

"Did you ever think that the fact that I'm small for a big folk and can see you means I'm one of you!" Tibs screamed.

The leprechaun took a step backward so swiftly that his hat fell off. He bent over to pick it up, and as he reached down, he kicked his hat down a hill. He stepped to catch his hat and fell down the hill. At the bottom he looked this way and that for his hat, not realizing he was sitting on it.

Despite himself, Tibs laughed. Then he turned his nose toward home and started dragging himself through the woods. He wondered if he wouldn't be better falling down a hill. *Maybe this stuff will be knocked off as a roll...No, if it doesn't work, I'll never get to my feet again.* Better not risk it.

At the manor house, his father exercised, slicing the air with his two-handed broadsword, for which he needed only one hand. Tibs appeared near the gate of the courtyard. What would you have thought seeing Tibs? A giant chicken attacking the manor? No, clearly this figure staggering down the road appeared human. The only explanation of a figure like this walking down the road had to do with tar and feathering. Tibs saw his father's puzzled face. Tibs didn't know if that was good or bad. And then his father screamed and came running at him. He saw his father draw the sword over his head. Tibs thought he would die, his head chopped off by his own father.

Tibs did what any ten-year-old would have done. He fell down. He would have put his arms over his face, but he couldn't move them. He did manage to repeat, "It's not my fault, it's not my fault."

He saw his father's sweaty face, a day's stubble on his chin. Sir Jesse's face shaking with anger. His father started beating on the sides, the legs, the arms and the head with his open palms. Tibs thought he was being attacked. "It's me, Dad, Tibs, it's me!"

Then he heard what his father sputtering. "Who did this, who did this?"

He looked up into his father's eyes.

"I, I—" he stammered. He hadn't expected his father to say that. Then he understood—"Dad, it's not tar. It's not TAR!" Tibs had to yell to get his father to listen. Sir Jesse went silent. He examined his hands. The stuff flaked off. Not tar.

"What happened?" Tibs's father demanded.

Tibs shook his head. "Don't ask."

"You're all right?" Sir Jesse prodded his encased son with his finger.

"No, I'm not all right, I'm stuck!" Tibs complained.

Then it started, like a trickle of water in a dead river bed. A giggle. Then his father snickered. Sir Jesse tried to cover his mouth but got feathers in his teeth. This made him laugh louder. With the giggles coming, he couldn't hold back the torrent of laughter welling from inside his lungs. It bubbled out of him, and then rumbled, and then cascaded out of him like a river. Sir Jesse fell over laughing on the ground next to his son.

"Stop it!" Tibs wanted nothing more than to kick his father as hard as he could in the shins, but he couldn't get up. Despite himself, he found himself laughing. Desperately, through his teeth, Tibs gasped. "It's not funny!"

His father struggled to his feet. He picked his son up as if he weighed no more than a loaf of bread, and still laughing, said, "Let's get you cleaned up."

Without any guidance, his father could only take him to the well. Maybe water would take the stuff off. He got a bucket and poured it over his son. Nothing.

Then Tibs saw Nathan.

Tibs's spirit lifted, and he yelled, "Can you get this stuff off?"

"It's alive!" Nathan covered his head in mock horror. "I came to get you. You were supposed to stay late after school, and I forgot." He examined the coating and the feathers. He poured water over the mess and watched it for a moment. "Nothing."

Nathan next tried to melt it with a candle, but that set the mud and feathers on fire. If they hadn't been right next the well, they would have been in trouble. "This is actually quite amazing," Nathan remarked. "Still caught fire when wet."

That was reassuring?

Then they went to the river. They plunged the boy into the water and waited. After twenty minutes, the coating peeled off very neatly, as good as an artist's mold.

"Is it magic?" Tibs asked.

"It's glue I would guess, I'm not really an alchemist," Nathan concluded, as he peeled off the last of it. "Not magic. They just changed the color. Or tried to. Maybe they wanted it to look like tar. Pretty ingenious."

Tibs's skin, now stained with brown stripes, had no hair and he looked like a raccoon's tail.

Before he could even gather his thoughts, his father cleared his throat and looked his son in the eyes. "Son, I'm going to ask you to do something that's going to be very difficult. But if you can do it, it will make you very powerful."

Powerful? That got Tibs's attention right away. "What?" he asked quietly. His father rarely spoke like this, and when he did he imparted some trick move.

"I'm going to ask you to do nothing to Sylas in return."

"What?" Tib clenched his fist shouting at his father.

"Hear me out, son." Nathan went back to scrubbing, trying to get the dye out of Tibs's skin while Sir Jesse continued to persuade. "I want you to try it my way for one week. I want you to do nothing. The next time you see Sylas and the Twins, I want you to look at them as though you were expecting them. Then slowly and deliberately cross your arms and smile. Stand there and do nothing."

"Father!" Tibs thought his father was making fun of him.

"Son. When an enemy is expecting a fight, they plan for it. They wait for it. They remain ready for the attack. Your job is to keep them in readiness. They lose sleep. When you appear, they tense up, they expect the attack, and none comes. This keeps them on the defensive, and you've wasted no effort. To everyone else, you look like the bigger man. And the waiting, the continual waiting for the attack, is the revenge. In the back of their minds, they always think the attack is coming. I know this will work especially well with Sylas."

"How do you know that?" Tibs asked.

"I know his father," his father smiled knowingly. "Try this for one week, that's all I ask, son."

Tibs thought about this for a moment. He could give his father one week. It would take at least two to think of a suitable retaliation. And this time he would have to be creative. *It might even be fun*, he thought. He nodded. "I didn't say Sylas did this," he told his father.

"I have no knowledge of Sylas doing anything." Sir Jesse winked. Tibs would wait for one week and then talk to his father before doing something else.

Tibs slept roughly, because his raw skin woke him. Nathan had tried to scrape the dye off using rocks in the stream. That didn't work. That REALLY didn't work. Still, it took him practically no time at all to fall asleep, and he felt fine when he woke up.

He had finished his chores and breakfast when he heard the bells. Tibs pulled on his tunic and rushed outside. His father, already in his armor, hauled out a double ax. "Fris."

"Here?"

"Get your head on, Tibs, it's only a few dozen, but they're hungry."

Tibs held on to Fibber's harness while his father mounted. "Do they have long handled axes or just the short."

"I'll tell you when I know. Shield."

Tibs picked up a shield to hand to his father.

"Do your job." Sir Jesse took the shield and readied his sword for battle.

"How do you know it's the Fris, couldn't it be Cimbris?" Tibs put a stool by the chair as if to make small stairs.

"Tibs, get the villagers into the castle! Do your job!" The knight pressed his knees and the horse tore down the road from stillness to full gallop in two or three steps. Sir Jesse didn't look back. He had no time to see if Tibs would do his job. He had to get into action to repel the war party come to take advantage of the sleepy village. If all went well, the barbaric Fris would be a small inconvenience.

Tibs knew he should be running for the castle, but he'd never seen a Fris before. All his life he had heard about them, and the Cambris and the Ruskas, but they rarely came this far inland. Last year when a group of six approached the village, the children waited in the castle till the knights drove them away. He begged for a job in the hopes he'd see battle. His father made him the head counter. He counted the heads as they went into the castle, to make sure no one was left in the fields. Not the job he hoped for, but still as a boy with an official job, no one would look for him if he went to the castle by way of village, and then he could see some of the excitement.

He ran out of the manor house toward the village. People ran toward the safety of the castle. He didn't see their faces. That didn't matter. Only the total number mattered. If his number matched the number of villagers, safety. If not, then they tried to find out the names of the missing. The names would tell them the likely spot they would be during the day, the village, the fields, the forest, the manor, and they would begin looking for them. He didn't count them.

Hearing the bells put all thoughts of his job out of his mind. He wanted to see the Fris. *How does he know who's attacking?* Tibs assumed his father could be wrong about such things, a Lord could place implicit trust in Sir Jesse, but Sir Jesse's son had to have proof.

As he ran toward the village he thought of what he would say if he saw his father. *I'm looking for villagers.* That didn't feel right. He passed villagers making their way to the castle as he ran toward the village. *My best bet is just to be fast.* He sprinted faster toward the town square. More than likely, the Fris would be looking for food and they'd be at the barns. Still he could get lucky. He planned on looking inside the houses around the village. That way if his father caught him he could claim confusion about his job.

As Tibs ran toward the village he didn't understand that now he had to be found, and that someone would have to be sent to find him, and when the head counter is missing, where does one look for him or her?

The houses melded together as he sprinted past them. He made the motions of looking inside, as if he had some concern about the occupants, but his eyes were on the street, looking for warriors. Anyone in the village would have heard the bells and made their way to the castle. The missing would be in the fields.

In any case, he never got further than the town square. He ran down the middle of the street and ran smack dab into a wall. *Wall?* His eyes focused down the street he didn't see the house. He looked up, his trousers soaking in the soggy street. *What an idiot, running into a house!* He hoped no one had seen him when he looked at the house. *House? This wasn't there yesterday.* Suddenly his wet posterior and bumpy forehead where the last things on his mind. He only thought—*I've found the house.*

CHAPTER 10

Not all fights are wars and not all wars are fights—

—FROM SENNACHERIB MACCAULEY'S *COMPENDIUM ON ARMOR AND WEAPONS OF THE PREVIOUS WARS*

TOO STUNNED TO do anything else, he sat there. He reached out and touched the house. His hand felt the gnarled logs woven together to make the wall of the house.

THE HOUSE.

Tibs had no time to tell anyone. The lure of the house outweighed any sense of responsibility he might have had. He didn't count villagers, nor did he clear out houses in the village. Instead, his jaw slack, his eyes vacant, he gazed at the house. It took up all his thoughts, all his vision, all his senses. Even still, he never would have seen the Fris running down the street, the invisible house which he could see prevented him from seeing the warrior, but the warrior could see him fine, it was the house he didn't see.

The Fris was draped in animal skins, except for the shiny iron cap with four horns sticking out of it. You might imagine warriors as hard men and women, scarred with battle blows and skin hardened and baked in the harsh sun. The Fris laughed at such ideas. They tried to look their best in battles. This one braided his long auburn hair and decorated his beard with bows for the battle. He might have been handsome if he had had all his teeth. Years of pumping oars at sea, of throwing axes and hammers, chiseled his body into perfection, but his smile made most women recoil as if from a bear. He spun two axes, one in each hand and laughed quietly to himself. He could hit a bee at a hundred paces, this boy in the village would be no problem.

His eyes measured the distance between his ax and Tibs. The boy loped down the street, ran into something and sprawled on the street. Then the boy stood and groped the air. Strange behavior, but then the Fris's rage and thirst for battle didn't demand his prey be smart or sane. He charged as quietly as he could.

Tibs didn't see the Fris salivate at the thought of killing a red-haired boy. He couldn't see the man stroke his beard with his wrist, or rush toward the boy to chop him with both axes.

"Oomph!" The raider's lungs expelled all the air in them. Tibs couldn't see the raider, but he could hear him. He just didn't understand what he had heard. *A bag of potatoes being dropped? No, that's not right.* He looked around and saw nothing. He approached the house. He knew touching the runes would send it away, but the porch seemed safe, and from there he could examine the boards in more detail, and maybe find a way inside. *Still*, he thought, *better get a good luck at them from here before getting on the porch just in case it disappears again when I step up there.*

The stunned Fris groped for his fallen helmet to cover his balding head. His long tresses only circled the rocky peak. He pulled on his helmet and looked for the boy. To his surprise, the boy hardly moved. He smiled. He could still smite him. He pulled his arm back and let the ax fly! A second and a half later, the ax bounced off something, and it hit the barbarian in the head, sending him to the ground again.

At this point three more Fris came running down the street. Their saw a fallen comrade and a standing boy. They screamed and charged at the boy.

Tibs heard screams, but glancing to his right and left, couldn't tell from where they came. *I don't see any Fris*, then he heard more falling potato sacks.

As the first warrior stood, leaving his helmet on the ground, the others sat on the ground and spat.

"Magic!" One of them hissed. In seconds the three latecomers ran out of the village, back to the river, to go back to their boat and to row back to the safe ocean where storms, monsters and pirates assaulted them with natural weapons of rain, teeth and swords. They would not fight magic. Still, one remained.

He picked up an ax. One ax, one boy. He didn't bother with headgear; he wouldn't need it with this bit of carrot, but now he took precautions. He moved forward, his left hand ready in front of him. His ax bounced off something. Then he touched the house and it appeared to him. When the ax had hit the house after he threw it, the house only revealed itself to the ax. When he had run into the house with his head, his eyes weren't working right because of the unexpected pain. Now he understood. A house kept him from the boy. He would quickly kill the boy and investigate the house afterward. Magic didn't scare him.

The Fris reached out and skimmed the house with his hand, running around it. He didn't scream or yell, he'd do that when he saw the boy, but he did laugh. A wild laugh, coming out with his breath and spilling through his nose. His mind filled with thoughts of blood and death, moments to relish for a seasoned warrior like himself.

Tibs heard laughter. *That's not right*, he thought to himself. He didn't want anyone from the village to see him, they might report him to his father. He walked around the house.

When the Fris rounded the corner of the house, he expected to see the boy. He found an empty street. He stopped for a second, letting go of the house. Then he saw Tibs and belted out his war cry, rushing right at Tibs, again, forgetting about the house.

Tibs heard the cry. *Oomph's, falling potato sacks, war cries. I'm in trouble.* Good sense demanded he run, so he sprinted down the street, as it happened, the direction he chose took him away from the marauder.

The Fris stood. He touched the house again, and ran around it. His prey would not escape. He laughed when Tibs came into sight, and now no house could save the boy.

Tibs heard the laugh and took a chance, he turned his head to see the warrior. The Fris had more muscles than he had hoped. Tibs tried to run faster, but he ran into his old nemesis, mud. It seemed that no matter where he wanted to go, mud plagued him. He slipped and fell flat on his face. He flipped from his stomach to his back like a sea bass. No savior stood between the boy and death. He thought about the things he should and shouldn't have done. *I should have gone to the castle, I shouldn't have stopped to look at the house. I should have brought some sort of weapon. I wish I wasn't lying in mud.* All his wishing helped him not.

An understanding played in the air between the warrior and the boy. The man nodded and smiled. Tibs grimaced at the sight of the smile. *I'm about to die and I'm thinking about his teeth.* The Fris wasn't offended.

Twenty paces separated them. Tibs heart beat faster. His mind raced, but running wouldn't help. The Fris sent the ax at the boy.

If this were another moment in time, or if he weren't facing death, Tibs might have marveled at the skill with which the Fris threw his ax. It spun in the air so fast it looked like a colorful fan. As it arced through the air toward Tibs's head, he found it hard to appreciate the Fris's skill. Out of instinct, Tibs brushed the air in front of him, like shooing a fly. He didn't use his hand, he used his mind, like playing a game with his imagination. What else did he have left to him? The ax hadn't reached him yet, but it moved in a new direction, hit the invisible house, and fell to the ground.

I don't know who felt more surprise, the seasoned warrior of a hundred battles, or the ten-year-old boy seeing his first combat. Tibs realized he had "felt" the ax flying through the air. Somewhere deep inside him he reached out and pushed the ax as if he were touching it, and it moved right where he wanted. He reached out again. He felt it on the ground. He lifted it with his mind. The ax floated in the air in front of him. He looked at the barbarian. "I think this is yours," Tibs said as he sent the ax toward the raider.

At this moment, the house disappeared. Well, it was always invisible, but now it vanished. It didn't leave without announcing itself. The boom hit both the raider and the boy so hard, it knocked them both over.

The ax fell at the barbarian's feet. Both boy and barbarian looked at the weapon. Whatever Tibs had felt before had now evaporated. He couldn't even feel the ax anymore. It had fallen at the warrior's feet, too far to grab with his actual hands, not that that really mattered. He had the feeling the warrior might have let him hack at him with the ax before killing him. The raider picked up the ax, turned it over in his hand, looked at Tibs, and stood over him. He aimed to cleave Tibs in half. He gripped that weapon tightly in his fist, the boy would not get the better of him, even if he had magic in him. He stood over Tibs, screaming, pulling his arm back, aiming at the boy's head.

Tibs couldn't move. He closed his eyes and prepared himself for the afterlife. Suddenly he heard a dull ringing, like a bell full of blankets. He could feel blood dripping on his face. It didn't hurt. He opened his eyes, waiting for a second blow.

CHAPTER 11

*The best diplomacy isn't done by diplomats, It is done by
the person who when told, this can't be done, decides to do it
anyway—*

—FROM SENNACHERIB MACCAULEY'S *CONTINENTAL
DIPLOMACY IN THE YEARS OF THE KHAN.*

THE RAIDER STOOD above him, smiling. The ax drilled Tibs's stomach. He felt the blood on his face and clutched his stomach. Then he realized he didn't feel much pain. He opened his eyes and stared at his attacker. The warrior smiled, and his tongue lolled out of his mouth like a worm in the grass.

He pushed the ax off his stomach. The Fris hadn't so much cleaved him as dropped the ax on him. It didn't even hurt. Tibs's wondered about his bloodied face, *Is this blood mine?* Then the warrior's eyes rolled back into his head and he crumpled onto Tibs's legs. The blood on Tibs's face dripped from the raider's shiny dome. For a moment Tibs thought the Fris had cleaved his own head, but that changed when he saw Nathan's smiling face behind the crumpled fighter.

Nathan waved a cooking pot, shrugging, "I was using it as a hat, and it occurred to me you might not want to be dead."

Tibs struggled to push the raider off his legs. "Did you see it?" he asked his teacher.

Nathan nodded. "Yes, yes, you did that with your mind?"

Tibs shook his head. "Did you see the house?"

"The house?" Nathan looked around, "No, I saw what you did with the ax." He pushed the Fris off Tibs's legs.

Tibs stood up and brushed himself off. He stepped to the place where he had felt the house. Gone.

"With the ax," Nathan prompted.

"No, no, the house..." Tibs kicked the dirt where the house had stood. He didn't think about the ax, the house filled his imagination. The ax happened. That moment lost in his head, the obsession still remained, still haunted him, the house. *How did it get here? Why today? Why does it leave, we didn't touch the boards, what made it disappear?* "It stood right here," he said. Tibs kicked the dirt where the house had stood.

Nathan shook his head. "What are you talking about?"

"The house, it was right here." Tibs felt the air for it.

"The house?" Nathan followed the boy. "It was right here?" He felt the air. Then turned to Tibs. "Don't tell anyone what I'm doing." He shook both hands, put them up to his eyes for a moment and hummed. Tibs felt an electricity in the air. The old man reached out with his hands, feeling the air that once contained the house, then stood as still as a statue for a moment. Nathan closed his eyes. His face darkened. He opened his eyes and they lost all color. They were completely white, nothing at all but a brightness. "I feel it. It's old, and it's young. It's here, and it's there. It grows deeper and lighter. It will be contained, it will be lost. The wheels are broken, my plans torn asunder. He will not win. He will be broken, he will be destroyed by the might of a thousand armies..."

Nathan slowly shook his head and his eyes returned to normal. "It's getting harder and harder to do that. Just not as funny as when I was younger." He looked at the boy. "What do you think?"

Tibs pulled in his tongue and shrugged.

"That's pretty funny. But not as big as I hoped. That's helps a bit." Nathan rubbed his face and looked around the square, and when he came around again to Tibs, he stopped and stared at the boy. "Tibs. I think the house is looking for you."

Nathan considered the boy for a moment. Which was more important, the boy having magic, or the house hunting for the boy? Best to put both aside and bring in the one person who could provide direction for both the house and the boy. *The world's changed*, Nathan thought to himself. *The boy has magic.*

Later, when Nathan had time to think about the implications, he would realize *Tibs has no aura, and haven't I seen him touch metal a thousand times in his father's kitchen? And he did this all without a wand or crystal, at eleven years old...magic he has, but of a kind I've never seen.*

But now they wandered the street, looking for some sign of the house. "This was the corner?" Nathan stood still in one spot.

"Yes, but it left no marks that it was here." Tibs studied the ground, well, he studied the mud, since it already covered him.

"It left a sign..." Nathan could almost feel it.

Sir Jesse rode up on Fibber. He looked down at the pair. "Do I want to know?"

Nathan shook his head.

Sir Jesse's imposing figure in his armor studied them for a moment. "The Fris have been driven back. Except for this one. They didn't get any crops or coinage, so all we've lost is a day's work." Fibber turned on some unseen command and they galloped toward the castle. Sir Jesse didn't celebrate victories—he endured them. He hated death, even the deaths of his enemies.

Tibs dragged his feet through the dirt as he made his way home, his tired body looking for a place to lie down. He ate alone, as he expected he would. His father drilled his men after a fight. *Best time to teach them how to do better*, he always said. He dragged himself up the stairs and fell down in the bed without undressing. Sleep had been stalking him and caught up to him as soon as he reached his bed.

Something in his dream disturbed him. He and Toraline walked through the woods looking for something they had lost. Something grabbed his shoulder. He pushed it off and started through the woods trying to catch up to the fast disappearing Toraline. It grabbed him again, a clawed hand just over his heart. He screamed and started fighting with it when he woke up.

His father stood over his bed. He could see the stars through his window. "What is it?" The boy rubbed his eyes, his body still sore from dragging shields through the street. Nathan stood behind his father, unsmiling. Tibs stomach turned sour. This was serious if both of them came to wake him in the middle of the night.

Sir Jesse motioned for him boy to follow. Tibs dragged on a cloak to keep out the cold and he staggered after Nathan and his father down the road toward the castle.

"What's going on?" He ventured, but the men said nothing and continued walking.

When they reached the castle gate, Saunders, a scarecrow with a metal hat, and Zips, an upright hippo with a spear, two of Lord Telford's personal guards, flanked the trio as they proceeded into the meeting hall.

The throne room looked bare because the shields had been stripped from the walls for the fighting. They had to be polished and cleaned before being replaced. Their absence made the tall ceiling seem taller and the dais with the five thrones smaller. Tibs could tell from personal experience that these were some of the most uncomfortable chairs in the village. If not for the power they implied, no sane person would ever sit in them. Lord Telford made it a habit to rarely do so.

Sir Jesse moved the tapestries behind the throne to reveal a "secret" door. Tibs knew about the door. Everyone did. But few had ever gone through it. Zips took out a key and dropped it. He bent over and picked it up again, pointing it to the lock, but dropped it again before he could get into it. Saunders roared, "Give me that!" Saunders then bent over to the pick up the key. With his massive stomach, this took effort, but he managed it. He pointed it at the door and then dropped it. They both bent over to pick up the key, bumping their heads together. Since they were both wearing helmets, it made a pleasant "ding," as they made contact.

"For crying out loud!" Sir Jesse barked. He pushed down the handle on the door, and it opened. "It isn't even locked!"

Sir Jesse barreled past Saunders and Zip, followed by Nathan, who pulled Tibs along after him.

Books lined the walls. Nathan's library consisted of scrolls, short writings on paper one rolled up and stacked. There were tomes of paper, hand stitched and encased in leather. The covers gave off a delightful smell. Tibs wondered what wonders these books told. From floor to ceiling, shelves, and each shelf filled with books, thousands. In the midst of this mountain of knowledge sat a desk, struggling under the weight of stacks of paper, vials of ink and a dozen quills scattered about, one of which struggled in Lord Telford's hand, scribbling away on a very large sheet of paper. He didn't appear to know they were there. He sighed, signed a paper and moved to the next underneath. The men arrayed themselves in a semi-circle and waited for him to notice them.

A minute passed. Tibs began to sweat. He had no idea why he had been brought here. He had been in trouble before, but nothing like this. Another minute passed, and Tibs started to shift from foot to foot. Sir Jesse put his hand on his shoulder and Tibs stood straight as a staff.

Lord Telford finally looked up at the five. "So this is the boy?" he asked Nathan.

The boy? Tibs thought, *He knows me, I've seen him often enough. Is this some sort of game?"*

Nathan nodded. "This is him."

Lord Telford stood and looked Tibs over. The Lord scrutinized Tibs's feet, eyes wandering his body to the top of head like he was a cow he was considering buying. Then Telford went behind the boy, presumably doing the same. "I don't believe it."

Nathan agreed, half-heartedly, "I wouldn't myself except..." He shrugged.

"Let's get started." Telford led them to the far corner of the room, where a spiral staircase slithered up.

Tibs knew the tower held prisoners waiting trials or executions. *Which for me?* he wondered. *All this for not counting people?* The only offense he could conceive worth all this trouble centered on not doing his job when the Fris attacked. He beat his brain trying to come up with something better. *Surely, the job wasn't that important,* he lied to himself as he struggled up the stone steps higher and higher. The guards remained in Telford's study. Lord Telford and Nathan ahead of him and his father behind, escape didn't seem to be an option. The steps were solid and smooth, worn down by the footsteps of hundreds of people who had come up the stairs before him, and the few that had returned to the ground again. They felt cold under his feet.

The higher they climbed, the darker it became. There were no conventional windows in the tower, only slits from which archers might send an arrow, but he'd never seen them doing that in his life. The meager light from them made everything more menacing. Nathan waited in front of Tibs, who wanted nothing more than to step backward into the arms of his father, but he didn't dare. A torch burned some ten feet above them as they made for a landing. At the top of the tower a dark heavy oak door, solidly shut, stood guard. Carved with rings and squares, the shadows danced in the light making it look like it breathed. Lord Telford unlocked the door and opened it. It opened silently and the room seemed to breathe on them as they stepped into darkness. It smelled of wet socks.

His father led him to the center of the room and sat him in a chair. Tibs could see nothing in the receding light, no furniture but the chair and a torch stand. He couldn't see the walls or any windows. Lord Telford put the torch into the stand, joining Sir Jesse and Nathan in the darkness leaving Tibs alone in the middle of the room.

He could hear Nathan pacing. He knew his father stood still as a spear. Nathan's footsteps echoed, making the eerie darkness more ominous. The room seemed huge.

Finally, with the silence stretching and stretching, he couldn't stand it anymore. "I'm sorry, I'm sorry!"

Tibs's father appeared next to his son. "Sorry about what, Tibs?"

"For letting the village down. I should have counted at the gate and not gone to the village, it's just, that well, it's so–"

Nathan appeared next to the torch stand, resting his hand upon it. "You think that's why we brought you here?"

Tibs's father scolded Nathan, "Let him confess, let him confess. I don't often have him this afraid of punishment and I could have sweated out a thousand confessions, you old fool!"

Lord Telford stepped up and looked down at Tibs again. "It's not possible." He took his knife and set it on Tibs's hand. "No sparks. This is a waste of my time."

"No, it's not!" Nathan insisted.

Telford angrily sheathed the weapon, and stepped back into the darkness. "Get on with it, then."

They all disappeared again.

All at once the darkness shattered. A row of torches in a straight line in front of him lit. Tibs saw the Fris again, ax in hand. The Fris gave out his war cry and threw the ax at Tibs. Tibs screamed, and as a reflex, he brushed the ax with his mind just as he had earlier that day. The ax spun into the darkness and the torches went dark, except for the one right in front of Tibs.

Tibs panted in fear, but he didn't leave his chair. A hand touched his shoulder. Tibs flinched, looking behind himself to see who touched him. Sir Jesse patted him reassuringly. "It's all right, son, just breathe."

"What happened?" Tibs asked.

"I don't believe it!" Telford came up to Tibs and looked him over again. "How could you have missed it?" Telford reached up and lifted Tibs's chin, looking into the boy's eyes.

"You think I missed it?" He'd never seen Nathan get so angry. "I'm not some novice attempting magic, the boy has no sign."

"Then what's going on?" Telford roared.

Wait a moment, Tibs thought. *What's this about magic?*

"Quiet!" Sir Jesse turned the chair so Tibs could see him. "Nathan created that vision of the Fris for you to see. I threw the ax at you, but it would never have hit you, it would have sailed over your head. We had to try to recreate what happened in the town square to see if what Nathan saw was real, or even if it was you."

116

"It's not real!" Sir Jesse handed Tibs a knife again, this time blade first. Tibs rattled brain didn't pick up that Sir Jesse never handed knives to others like this. One always hands a knife by holding the blade and offering the handle, it's safer. Tibs took the blade.

Nothing happened, and Telford looked confused. "No wizard can handle metal" Telford took the knife from Tibs and examined it. He threw at the wooden torch tower, it stuck there. "Nathan, explain!"

"Telford, the lowest novice from Congrey can see magic in a ten-year-old if it's there. Tibs has no color. And apparently he can touch metal with no effect. The signs of magic are not in him. I missed nothing," Nathan hissed.

"I don't understand," Tibs protested.

"Nathan, show him," Telford ordered.

"He understands," Nathan said simply.

"Nathan!" Telford rebuked the hairy enchanter.

Nathan sighed and walked over to the knife. He closed his eyes and took the handle in his hand. He walked back to Tibs, showing him the knife. "You've seen this before, Tibs." Then Nathan touched the blade. Sparks went in every direction, the knife spun of Nathan's hand, and Nathan fell backward to the ground.

"Magi can't touch metal." Telford's voice menaced. "Why can *you* touch metal?"

"I'm not, I don't, I have no magic." He looked at his father.

Sir Jesse shook his head.

"I'm not a wizard," Tibs said louder.

"No aura, he can touch metal, I've never heard of it." Telford spat.

"Telford, he made the ax move and he has no wand or crystal or anything," Nathan sat up, recovering from touching the metal.

"What's that?" Telford probed.

"Most of us, ah, magi, need something to help us focus our magic, an object through which we do what we do." Nathan stood and came up to Tibs again. He showed Tibs his burned fingers, "You owe me for these." He pulled back his sleeve as the burns crawled up his arm. "Iron hurts, silver can kill. Some wizards can't handle gold or mercury. It's what keeps us humble servants instead of kings."

"Have you tried gold or silver?" Telford puzzled over Tibs.

"Of course," Nathan sighed.

However, Lord Telford reached into a bag around his neck and tossed Tibs two coins. Tibs caught them.

"Is that silver?" Nathan retreated into the darkness. "Telford, I swear I'll forget your nobility unless you get that stuff out of here!"

Looking down at the two coins in his hands, which were obviously doing nothing to his skin or body, Tibs interrupted. "Stop it! I don't have magic. I'm going to be a great knight like my father." He had to be like Sir Jesse. He had to.

Telford glared at Tibs's father. "A magus is worth a hundred knights to a lord, depending on his power." Telford glanced at Nathan. Telford had little regard for Nathan's abilities, but perhaps Tibs could be useful.

Telford took the coins, which had no effect on Tibs and put them away. They surrounded the boy, staring at him, studying him, as if he might change any moment.

"It doesn't make any sense, and yet here he sits," Nathan turned away from Tibs.

Tibs's father whistled. "Sy's domain is nature, what is Tibs's?"

Nathan shrugged. "You think I know? He has no aura, that tells you his domain. Tibs is something I've never seen before. I've never even read about something like this. If he had an aura, I'd know his gift, his strength, and, well, I'd know more. Sy's aura is green, and he controls plants. Brown is usually for animals, gray for stone and minerals, light yellow for the air, blue for light or sometimes water or ice, and hundreds of others. There are men in the Congrey whose sole task is to record colors and powers, trying to understand what it all means."

"What's yours again?" Lord Telford asked matter-of-factly.

"No, no, no, you'll not catch me that easily. And besides, the aura is like a jumping-off point. It shows your strength, where things will be easy. But a gifted one can, ah, expand the skill set, so to speak. Like a knight being good at sword-play can learn to handle an ax without embarrassing himself." Nathan winked at Sir Jesse.

"I'm not going to be a magic-thingy, I'm going to be a knight," Tibs said. The three men turned and stared at him. He realized he might not get a vote in the matter.

"We only know about his powers because of an accident. Most children feel the powers around the same time we see the aura. Tibs doesn't feel his powers." Nathan walked in front of the boy. "Do you, my lad?"

Tibs took this moment to try to set the record straight, "No!"

Nathan squinted at him. "Is that 'no' as in you do feel your powers and disagree with me or 'no' as in you don't feel your powers and agree with me?"

"What?" Tibs asked confused.

Lord Telford barked, "Do you feel your powers, boy!"

"No," Tibs said.

It finally dawned on Tibs what they were all saying. *NO, no! I will be a knight, and then a great general, like my father!* He stole glances at his father's eyes. *I have a mind for it, and my body will grow...* He knew his small and weak body had to change so he could realize his dreams. "Why can't I just be a knight?" he finally asked.

"We have to hide him on testing day." Sir Jesse pulled at his lip.

"Why?" Nathan challenged. "He can touch metal, he has no aura, there's no reason for them to suspect he has magic at all. And if we hide him next year, we have to hide him every year. That never turns out well. Plus, the Congrey know how to track people in their domains, they've been doing it for centuries, you remember how they knew Toraline was the daughter of the blacksmith? They know Sir Jesse too well to forget about Tibs here."

"Nathan is right, those wizards can't be trusted." Telford stamped his feet.

"Present company excepted...?" Nathan gave the Lord a lead.

"We keep him secret, at least for now." Telford was adamant.

"Present company excepted?" Nathan prompted again.

"He needs training." Sir Jesse thought along practical lines.

"At eleven?" Nathan objected.

"He's ten," Sir Jesse corrected.

"Oh, joy." He clapped his hands sarcastically.

"Am I going to get in trouble for the raid?" Tibs asked timidly.

"Of course you are." His father smiled and tussled his son's hair.

Tibs smiled with him for a second. Then he realized that meant he would be showered with punishments. The smile drooped into a frown.

Lord Telford turned toward the boy. "Tibs, you can't tell anyone what we've talked about here today, or about what you can do."

"Just Toraline— " Tibs felt Telford's hand on his face.

"No one." Telford grabbed him by the chin and looked straight in his eyes. "You can't tell anyone what we've discovered here today."

"Because then they will find me." Tibs posited.

"And take you away, and ..." Nathan choked on something and then knelt next to Tibs, "You are not a noble so you have no protection under the law. If they discover you're different, they may want to conduct tests on you, which would mean..." Nathan's voice trailed off in that way that teachers used when they wanted you to finish their sentences.

"I would die?" Tibs finished.

Nathan shook his head. "No, worse, much worse..." Nathan touched a place just below his neck on his shirt. Tibs could see something concealed there under the cloth. "What if..." Nathan pulled something from around his neck. A yellow, squarish stone hung from a tattered leather string, about the size of Nathan's thumb. It glowed, very faintly. "Most magi need a focal point for their magic. A stone, or wood through which we push our magic into the world. You did magic without one. That's very rare. I keep mine hidden because I like people to think I don't need anything to help me with my magic."

Tibs reached out and touched the stone. It grew brighter and whiter. It glowed until it lit the entire room.

The two men looked at Nathan, who quickly stammered. "Well, don't look at me! It's never done that before!"

Tibs pulled his finger back, still looking at the stone. Somehow, he knew he was still connected to it. He could feel it floating as if it was still in his hand. With nudge, he realized he could feel every object in the room. He turned toward the stand and the torch sitting inside it. He thought and they flew into the air. Tibs separated the torch from the stand. He started making the stand attack the torch.

Nathan reached out and took the stone with two fingers. Then he cupped his hands around it.

The stand and torch fell to the ground and the room went dark, as did Tibs's mind.

Lord Telford's breath hissed in the darkness. Tibs couldn't hear his father at all. Nathan giggled.

Tibs didn't like the darkness. With a small part of his mind, he could still feel the torch and stand. The torch, still hot, burned in his mind even if it didn't give light. He nudged it with his mind again, and it flamed into life.

All three men were startled as the light flooded the room.

Nathan pointed at Tibs. "Did you do that?"

"Do what? Do what?" Telford asked.

Tibs nodded.

"He lit the torch." Nathan smiled.

"What does this mean?" Telford asked the wizened magus.

Nathan laughed. "I have no idea! Isn't that wonderful? But he's not supposed to be able to do that."

Telford scowled. "Nathan, you are an idiot."

"I aspire," Nathan sang as Telford stormed out.

As he slammed the door shut behind him, he barked, "Tell that boy of yours if he tells anyone what he can do, I don't care what I have to do, I promise, he'll never see the light of day again!"

CHAPTER 12

Enemies to the left of me, enemies to the right, surrounded by enemies. What could I do? I did what any hero would have done in my circumstance, I invited them in and we all had pie. At the end of the pie, my enemies were vanquished and I was surrounded by friends. Good pie conquers everyone—

—FROM SENNACHERIB MACCAULEY'S *LECTURE ON HIS OWN LIFE*

THEY LED TIBS back down the stairs, through the library and, the throne room to the gate. Morning surprised him. How long had they been in that room?

Tibs looked up at his father.

"I'll discuss your punishment later." His father motioned for him to go.

Tibs ran as fast as he could toward Toraline's house, but then he realized he couldn't tell her anything about what just happened. He slowed down. Maybe he didn't want to tell her. He had no idea if he could really do any of that stuff again. He slowed down to a walk. He imagined her in the smithy. He pictured the fire, and bellows, the hammers and other tools. He reached out with his mind to a bucket outside the blacksmith's shop. Toraline's father had put buckets of water everywhere since the smithy burned. He couldn't feel it. He couldn't feel anything like he had in the room. Whatever had happened in the room, he left it in the room.

Then he noticed he had a headache. A big one. *Perhaps it might be better to go home.*

Then he noticed Sy and the twins on the street.

"What are you doing out here?" Sy sneered.

Tibs stopped. He remembered his agreement with his father. He slowly smiled at Sy and crossed his arms over his chest. "Nothing, nothing at all, just going home." Tibs sauntered down the street toward the manor. He knew that Sy watched him. He took great care to go very slowly. He took a casual glance behind him and noticed that Sy and the twins were very careful about where they walked, looking for a trap.

Maybe my father was right—Tibs thought.

He slept all day.

He slept all night.

When he woke after sleeping almost twenty-four hours, he came down to breakfast and felt like nothing had changed. Had he even done those things in the tower of the castle? Or maybe he dreamed it. Without being told, Tibs started in on the chores and punishment. He moved manure.

After his chores, he made his way to Nathan's school. No one treated him differently. Nathan asked him to stay late to look through scrolls for information about the house. All that practice actually made him a good reader.

The week passed quickly; routine comforted Tibs. Maybe he did dream everything. Maybe he could be like his father, be a knight, a general, serve his king and have people respect and fear him like they did Sir Jesse. Then came a miraculous afternoon. He finished his chores, school ended early, and they had nothing to do.

Tibs found himself laying on a grassy hill with Gabe and Toraline. They looked up at the clouds, bored out of their minds. Bliss.

"Ah, ah, oh, Tibs, ah, never mind—" began Gabe, but he cut himself off.

"Go on," Tibs said, a bit too royally.

"No, no, it's not important." Gabe rarely finished sentences well.

"Don't worry about it, ask whatever you want." Tibs sat up to his elbow and looked at the other boy.

"It's just that..." Gabe muttered. He looked away from Tibs.

Toraline now took an interest. "Tell him! It's not like he's going to hurt you."

"I forgot." Gabe's face surged with a deep, deep red. Gabe blushed better than anyone they knew. "Wait, I remembered!"

They waited for him to speak, instead they heard more silence. Toraline kicked Gabe to get him going.

"Yes, yes, it's about the war. I wonder, you know, if, if, well, if you needed help."

"The war?" Tibs had almost forgotten his private war with Sylas. "Oh, well, I'm doing something even as we speak."

"What?" Toraline seemed unconvinced.

"I'm doing nothing," Tibs laughed.

"He's lost it." Toraline shook her head.

"I don't understand." Gabe astonishment drove his stammer right out of his mouth.

"Look, here's how my father explained it. Whatever I do next, whatever wild thing I do, and believe me, the next move would be so big as to make him think twice about any retaliation, I'd be grounded for a year, right?" The others agreed, dumbly, that is, in silence. And then he said, "What Sy did requires action, so Sy will be on the lookout for my next move, right?" They agreed again. "Since he's looking for something big, for the time being all I have to do is show up in this place or that place and smile at him."

Gabe cocked his head, not yet understanding. "Your revenge is to smile."

"Yes!" Tibs was now quite excited. "Just yesterday he came through the village square and I stepped out on a porch and smiled, watching him walk down the street. It was fantastic. He couldn't take his eyes off me and fell into the horse trough." A horse trough is a big wooden box set out for animals like horses so they can have water when they need it. Plenty big enough to douse Sylas.

"I saw that," Toraline laughed. "He fell in because of you?"

"Yes!" Tibs stood up. "He was looking over his shoulder and didn't see it."

"All you have to do is nothing," Gabe gushed. "It's brilliant."

"Now, I may end up doing something big, but right now, all I have to do is nothing. And it means I get to sleep at night and walk down the street without watching my back. He has to watch all the time, everywhere, because it's my move and he knows it."

"How long do you think you can keep this up?" Toraline said. She stared at Tibs and he looked into her eyes. She knew him, perhaps better than he knew himself.

"I don't...know?" Tibs didn't know, he hadn't thought that far in advance.

Toraline turned away, hiding her face behind her hair. "I'm just sick and tired of having Tibs always doing extra chores."

Tibs laughed and poked her in the side to make her laugh.

"Tibs, the next thing you do is likely to get you in more trouble than we've ever seen. The punishment they give you for that will be bigger than anything we've ever seen. It won't be moving manure or polishing the shields or anything like that. This is a hostage son, they might banish you or worse. And when you're gone what will I do for a best friend?" Tears welled up in her eyes and she ran off.

Tibs looked at Gabe. Gabe shrugged. Tibs had no understanding at all of what had occurred. He told her he was doing nothing and she ran off crying. *Best friend? What just happened?*

CHAPTER 13

How does one put it? It cannot be emphasized too much
that history is nothing more than trying to explain people.
Explaining people is difficult because more often than not, they
behave like people and not neat little boxes in which one puts
a few character traits and nothing else. Trying to explain the
contradictions, the stupidity, the brashness, the pure luck, or
providence is the hardest job an historian can undertake. And
most historians, this writer included, fail.
That's because we too are 'people.'—

—from Sennacherib MacCauley's preface of the
History of the 11 kingdoms, 2ND edition

Tibs' boredom loomed over him like a black cloud in a blue sky. He wanted revenge on Sy in a big way, and didn't want to wait any longer. He couldn't act on his desires without a plan. A good plan. A great plan. None of things he came up with were worthy. They didn't have elegance or enough humiliation.

He couldn't think enough to read, so he stared at Sy contemplating any plan. Sy's mouth moved as he read to himself. Tibs smiled. He read better and everyone knew it. He'd rather be known as a good jouster, or swordsman, but at ten that wouldn't happen. And Sy would never know the joy of battle as a wizard.

Nathan came up behind Tibs, "No, no, that scroll is much too hard for you, Tibs," pulling a scroll out of his hands and replacing it with another. "Try this one. It's much easier."

Tibs glanced at it. He didn't know half the words. *This is easier?*

Sy read something intently. They never discussed between themselves what they read. Tibs wondered what could fill Sy's head with such interest. The history of kings? Magic spells? Tibs had been looking at scrolls on magic, but they didn't help him tap into his power. He spent a couple of hours staring at a rock by the stream trying to get it to move, nothing. He also spent fifteen minutes trying to light a fire in the kitchen, no fire. Whatever happened to him, he left it in that room with Nathan, Lord Telford and his father.

Tibs tried to read his scroll.

...Some wizards use words to focus their spells. Words are not important in making a spell work more effectively, of course, but the words calm the thoughts and focus the energy, so some wizards use them as if they are necessary, and teach they create the magic...

He hadn't tried words to trigger his magic. *Couldn't hurt, I suppose.* Scrolls like this seemed to make everything worse. Magic or no magic, why could Sy do whatever he wanted and say what he wanted to anyone and Tibs had to keep his mouth shut.

...Then there are potions and talismans. Magi infuse the liquids with their own magic, which is then unleashed at a command, or a touch or some other prearranged signal or device. Unlike words, the ingredients of such objects are very important, varying them in the slightest can have catastrophic consequences like destroying a village or building or making everything just vanish. Recipes are passed down in noble families because relatives tend to have similar powers...

Why is Nathan having me read these? Tibs fumed. Reading about all this magic only made him more frustrated. At least he could be reading something related to the house, that would take his mind off his suddenly ruined future. He was to be a knight and now what was he?

...One must never mix potions or allow talismans come into contact with each other. The effect is quite unpredictable. Of course, surprises can be good as well as detrimental. The first flying carpet developed when two talismans came into contact with each other. However, we all remember the three headed, giant dog that plagued the coast for decades, the result of a potion and a talisman combining unpredictably. These "recipes" are highly sought after, especially by the Congrey for the magic hoard...

Flying carpets are just dream rugs, Tibs thought to himself, pushing the scroll away.

Tibs wondered, *Is Nathan training Sy?* Most boys didn't begin training until they were twelve or thirteen. *They gave him a wand, doesn't that mean he started training, if only not to hurt himself? I don't want training, I want to be a knight.* He poked at the scroll angrily. *Magi never became knights.*

Nathan swatted Tibs on the head with a scroll. "Get your mind on your reading." He looked critically at Tibs for a moment, and when their eyes met, Nathan winked and looked away. Tibs didn't like sitting at the same table with Sy and the twins. *Still, I have to trust Nathan. What choice do I have?* Tibs leaned back in his chair. *Still, Nathan's afraid of something or he wouldn't be here. That's what people say...*Did he believe it? That Nathan's fear kept him here? *Is Telford afraid of Nathan?* He didn't think so. *If Nathan is hiding, he must be hiding from something? What? Who? If he's hiding, everyone in this room is danger.* His thoughts ran like his father's.

Nathan rapped Tibs on the head again. "Get your mind into the scroll."

Tibs looked at Nathan again. He could see the wrinkles around the old man's eyes. Nathan worried, a lot.

Nathan looked seriously into Tibs's eyes. "My hands are wet, Tibs. Can I dry them in your hair?"

"No!" Tibs didn't want wet hair.

"Did you say, 'No?'" Nathan said.

"Yes," Tibs replied.

"Oh, Yes?" Nathan rubbed his hands all over Tibs's hair. Indeed, they were very wet, and now his hair dripped of dew. Duped again.

⁓

A few days later, Toraline and Tibs cut through the tall grass below the trees. "First to class!" Toraline shouted.

What they found startled them. There was no house in the clearing.

"Did he move it again?" Toraline surveyed the clearing while slowing her walk.

"Why would he do that?" Tibs pulled some grass and stuck it in his mouth. "Do you smell that?"

They both sniffed the air deeply. "Burnt hair," Toraline's certainty left no room for doubt. Her experience in her father's smithy made her an expert on smells of things burning. They walked into the clearing a few more steps when Tibs saw him.

Nathan lay on the ground, his beard still smoking from fire. They ran up and patted his beard out.

Gabe came up and stood over them. "I didn't do it."

"We know that," Tibs shook Nathan. "Wake up! What happened!"

Nathan stirred, groggy. "I tell you I don't know how to ski."

"That's obvious." Toraline helped him sit up.

"What happened?" Nathan shook his head and looked around.

"We don't know." Tibs sat back and looked around the clearing again.

"What happened to my house?" Nathan stood up. Everything in the clearing was the same, except there was no house. "Where's my house?" He said it louder as if that might bring an answer out of thin air. "My house!" And finally, he whispered it, "my house..."

The children didn't know what to say, and miraculously, they remained silent.

CHAPTER 14

Whenever you lose something, it's always in the last place you look. Because if you look any further, you're pretty much a fool—

—SPOKEN BY SIR WARD KAY (PARAPHRASED) DURING ONE OF HIS LECTURES AT WHAT GREW INTO THE UNIVERSITY OF GRANDFORD

TIBS SHOOK HIS head. If you made a list of things Tibs would never say in his life, thing like, "More grubs for my porridge," or "That puppet is stealing all the cucumber sandwiches," this next sentence would be so remote and inconceivable, it would not make the list. "When did you see your house last?"

The clearing looked peaceful, with hints of the end of summer. Leaves littered the ground, like always. The wind pitched the branches this way and that, but no pollen, the flowers long gone. The overcast sky didn't even hint of rain.

"What day is this?" Nathan tried to get to his feet, but fell back to the ground.

"We saw you yesterday," Toraline looked around the clearing as if the house might be hiding behind a clump of grass on a second look.

Gabe walked in a few steps. "This can't be the c-c-clearing."

"Did someone take it?" Toraline stepped into the clearing and looked closer at where the house had been that morning.

"How can someone take a house?" Gabe inquired.

"Well, something happened to it!" Toraline grew impatient.

"Help me up!" Nathan insisted. The three children pulled him to his feet, and he swayed there for a moment before getting his equilibrium back. "Now, stand back." He put one hand to his chest, Tibs knew he was holding his stone, the one that focused his magic, the other he held out in front of him as if feeling for something close. "It has to be here." He stepped forward, eyes closed, looking for some hope, "I know it's here."

Sy and the twins brushed by Tibs into the clearing, almost knocking him to the ground.

Hearing them, Nathan turned and screamed, "Stop, Stop!"

"Where's your house?" Sy asked looking around the clearing.

He rubbed the back of his head. "Why am I outside?"

"Maybe you just moved your house," Gabe suggested pleasantly.

"No, no, I didn't move it." Nathan denied, "Something went wrong."

"Anyone can see that," Sy snorted.

"I was pouring out power, feeding it, feeding it!" Nathan snapped his fingers.

"Your house was eaten by something?" Gabe gasped.

"No, no!" Nathan touched the rock under his shirt again, this time pointing his finger in the general direction the house had been the day before.

"It's not there, you must have moved it," Tibs insisted.

"No, no, no. If I moved it, I'd still feel it. If it shrank, I'd still be able to feel it. I don't feel it. Not at all. This is something else."

"Then it's not invisible?" Tibs hadn't wanted to mention invisibility, he didn't want to leave any hints about his hunt for the mysterious house for Sy to pick up on.

"Invisible, then, I'd, I'd, still feel it? Wouldn't I?" He turned to the children as if they knew. "I move it, sometimes I shrink it, but to make it invisible, that's something else. In order to make it invisible, you have to move the light all around from every conceivable angle. That's using a bit of infinity. A neat trick. I mean, even half of infinity is overwhelming.

Ask any mathematician. Do you know how many different angles you can look at something from? It's quite staggering to think about it. I mean, I can easily make it invisible from one or two angles, but from thousands of angles? From millions of angles? And from every place a person stands, you have to bend light perfectly. I mean, every place you stand would have its own rules governing how the light should bend. The mathematics alone—"

"What were you trying to do!" Tibs stamped his foot to stop this lecture.

Still agitated. Nathan walked out into the clearing. "If it was invisible, I'd feel it? Wouldn't I?" It had vanished. Nathan looked forlorn. "I think I've lost my house forever."

Sy laughed.

Tibs shot him a look.

Sy defiantly chirped, "It was an eyesore anyway."

"I thought it was special." Nathan hung his head in defeat.

"Where are we going to learn to read?" Gabe asked.

"No one cares about finding your old house, just build another one out of sticks this time." The twins laughed at Sy.

Nathan puffed out his chest, "The real question is, whose bed am I going to share tonight if we don't find my house." He looked from one face to another.

"What are we waiting for, the house has to be here somewhere." Tibs got on his hands and knees and felt the grass for the house. That's when he noticed little people. They surrounded the clearing. Nobody else saw them, of course, but they stared at the children and Nathan in a way that made him nervous. He had never seen so many together. In fact, he'd never seen more than two leprechaun's at once before. He found it hard not to look at them.

"He can see us!" One hissed at the others, pointing at Tibs.

Tibs brought his finger to his lips, telling the little green folk to be quiet. A few disappeared behind trees. He had no way to tell if they were leaving or hiding.

Nathan stopped, screaming, "Wait, wait, WAIT! Let's not get ahead of ourselves. We must be systematic. If I step on the house because I accidently shrunk it, that's one thing, a tragedy, but if you step on it, you'll have a donkey's tail till the day you die." They stopped. He motioned to Toraline. "You go around the edge of the clearing till you come opposite me. Tibs, you go the other way and stop over there." Making them walking around the edge of the meadow, he arranged them in a sort of circle. "Yesterday, the house sat inside this circle." Nathan began, "We will step slowly, one at a time. Sometimes, when people gather like this, they can disrupt magic. Maybe it will give us a clue to where the house went or what happened to it." Nathan lifted his hands and said, "When I put my hands down, you will all take one step toward the middle with me." He put his hands down, and they took a step. He lifted his hands and dropped them, and every time he dropped them they took a step. They felt the ground with their hands.

He made them move slowly, and slowly they stepped. Minutes changed into half an hour before Tibs gauged they were actually near where the house stood.

"All right, extend your hands." Nathan said for the tenth time, holding out his hands as an example, again.

"We got it!" Sy scolded.

"Shuffle your feet! Don't lift them!" Nathan instructed. "Less chance of stepping on it if I accidently shrunk it."

"We understand, Nathan!" Tibs moved into Sy's camp without even realizing it.

They groped and shuffled forward.

Suddenly it happened. The house flickered into existence. It appeared before them, out of focus, the way a person sees when they get hit between the eyes by a wooden ball.

Everyone jumped back in surprise.

"There, it's, I, step baaaack!" Nathan reached out. Then he stepped back. He found nothing. No house, just air. "How is that possible!" He kicked the air and stepped back. He snapped his fingers. "Tibs, I want you to reach out just as I did," Nathan commanded.

Tibs reached out with his hands. Then he stepped forward and reached out again. Then he took a third step. Nothing.

"Step back, back, back! Let's give the lady a turn," Nathan barked.

Sy cried out, "No me!"

Nathan sighed, but nodded, and Sy took a few steps in. "The house was here, I saw it." He stepped forward, one, two three.

"Stop, stop!" Nathan ordered but Sy took two more steps," Stop! What does Stop mean in Cush! Now move back and give the lady a turn." Nathan waved at Toraline to proceed.

She took a step forward. For a moment, the house flickered into sight. It shivered. It wasn't out of focus, it was vibrating, faster than a humming-bird's wings. She tried to keep touching the house but a sound came with it. High pitched, louder, and then louder it forced the children to cover their ears. As soon as she drew back her hands, the house and the sound disappeared with a bang, driving Toraline backwards. She sat up, her nose bleeding. She didn't notice till the blood dripped down her chin.

"Don't just bleed there, do something!" Nathan yelled. "I mean, you, boys, help her!" The boys walked directly toward her, "NOT THROUGH MY HOUSE!" They all stopped, milling about where the house had stood wondering if they should go back or forward, "Just stand around her."

As they reached for her, she batted their hands away, "I'm all right. You'd think none of you have ever seen a little blood."

"I'm sorry, are you all right?" Nathan got on his knees beside her.

"I'm all right." She nearly yelled at him. "Let me stand up."

Nathan probed, "Did you run into it?"

"I touched it, you saw me." The bleeding stopped.

"Well, that's something." Nathan stood and brushed himself off.

"Let's do this again." She reached for the house once more.

"Stop!" Nathan put his hands up, "First, everyone stand behind her, Tibs and Sy first and then the others behind them. Toraline, when you see the house, grab it. Boys, when you see the house, grab her. And don't let go, whatever happens!"

Toraline took a step forward.

"Not yet!" The wizard came up beside her now. He closed his eyes and held out his hands. "I can't even sense it, it's as if it is not here at all." He opened his eyes and took Toraline's hand in his, guiding it toward the point the house had appeared. It flickered in front of her. She screamed and pulled back her hand, wrenching her arm out of Nathan's grasp, sending the man forward, onto his face, on the ground. The house was gone.

"Sorry," she apologized. "Just took me by surprise."

Nathan spoke while still lying down. "Toraline, my darling, can you hear me?"

Toraline nodded.

Tibs snorted. "He can't hear a nod."

"I can hear you," she chirped.

"Then DON'T LET GO OF THE HOUSE!" Nathan stood. "I'm going to have to go in."

"Is that safe?" Gabe sheepishly questioned.

"Safe? Good heavens, no. Not in the least. When she grabs it, you all have to hold onto whatever you can find! You have to keep your hands on it the whole time I'm inside. Or I might disappear with the house."

Nathan guided her hand, the house flickered into sight. This time she grabbed the railing on the porch and all the children reached out and grabbed her.

"Good, good!" Nathan now touched the house himself. They could all feel it vibrating. He stepped on the porch. "Remind me to wash the house when I'm done."

"Wash it?" Toraline asked.

"I don't know where it's been!" Nathan shook his beard. "Haven't you been listening?" Nathan walked to the front door and stepped inside.

A few minutes later, they felt the house shudder and it seem to, for lack of a better word, settle. At least it stopped vibrating and just became a house. Nathan stepped outside again, his robes and beard flaming, which he promptly put out. Two birds flew out of the beard angrily as he did this.

He inspected the house. Someone scarred the pristine west wall with a childish painting. Nathan groaned, "who did this!" He waved his hand and the house returned to its former glory, or lack of glory.

The children were all still as statues. Nathan surveyed the crew, all still holding on as hard as they could. "Come inside, you look cold." They *were* cold. They rushed inside.

Instead of school, Nathan decided they should have another breakfast. No one complained. They had so many questions, but Nathan would answer none of them while cooking. "You dare distract an artist!"

Tibs walked to the window and looked out. The wee folk pointed at the house but began to wander off as the humans ate. Tibs started to ask Nathan about the little people when Nathan, flour in his hair, reminded him again not to distract the master chef at work.

The eggs finished, the toast buttered just right, and as Nathan slid a plate of hot bacon onto the table, the children realized hunger gnawed at them.

Nathan took his food. He bowed over it silently, closing his eyes, as usual.

Toraline looked around the table. The boys stuffed their mouths till they could get no more food inside. Normally, as the blacksmith's daughter, she would have followed suit, but something inside stopped her. She picked up her knife to go with her fork and ate half bites.

"Out with it," Tibs said. "What happened!"

"Yes, I'd like to know, too," Sy prodded.

"That's not important," Nathan mumbled.

"NOOO!" They said in unison.

"All right, all right. I just wanted to see if I could, you know, make the house disappear. It's puzzling. I can make the house move, but not be invisible." He contemplated it for a moment. "As you can see, I almost lost my house."

"How did you do it?"

"Talisman." Nathan said that in such a way as to make them all think it should have been obvious.

"Talisman!" Sy said, "An object set to make something happen."

"Yes, I tried to make my house one. Obviously, I don't really have a talent for making those, but I tried, just to see." Nathan poured himself more water.

They finished the meal as if that answered all the questions, but of course, it didn't.

Sy and the twins left, and Gabe lingered until Nathan shepherded him out of the house.

Nathan sat down in front of Toraline and took her hand.

"Let's see the truth." He looked into her eyes.

"Is there something wrong?" Toraline worried.

"I don't know." Nathan licked his mustache. "I hate to do this, Tibs."

Tibs moved his chair closer. "Use your knife to touch my hand." He indicated the one holding Toraline's hand.

"Knife?" Tibs's innocently said. "What knife?"

"Don't give me that, I feel it, it's in your boot." Nathan didn't even look up.

Tibs drew out his knife.

"Now, touch my hand with it." Nathan closed his eyes.

Tibs touched the knife to the wizard's hand expecting an arc of power to explode and throw everyone a few feet backward. Nothing happened.

"Now, put it away." Nathan instructed. He let go of Toraline's hands.

"What is it?" Toraline said.

"You dampen magic." Nathan stood up and scratched his head. "I've only read about that power once. The Congrey says you are a myth."

"I *am* a miss," Toraline said, laughing.

"No, a myth, myth!" Nathan chided her for her joke. "A fairy story, made up to frighten children. I suspect the myth is their story, meant to deceive the rest of us and you are the fact."

"I am a magician?" Toraline suggested, hoping the old man would get to his point.

"NO!" Nathan barked. Then he smiled. "You children may as well learn right now that a magician is a person who appears to have magic but actually has none. They create illusions through sleight of hand and deception. Great skills to have, but their power is deception. To be sure, real wizards use that too. The best use it more."

"I have magic, then?" She leaned forward.

"No, you're not a wizard or a witch," Nathan snorted. "You suppress magic. It takes a lot more effort to do magic around you. It explains a lot. I thought I had been losing my touch." Then his face changed. He became serious. "You must never tell anyone. Not even your parents."

"I tell my father everything." Toraline tried to be truthful with her parents.

"Of course, certainly, I, I." Nathan stroked his beard. "I don't want you to keep secrets from your father, and certainly if he knew I suggested it, he might tear off my ears. But this isn't that kind of secret. You can't tell anyone because you're protecting them, not yourself."

"What?" Toraline prodded.

"If the Congrey finds out about you, they'll experiment on you. And your friends." Nathan waited for her to say something.

"How would they know?" She looked at her hands.

"How? Let's say, there are wizards who have the gift of knowing what people know."

"Kill them, wait..." Tibs started but then he realized, *They'll kill Toraline.* "She can't be, a, a, whatever this is. You've done magic around her."

Nathan turned to Tibs, looking the boy in the eyes. "What did you say?"

"You changed the house back," Tibs said simply. "You moved the scrolls. You changed your clothes."

Nathan laughed. "Just when I thought no one could teach you any-thing! Around her, I struggled to do magic. Normally, I don't have to work at it at all. Toraline, I will tell no one about this, not Lord Telford, whom I should tell, nor Sir Jesse, whom I tell everything. This is your gift. Wait one day, and then do as you see fit."

She nodded.

"And the house?" Tibs prodded.

Nathan nodded vigorously. "Yes, talismans. Only by bringing many talismans together could someone make a house invisible and move it from place to place. The house you've been seeing has to be a giant talisman. Has to. We know that when you combine two talismans they create wondrous or dangerous things, I think that the person who made this brought together two or three or more."

"Which means...?" Toraline knew Nathan was leaving something out.

"That the person who made this is very powerful, or very stupid, or completely uncaring. Probably all three. I think, if Toraline hadn't suppressed the magic, my house would have been gone forever. I mean, it would have been here, right here in this place, but no one would have been able to touch it. Thank you."

"I didn't really do anything." She protested.

"You held on." Nathan suggested.

"I did do that, and that hurt." She agreed.

"Time to leave!" Nathan clapped his hands. The door opened and the lights went out. "I've been up all night and need a nap."

Within seconds their plates, cleaned of food, disappeared, and Tibs and Toraline ran through the woods back home.

He could see Sy and the twins ahead of him. They didn't go straight home.

"What did the enlightened Nathan pass on to Tibs the favored one?" Sy asked.

"Favored one?" Tibs confused look made Sy laugh.

"He spends more time with you than any of us, or hadn't you noticed?" Sy threw a rock, it zipped by Tibs head, perhaps a half an inch away from his ear.

Tibs spun around to see where it went when he noticed the leprechauns. They stood behind him, in front of him, near trees, bushes, they were everywhere watching. *Why would they all be out here?* Tibs thought. He started to walk away, he didn't want the others to come in contact with them when they all started making hand motions. *It's odd to see them and this odder still.* One made a slashing motion across his throat. *Does that mean the same thing in leprechaun as it does in human?* Tibs wondered. Another rock went by his head, he could hear it. He spun around and looked at Sy and the others. Now, Leprechauns don't bother the birds or squirrels or insects. Tibs noticed no sounds of wild life, which could be because of them. *But maybe...Are they trying to warn me about something? Why would they do that?*

Tibs moved back the way he came, they motioned, 'No.' He moved toward the village, they motioned 'no,' again. The others just stared at him.

"Is something wrong with your head or your legs?" Sy smirked.

Can't go back, left or right, there's only once choice. So he made it. *And if it's wrong, let's make it big.* "RUN!" He yelled and sped off through the woods, past the twins. He didn't look to see if they followed.

He rounded a tree and found himself flying through the air. Now, this sensation is sometimes mildly pleasant. When dreaming, soaring is delightful. When diving into the river on a hot day, anticipating the delightful shock of cool water, flying through the air gives one joy. His leg, grabbed by an unseen rope, pulled him off the ground for a moment, smacked his head down and the ground, and then dragged the rest of his body behind it for ten feet and then pulled him back into the air. No joy in this journey.

Upside down, he first tried to pull at the ropes around his ankles, but he lacked the proper strength. It was too tight. Then he looked around. Three men glowered. They wore animal skins and smelled like over ripe fruit. He had been captured. "Something tells me you don't know Sy, do you?" He smiled weakly.

They scowled, angrily.

"This isn't going to be good, is it?"

CHAPTER 15

───────── ᧁ ─────────

You did what? Didn't you know what was an idiotic idea?
How could—
you must—
you could have been killed!
I may kill you!
AHHH!"

—Sennacherib MacCauley talking to a young
boy—We must remember the even Historians
are human too.

A good question to ask right at this time is this: "Who would want to capture Tibs?" It's a very good question. The answer comes back: no one. Tibs, the son of a poor knight, had no value. As a wizard someone might risk trying to capture him, but no one knew about that, at least no one who had any reason to kidnap him. He got into trouble a lot, so it could be argued that at times his father might have wanted him captured, but this was not one of those times.

"Here now," one of the bandits exclaimed, "this ain't the one we was aiming at!" The bandits made a mistake. Not their last, I'm afraid.

Sy and the twins were coming up behind him, and as Tibs swung into the air, he could just make them out.

"RUUUUUUN!" Tibs screamed.

The three took off through the woods toward Nathan's house.

The bandits wasted no time trying to fix their mistake. "Don't worry about the girl! He's got to be one of the boys!"

They ran off after Sy and the twins. He squirmed as hard as he could and found himself swinging. A pair of hands tried to steady him. He fought off the hands as hard as he could, twisting himself and flailing his arms this way and that, but lost against the superior strength of his attacker.

Which turned out to be Toraline, "Would you sit still so I can get this thing off of you?"

Relief turned to embarrassment for Tibs. "Don't worry about me, you squeak-pig," Tibs hissed. "Find my father!" Toraline let go of Tibs and ran off.

Tibs immediately regretted telling her to go. First, Sy and the Twins probably ran toward help. Second, his head started pounding from all the blood pouring into it because he was upside-down. He bent himself at the waist trying to get to the rope off his legs. He struggled with the knot. *Too tight.* Suddenly, he could hear footsteps again. He twisted his body around thinking it might be his father.

A dark figure grabbed him by his hair. Tibs grabbed the hand. Pain shot through his head right to his toes.

"I should kill you right here." He could see the man's blood shot eyes. He wore a silk hat, colorful, and had a waxed mustache, straight as a knife on his face. "That would take too much time." He gave Tibs a shove and sent him spinning around and around.

"Come on boys, the fox has escaped," he yelled. "There's always another day. Don't want to wake the whole village!"

The men ran off leaving him swinging wildly. He struggled to untie his feet again. At least when he tried to do that all the blood didn't pool in his head.

He heard Gabe's voice. "I'll pull at this rope, shall I?" he asked helpfully.

"Gabe!" Tibs yelled gratefully. He saw the rotund boy standing by the tree where the men must have tied the other end of the rope. Gabe held one end of the rope. To get Tibs down, all he had to do was give that rope a good "yank."

"NO!" Tibs started to say, but Gabe pulled it. The rope came undone, Tibs fell on his head, and everything went dark.

When Tibs opened his eyes again, his body was bundled in an old blanket in front of the kitchen fire. Water dripped into his eyes from a cloth in his father's hand.

"Stop it!" Tibs protested.

"I have to clean the wound," his father explained.

"What wound? I wasn't hurt," Tibs babbled.

"You landed on a rock when you fell out of the tree." His father finished and dried off Tibs's head, which hurt something awful, then started wrapping it up.

"Can you tell everyone this happened because I fought the kidnappers?" Tibs asked.

His father laughed. "No, I will not tell anyone that. They already know the truth."

"What's the truth?" Tibs asked, still confused.

"You fall down and go boom." Wounds never bothered his father. He smiled down at his son and Tibs knew his father didn't describe it in that way. Then Sir Jesse's face became serious. "They weren't after you."

"Sy." Tibs knew. Sy's father had money.

"It was lucky that you were first," his father said.

Lucky? Tibs thought about it. Wee folk making hand motions. Sy and the twins waiting for some reason he didn't know. He made it through the wood faster than Toraline. He didn't know what it all added up to, but it couldn't be luck.

—ᖇ—

A few days later Tibs had a chance to speak to Nathan alone. After classes, he made an excuse to go back into the house.

Nathan sat at the table with his back toward Tibs. He didn't even look up when he spoke. "Well, out with it. I know you want to ask something."

"Why don't I have an aura?" Tibs asked.

"You are," Nathan paused and thought about what word to use, "how can I put this? Different." He pushed his chair back and gave Tibs his full attention. "But you already knew that! Still, no one that I've ever studied has been without an aura. You are the first. Can you see them?"

"I think so." Tibs thought for a moment. "Sy is green."

"Exactly. Green. Sy's magic is probably the power that's the most coveted." Tibs snorted, but Nathan shushed him with a wave of his hand. "Making things grow is the most useful power to have. With his magic, his father's lands will always have big crop yields. It will make him rich and rich means influence." Nathan stoked his beard thinking. "There may be as many colors as there are, well, colors, I suppose. The color gives us an idea of the main strength of the wizard. The only warning I have is that if you see one in black, go the other way."

"Black," pondered Tibs.

"Black means death, boy. There are two things that you need to remember about wizards who work in death. One is that they may kill you with a look. The other is they never started out black. That's the color that comes when they purposely corrupted their power. Once I faced a black wizard. More properly a witch, I suppose. Her power, her anger, her desires were terrible. It took all my strength to leave alive."

"Is she still alive?" Tibs asked.

Nathan sat lost in thought and then shook his head and mumbled something. Then sat up and spat, "I pray she's not. Black magi don't live lives that are...It's hard to explain. I suppose I could just say they are never happy—and can never be happy."

Tibs nodded politely. He didn't understand.

"Back to you. You have no color. What does that mean? I've never heard tell of it, I've never seen it. Maybe there are thousands of you out there, and we don't know because we've never tested any of you, at least seriously. I just don't know, and when I find something I don't know, you know what I do?"

Tibs shook his head.

"I'll show you." Nathan leaned back in his chair, clapped his hands to his knees, and laughed. Not a typical laugh. The laughed filled the room with delight and mirth and humor and love and well, just about every joyous emotion one can think of. It infected Tibs. He tried to stop, but after two or three test chuckles, he had to laugh with the old man.

He didn't know how long he laughed, but when they finally stopped, Tibs felt disappointed. He hadn't laughed like this for a long time. He felt Nathan's hands on his shoulders. Nathan eyes contained no laughter now. "To find something totally new at my age is a joy. I'm just glad we found you, and not the Congrey. You must stay away from them, my boy."

"Why?" Tibs asked.

"What?" Nathan didn't understand.

"Why stay away?"

Nathan shook his head. "The Congrey is only interested in the Congrey. Not helping people, only helping themselves. They want to control magic. They look upon people as, oh, let's say animals. People without magic are cattle, fit only to serve those with powers. They say they want to domesticate people, they say they want to bring them peace and help them stop war and disease. But really, they want to control, dominate and rule. They are no better than the Lords and Ladies who sadly rule now, or the Black Heart. The difference is that the nobles and such want money and power, the Congrey want to fundamentally change people into something else."

Tibs didn't feel so well after hearing this. "And they'd want to kill Toraline?"

"Toraline? First and foremost, anything that threatens their power they destroy, but you they'd study and then kill you. Toraline's death would seem a blessing."

"I can't even use my powers."

Nathan playfully slapped him on the head. "Let us take a step backward and say what we do know. You can move things with your mind. That's usually a light blue kind of power."

"I've tried. I can't do it anymore," Tibs interrupted.

Nathan looked down at him again, his eyes betraying that he might start laughing again, but instead he spoke. "Tibs, you're not even eleven-years-old. I've never seen anyone under eleven manifest any power before you, and I've seen a thousand if I've seen one. And since you are one, I've seen a thousand." He pulled at his mustache absentmindedly, twirling it around his finger. "This means two things. One, that you're powerful. Two, you did it in a village with a suppressing aura. Which means you're probably even more powerful. And three, well, I'm working on three."

"Aren't we supposed to do some training or something so I can use my power?" Tibs suggested.

Suddenly Tibs saw fear on the old man's face as the room went dark.

"What is it?" Tibs asked.

"Shh!" Nathan hissed. "One of my defenses went off."

"It's dark," Tibs hissed back.

"I can see that, kidling, I'm not an idiot." He could hear Nathan moving quietly in the dark.

The hair on Tibs's arms began to raise and vibrate. *This wasn't going to be good.*

"Don't move, Tibs." Nathan's voice quivered.

Tibs heard something scrape the floor in a strange way. "Why not?"

Tibs could feel breath on his face, like some large creature waited for him to move or speak so it could eat him. Fear filled him from head to toe. He wanted to see, he wanted to see, he wanted to see. He felt with his mind a candle right near him. He didn't know how he knew, but he could feel it. He filled it with fire, and the candle lit. The whole room filled with light. And when one candle lit, all the light came back. Nathan sat in his chair by the desk, and Tibs sat in his chair holding a candle that burned brightly. Except for the two chairs and the desk, the room was now empty.

Tibs looked around the empty room. He looked back at Nathan. Nathan's eyes betrayed his fear. They weren't blinking. He clung tightly to the chair.

"Is it still here?" Tibs asked his teacher. He could see Nathan's hands unclench.

Nathan cleared his throat. "I am."

"You?" Tibs wondered.

"With a little help from the gentleman with the magic." Nathan smiled. "A test. I suspected, I thought, it, it." He shook his head. "You have no aura, so that should mean you have no magic. You can touch metal, again, no magic. But you have something in you, and I thought, why not try out a few basic tests they give to all new recruits for the Librarians."

"You mean the Congrey?" Tibs asked.

"Of course," Nathan nodded. "Most new magic users would never be able to light a candle, but they might make it warm, but you..." His voice trailed off. He twirled his beard. "I think you'll have to begin training soon, or you'll destroy the whole village. You can't contain all that inside you without consequences."

Tibs left Nathan's house excited. He made the torch light again. He didn't look where he traveled, he didn't have to. He knew these woods so well, he could get home in his sleep.

Sleep. That idea floated in his head as his feet made their way through the woods.

At home, his bed was stuffed with spring heather. *Soft spring heather,* he imagined himself in the bed. He remembered where he had gathered the heather, the slopes of the nearby mountains. His father took him by cart and horse, a treat in itself. They brought them home and put them in the mattresses. The fresh heather meant a soft bed, a delight, especially after winter when the beds became hard and prickly, heather lasted only one season and they used it for four. He smelled the fresh heather in his nose as he walked toward his house, even though the spring was long past. He wanted to feel his bed under his body, his eyes dropped in sleepiness as he walked away from Nathan's house.

He didn't notice his gait turned to staggering. He looked for home, but his feet wouldn't walk in a straight line. They zigzagged. He believed he could now see the manor through the trees, but when he blinked it would disappear again. He shook his head to fight the sleepiness, plodding one foot in front of the other. He stumbled as his mind fought to keep his eyes open. Then he discovered it was easier to walk with them closed. He kept walking, his hands out in front of him, and when he touched a tree, he would push away from it and move forward, all the time his mind sought his bed.

He didn't remember falling asleep, but he did. He didn't remember walking anywhere, but he never told his feet to stop. He dreamed about walking. In that dream, he walked with his eyes closed through the forest past trees he'd never seen. His walking turned to running, and though his eyes were closed, he didn't hit any trees! He felt alive in the dream, delighting in the running. He ran. He ran.

He screamed.

And opened his eyes.

His face meshed with the dirt on the ground. *At least it's not mud.* He lifted his head and looked around.

How long had he been walking?

Little torches burned, attached to the walls. The walls were made from timber, as if the whole room was carved from a single piece of wood. They sloped up into the darkness, he couldn't see the ceiling but imagined it came to a point above his head somewhere. He felt like he was still outside, even though he couldn't see anything beyond the room itself. The doors were obscured in darkness. A chair was thrust into the light.

"Is this another test?" he screamed at the walls. *Nathan's behind this.*

"I'm sorry, but the king wants a wee word wit' ye." A tiny man with red hat stepped into the light before Tibs. "Ye've, ah, you've, ah, been brought, broughten? This is his throne room and ye've, ah, oh, Ye may sit before the king, not many have been given that boon, let me tell ye." The man took off his hat and motioned for Tibs to sit.

Tibs sighed. He stood up, and hit his head on the ceiling. It looked like a high ceiling because of the darkness. *Permission to sit?* They let him sit because he couldn't stand, even if he wanted to, the low ceiling prevented it.

He looked around the so-called room. The grains of the walls smoothed by hundreds of hands soothed. They carved the room inside a tree. From the looks of the wood, they used an oak tree.

He heard a large sigh. The man in the red hat nodded and stepped into the darkness.

Tibs tried to stand, but hit his head, and the room filled with whispering. He sat down, holding his head. The voices got louder, but he couldn't understand anything they said because they all spoke at the same time. He noticed the man in the light fled. The voices argued.

"All right, all right, keep your hats tight!" He finally heard.

Then another of the wee folk, with a long beard, all white instead of the usual reddish orange, stepped into the light.

"I'll be thanking ye to treat me like you would any king of those eleven kingdoms." His hat had a gold medallion on the front, but otherwise his dress was like any of the other leprechauns he'd ever seen.

"I've never met a king before. You're the first." Tibs said, staring at the little man, and then added hastily, "Your majesty."

"Our kingdom prefers to go unseen, unwatched and unnoticed. But as ye have noticed us, and I'm here to determine whether ye should live or die for crimes against the wee folk." He didn't seem at all sure about himself, but his words worried Tibs.

"His life for his crimes! Be ye daft?" A little lady stepped into the light and pulled on the king's nose.

"I'll have ye know there's not an unwise bone in me body, woman!" He felt his nose all over to make sure it was still there.

"If ye be the king, I be the queen, and because of that, I'll have ye treat me with respect!" She stomped on his foot and he began to jump on one leg, howling in pain.

"Don't you be doing that in front of the giant!" he said between howls.

"Giant! Hmph, look at him. He's a wee boy and more scared of we'en than we are of him, I'll warrant." She turned to Tibs and smiled sweetly. "Did ye have a wish for anything to quench your thirst at all, at all?"

Tibs didn't know what to say.

"Don't give him civility! He can see us." The king jumped in front of the little woman.

"I can see ye, and I'm not on trial. Though there's more'n one told me I needed me eyes examined when I married ye." She walked into the darkness.

"Never did, I, you didna, I!" It was if the king filled with angry air, and then hissed at the end. He turned toward the boy and waved his finger. "Excuse the woman, she doesn't know about affairs of state."

At that moment another little man stepped into the light. "Charlie, if I could just step in here—"

"Charlie! I'm king, if ye haven't forgotten!" He punched the other little man in the stomach.

"King!" Another lady stepped into light. "Because of that hat!"

"Don't you start in. Someone has to be king, and I have the hat!" He pointed importantly up at his chapeau.

"Not for long!" Another wee man stepped into the light. Stepped is actually the wrong word. By the time he entered the light, he was a good foot in the air, quite a height for someone of his size, aiming for the king's head, which he hit at a good speed, knocking over the king, and the man behind him. Two more men jumped into the ruckus, and a half a dozen women stepped out to pull them apart, followed by three more men, more women, and the whole room erupted into fighting and pulling and jumping and yelling.

Into the mess, walked the woman who Tibs guessed to be queen, carrying an oversized tea cup. She stepped lightly around the fighting people as if it was the most natural thing in the world. Amazingly, she sidestepped through the whole crowd without spilling a drop and held the cup up to Tibs. "Here boy, drink up. You must be tried from all these affairs of state." She winked as he accepted the cup and took a sip. The tea tasted very good, with a whisper of honey.

She walked into the middle of the fight and put two fingers in her mouth, whistling loudly. Everyone stopped fighting. "He has tea!" She pointed at Tibs. "He's now a guest, and anyone who says different will feel my wrath!" She held up a fist.

They must have forgotten what started the fighting, because they all just stopped, picked up their hats, brushed themselves off, and then came up to Tibs and said things like, "Good to know ye," or "Welcome ye are to our hospitality," or "Will ye be needing anything with that tea?"

Tibs nodded and tried to smile, but he still had no idea why they kidnapped him.

"I think you'll not be forgetting this soon." The king stood up and put on his hat. As he did so, the first of the wee folk, the one who had been following Tibs, came up and whispered in the king's ear. "Oh, that's right, that's right. Cubert here tells me we still have a problem. Ye can see us."

"I've always been able to see ye, ah, you." Obviously, Tibs felt that needed saying.

"Human children can see us, but they outgrow it. The few that don't learn not to see us—They ah, they…" The king scratched his head. "Some think they shouldn't, and so they don't, but you can see. You're the only one. You haven't outgrown it, and that's a kerfuffle." The king slapped his thigh sternly, then walked in a circle trying to make the pain stop. "I wouldn't be a risking telling the big people, yah hear?" He looked Tibs right in the eyes.

Tibs nodded.

"They won't believe that we exist, and it will get ye in a bee's bumble. That ye know for certain, am I right?" The king spread his hands, and the crowd cheered as if he had made some big point.

"They don't believe me now," Tibs stated.

The king finished brushing off his clothes.

Tibs sipped the tea. He looked around. He felt courage inside him. A certainty of purpose, plan and execution. He felt as if he could do no wrong. If he had known what it meant to share food and drink with the little people, he would only have pretended to drink the tea. If it had been a drink with spirits instead of tea leaves, he might have stayed with them a hundred years and never felt he missed a day outside the tree, but as he was a child, they gave him only their tea, which was strong enough to turn the meekest pigeon into an eagle, at least in thought. Either by drink, or circumstance, or a bit of both, he knew the situation called for diplomacy. He might be able to beat them at arm wrestling, but they come on him by the dozens, and how would that help his situation? He cleared his throat to get the king's attention. "Oh, great and mighty leader," he began.

The little man with the badge on his hat looked behind him for a moment, not realizing that Tibs meant him. Then he pointed at himself and said without making a sound, "Me?" He folded his arms over his chest and gave Tibs a condescending glare and a little nod.

"Your kingdom is a delight to behold and your people are mighty. To reveal you to the big people would give me no pleasure, since they would compete for your favor. Consider me your servant and devoted follower, with only my obligations to my own lord, king, and family ahead of your state and wonderful people." Tibs tried to bow, rather difficult from a sitting position.

"What a pretty speech." The king's wife stepped out of the shadows. "Do ye know what he's a mind to be saying?" she asked her husband.

"Of course I have a mind to know what he's saying!" the king yelled. He pulled on his lower lip. "He's saying, ah, he's saying." He pulled off his hat and scratched his head. "What are ye saying, boyo?" He looked at Tibs.

"I am your friend and I'll keep your secret if you keep mine," Tibs cocked his head and winked. He'd seen his father do that a thousand times in tense situations and it seemed to make everything better.

"Your secret? What secret is that?" The king looked suspicious.

"That I see little people." Tibs sipped the tea.

Cubert roared with laughter. "Then take the hand of the king, and we'll say no more about it. We'll have a drink on our newfound accord!"

Cheers exploded out of the little people. Torches flared on the walls. Tibs cowered for a second, the walls were lined with wee folk. *There must be a thousand.* They appeared to his left, his right, his front, his back and even above his head. The cheers had hardly subsided when the music started. The infectious beat drew Tibs to his feet. He started dancing, which, before that day, he hated, but now, because of this music, delighted him. His feet moved of their own accord, stepping and stamping in time with music and never did he come close to the little people all around him. He felt himself clapping and his knees moving, all under the influence of the music. They began to sing, and to his surprise, he joined in, even though he didn't know the words. They were in his head whenever he needed them. Truth be told, this magic was the same that took him into the old oak tree from his path to his own home. They played and led him to this place and with this music they will lead him away to his home. He gulped his tea as it cooled, and they drank a very different kind of drink that frothed and billowed all around him. They didn't offer him any of their brew and he didn't think to ask, he couldn't, the spirit of the dance possessed him. The last man who sipped that drink slept for twenty years, but he had sweet dreams.

It's clear now that, sometime during the party, the king touched Tibs in the middle of his forehead, between his eyes. He left a mark there. A leprechaun seeing it would know Tibs as a friend.

Tibs's exhaustion drove him home. He didn't want to leave. "The party is just beginning," he begged the king. He fell asleep before getting out of the tree, but they knew it was time to return him to his kin so they wouldn't get suspicious so they returned him the same way they took him, sleepwalking.

The next thing he knew, his eyes opened and he stood in the kitchen, six hours late. His father sat at the table. Tibs tried to smile.

"Something wrong?" Sir Jesse scowled in confusion.

Tibs managed one smile before collapsing on the floor, his legs rubber from the dancing, every ounce of energy gone and his feet blistered. He fell asleep a second before hitting the floor.

Late the next morning, Tibs woke up. Two things came to his mind. One, his stomach demanded food! And lots of it. The other, noises came from the manor courtyard. He pushed the blanket off. He still wore his clothes from the night before.

He leaned out the window to look. *What are the noises?* There in the courtyard, two men threw rocks at Old Gus. Bam! Not men, really, William and Sidney barely scraped nineteen, poor fighters and thinkers, they wouldn't make Lord Telford's guards proud. They excelled at making fun of people, and their favorite insults and tricks, like so many others in the village, found Gus. He'd never seen them attack Gus before.

One connected with his head and Gus fell to the ground. They yelled and threw, and yelled again. Tibs saw blood on Gus's head as he got to his hands and knees. They kept throwing. He didn't know the details, he didn't need to know. *They're gonna pay.*

CHAPTER 16

━━━━━━━━━━ ⌐ ━━━━━━━━━━

It's not really wise to bring two talismans together. On their own, they may work perfectly, but we've discovered that when two or more are brought together, they have unpredictable outcomes, many of which are destructive. The simple truth is this. A ward for evil in an acorn being brought together with a ward for good in a lump of coal means both will explode. Fun at parties, until someone gets hurt, and someone always gets hurt—

—Nathan, addressing his novices at the University of Grandford

Tibs didn't think. It just happened. William and Sidney's clothes caught on fire. Tibs fell backwards, as if the explosions happened right in front of face. *What happened?* He heard them screaming. He looked out the window and saw Gus trying to put out the flames with his hands.

"Fire's hot," he heard Gus saying as the now flameless boys ran down the road toward the village.

How did that happen? Wait, I did it. He knew he made the fire appear on the men. His anger must have triggered something. The fire hurting the boys knocked the anger right out of him. *I wonder if I can get angry again?*

Old Gus interrupted Tibs's thought, screaming, "It's time, time, time! You have to get going!" The old man ignored his bleeding head. His normally serene face desperate as he made his way into the manor like he owned the place. At the bottom of the stairs, Tibs could hear Gus jumping up and down, yelling, "You have to come, come now, it's time!"

Tibs turned from the window and yelled through his bedroom door, "I'm hungry. I'm not going anywhere without food." Tibs didn't have to dress; he was already dressed. So he wandered to the kitchen, despite Gus's urgency, and looked for food. He hoped his father had left him something. He couldn't remember eating dinner. He had eaten with the leprechauns, but their servings were so small, he needed four or five servings just to make a mouthful. It didn't seem polite to eat half the feast meant for the whole clan, so he had held back.

"You have to come, it's time. It's time!" Gus said over and over as Tibs plodded down the stairs.

"I have to eat." Tibs continued his walk toward the kitchen.

Gus stood still for a moment. Then he shook his head up and down like he was agreeing with something or someone. "That's right, that's right, food!"

The old man rushed into the kitchen. Tibs staggered in to see two things. One: a cold breakfast of ham, fresh bread and delicious, sweet carrots. This told him his father loved him. Two: A frenetic Gus filling a sack with food from the pantry. Tibs sat down and started to eat.

Between mouthfuls of the best tasting breakfast Tibs could remember, he muttered at the village idiot. "I don't think you should be taking that," then again, "My father will kill you if he sees you in our kitchen, Gus." Tibs didn't stop the old man. Unpredictable things happened when people interfered with the old-timer. Tibs knew to wait until an adult came around.

Tibs pushed back his chair and sighed. He felt great. He couldn't remember anything being so satisfying. His feet didn't hurt so much now.

"Come on, we have to get going." Old Gus grabbed Tibs's arm and pulled him up.

"I have chores," Tibs snapped. He had had enough of these strange games.

"You don't understand." Gus sobbed.

"That's funny, coming from you," Tibs laughed, even though he knew it was rude. "I have to get to work."

"The house won't last long. It will move soon. We have to get going." Gus pulled on Tibs's hand again.

Tibs only heard one word. House. He grabbed the old man's shoulders and looked into his eyes. "How do you know you about the house?"

"It's in the field. You have to get there before it goes. Today is the day. Today is the day."

The house? Could Gus mean the raven house? The one that disappeared? How could the old man know about it? Still, a house in the fields, what else could he mean? Tibs had to act now, but he didn't have to act alone. He had to get Toraline. Where was she? "I need Toraline," Tibs mumbled as he organized his thoughts.

Gus looked into Tibs's eyes for a moment and then smiled. "Of course, we were all there. Come on." He threw the bag of food over his shoulders, grabbed a fur wrap and trotted out of the kitchen, through the house, and into the courtyard to the road to town.

"You don't need the fur!" Tibs reminded the old man. "It's not really cold and won't be for months."

Gus ran down the road, halfway to the farms before Tibs had a chance to really get in gear. *I've never seen him move so fast.* He sprinted to catch up to the old man. "You're going the wrong way, Toraline will be in the smithy!" Still, he followed Gus instead.

To Tibs's surprise, Gabe and Toraline weeded in the fields. Gus ran right there like a bloodhound on the scent of a deer, or dinner. *How did he know where they were? Does he have magic too?*

"It's time. We have to get going!" Gus repeated.

"What about our, our, our, argh, work," Gabe sputtered, stamping his foot, clearly having a bad day putting together sentences.

Tibs ran up, collapsing on his knees. His feet still hurt from the dancing.

"What's with Old Gus?" Toraline asked in that demanding way she had.

Tibs panted, trying to get words out, but his breath eluded him.

Old Gus stood straight for a moment, listening. He scowled like a rabid wolverine. "He's just been taken," he murmured.

"Taken? Who's been taken?" Tibs demanded.

"Sylas." Gus let go of Toraline's arm. He took a step toward the wood. "They're back." The bright morning had succumbed to darkness. The sky filled with clouds, menacing the forest and the farms. The wind picked up from the ocean, battering the trees into losing leaves early. They bent in protest, struggling to right themselves. The old man took a step toward the forest. "Come." He ran across the field, barreling down the wheat as he made for the woods.

Gabe stood and ran after Old Gus leaving Toraline and Tibs alone.

"He says he's found the house," Tibs said.

"The house? How does he even know about it?" Toraline questioned.

Tibs shrugged, "Shouldn't we at least check it out?" He pointed down the path Gus created through the field.

She smiled, "Couldn't hurt, I suppose," and took off after them.

Tibs followed, trying to organize his thoughts. *Sylas? They're back? Who? If Gus is out of his mind, we'll only be wasting a little time, and if he's not...hard to think about.* He ran down the road, trying not to be last, but Gabe had a huge head start and Toraline's long legs made it impossible to catch up to her. They headed into the woods. *Why would Sy even be out in the woods? He'll have guards or at least the twins with him. No, it can't be him, Gus must be an arrow short of a quiver.* Still, he followed them all.

He moved after them from the fields into the woods. The springy branches brushed him as he passed into the thickness. Ahead he heard twigs breaking and whispers, they slipped through the woods fast. Gus ran like a deer, *Incredible,* Tibs thought watching the old man move like he never had before. The old man pushed the ground away with his toes, as if he knew every rock and log he passed over, like a rehearsed dance.

Suddenly, Old Gus stopped.

So suddenly that Toraline ran right over Gabe and right into him. He moved as much as a mountain might, that is not at all. She fell into the leaves, rather than on top of Gabe. Gus held up his hand as Tibs came up silently behind them. The old man meant for them to stop and observe. "I want to get this right," he whispered to the trio, as if that explained anything. He pushed silently through the undergrowth. The children tried to follow in like manner, but Toraline seemed to laying on a pile of twigs, which were breaking with every movement as she tried to stand. Gus turned to the girl and held his finger to his mouth for silence.

She couldn't apologize, that would make noise. She stood and brushed nature from her clothes.

Gus stepped up to a tree and looked from behind it, deeper into the woods.

Tibs saw Sy leaned against the stump of a fallen tree. Sy didn't appear to know they were there. They could still hear the incoming storm in the treetops. Below the canopy they were protected from the worst of the wind. The light grew dimmer as the clouds gathered overhead. Still, Sy didn't move. A more trained eye would have suspected something wrong.

Tibs snorted, stood, and then took off toward the hostage-son.

Gus followed, taking the same precautions as Tibs, that is, none.

"SY!" Tibs belted. "My father will have you flogged if he hears you're here alone!" Finally, a chance to get the great Sylas into trouble.

Sy's head moved as if to look at them. Then he fell over behind a log. Tibs stopped. *Strange.* He couldn't see Sy now. He'd fallen behind the trunk of the tree. *Why would he hide? Maybe he's planning a prank. But it's my turn...* It didn't feel like a jest to Tibs. Tibs stopped and looked at Gus. Could the old man be a part of a prank? It didn't seem likely.

Tibs cautiously jumped up on the log and rounded the tree, ready for some sort of trick. He looked down at Sy. Sy didn't want to hide. Ropes wrapped his arms and legs. His mouth stuffed with cloth, he couldn't even speak. *Why would Sy do this to himself? Wait, he didn't do this to himself. The kidnappers are back. That's what Gus meant when he said, "they're back," he meant the kidnappers.*

The others came up behind Tibs. "What's going on here?" Toraline asked, confused.

Sy opened his eyes. His face filled with fear. From out of the forest appeared four bandits, swords drawn and smiling.

"This makes things a bit complicated since I don't like witnesses." The tall bandit, clearly in charge, waived his sword with one hand, pulling his mustache and twirling it at the same time, as if the two actions were somehow related. He wore a silk shirt covered by a thick embroidered coat trimmed in lace. His boots were black leather that went up past his knees. If clothes meant anything, he was successful.

"That's right! Lor don't like no witnesses," laughed the big one dressed in light chain mail and brandishing a rusty sword and a shield with the coat of arms blackened out.

Lor screamed at the other bandits. "How many times do I have to say: Not our real names!" Lor grabbed his goatee and pulled it in frustration. "I could have had anyone help me in this, and I choose you three, I must..." He closed his eyes and counted to ten and then opened them again, smiling at the children.

"Still, he's right, I don't like witnesses." He motioned for his men to restrain the children and Gus, and in a moment they were roped together.

The big one finished tying up Tibs flicking his nose toward him, "Lor, here's dat brat who's tripped our trap."

Lor glared at the fat one again, "No names! no name, NO NAMES, Fats."

"You said you wouldn't call me dat no more." Fats hit his shield with his sword.

"Fats, I'll remember that when you don't call me by my name."

Tibs tested the ropes, tight and tidy, he wouldn't get out of them soon. *Should have gone for my father or Nathan.* Tibs wished. *Too late now.*

"The one who tripped out trap the other day. Good. All the more reason to kill them all." Lor ran this thumb along the blade of his sword.

Really wish I had gone for my father.

CHAPTER 17

*Throughout history people have attacked problems in one of
three ways. Some hide and pretend the problem doesn't exist,
which works only for mice, and not very well for them. Others
use footwork to avoid the problem for as long as they can, which
works until you run out of breath, and the problem overtakes
and controls you.
And then there are those who confront the problem head on,
hurtling themselves at it till only they or the problem exist.
These people tend to rise to the top of leadership, not really
because of skill, but because the other two groups are perfectly
content to let someone else get his head battered.
And that's how kings are chosen: they have the hardest heads—*

—FROM SENNACHERIB MACCAULEY'S *HISTORY OF THE
UNIFICATION*.

TIBS FELT HIS legs shake a bit. *Lor and his friends won't notice* he told
himself. He didn't believe himself. Whatever happened, Sy would live. Sy's
parents would spare no expense to save their son. That's what these men
wanted—booty. But the others had no family with money, so they had no
value except as witnesses, and they didn't want more witnesses.

"We all go to the house now," Gus sputtered.

"The house?" Tibs repeated. *Of course, the house! Maybe that was the
key to getting out of this mess.* "You don't want to kill us!" he shouted to the
bandits.

Lor swaggered toward Tibs. "Why not. You look ripe enough." The others laughed.

Tibs looked squarely up into the leader's eyes. "We know of a magic house."

Lor's eyes narrowed. "Magic house?"

"He can take us to it." Tibs pointed at Old Gus. "We were on our way there when we found you. The things in that house would get you more money than a little ransom."

The other bandits shifted uncomfortably. Magic could be good or bad, but always it was dangerous. However, talismans and potions could be worth a lot of money, a lot more than the ransom they would get from a lord's son and a lot less dangerous to sell if they could get them.

"You're lying." Statement of fact, but the way Lor said it made Tibs think Lor didn't believe it even as he said it.

Tibs knew it sounded too good to be true, but he had to sell Lor on the idea, it was their only chance. And the best traders walked away when the deal was good. "What do you have to lose?"

"You're going to lead us into a trap," Lor suspiciously looked the boy up and down.

"We're going away from the village, and he'll lead us." Tibs motioned at Gus. "He's not right in the head. How could he trick you?" He knew the bandits had been watching the village. For weeks. They knew Old Gus.

"I don't like it, Lor." Fats chimed in.

"NO NAMES!" Lor kicked dirt onto Fats feet. Fats looked confused by that, but said nothing. Lor continued, "No name, and no one asked your opinion. I'll make this decision. I'm the leader."

"Look, Gus, where is the house?" Tibs asked.

Old Gus pointed deeper into the woods.

"What sense would it make for us to take you deeper into the woods? If there's no house, you'll kill us all anyway; and you haven't lost anything but a little time, but if there is a house, you get inside and let us go. No one needs to know." Tibs could see two of them nodding.

"You'll turn us in." Lor pointed his sword right at Tibs's heart.

"I give you my word," Tibs vowed and then pointed at Sy. "And so will he. We will not come after you or try to find you."

Sy, still gagged, nodded.

"Oh, your word? Well, that settles it." Lor laughed, "But we'll try it your way for a bit. Chemise!" Lor pointed to the tall thief with the red shirt and scar over his eye, "Tie their hands. It wouldn't do to have bunch of children wandering the woods alone, would it?"

The children found themselves linked together in a line, with Gus at the head and Gabe at the rear and Sy on the ground still bound. Lor couldn't help talking, it seemed, prompting his men to laugh at his little jokes, "I know you may be lying, right men?" They laughed. "Still, the hostage won't be missed for some time and I imagine they won't miss the rest of you until nightfall, so we'll indulge your walking tour of these woods a bit and see if we can't make some bigger profit, you'd like that, right men?" They laughed. "What's so funny?"

"Nothing, Lor." Fats tried to remember what Lor had been saying.

"Amateurs, nothing but amateurs." Lor shook his head.

The one Lor called "Chimese" put Sy last in line, then cut the ropes around his legs so he could walk. Sy managed to get the gag out of his mouth. He came up behind Tibs and hissed, "I hope you know what you're doing."

"Right, because you're doing so well without us," Tibs hissed right back.

"At least I didn't get all my friends killed," Sy said.

"Where are the twins?"

"I'm out here alone."

"Why are you out here anyway?" Tibs had wondered about that since finding him there.

"Practicing." Sylas scowled.

"Practicing, where's your sword?" Tibs asked.

"I can't use a sword, idiot." Sy pouted.

"Then..." Tibs understood, he was practicing magic. "Oh, didn't want people to see you making mistakes."

"I leave that kind of thing to you, Tibs." Sy jibed.

Tibs didn't react. He concentrated on his walking. If there was mud, he put his foot in it. Then he dragged his feet through dirt and rubbed his body on the thorns trying to leave bits of cloth on them, all this left for his father to follow. The bandits didn't appear to care. They were right, no one would miss them till nightfall or maybe a little before, and they wouldn't worry till darkness covered the village completely. Hours. Hours before anyone noticed their little group was missing and still more hours before any suspicion something was amiss.

By that time they would probably all be dead.

CHAPTER 18

The question isn't what makes men bad. That's easy to see.
Hunger, greed, hatred.
All these can darken the soul. All men are evil, that's obvious.
The question is why do some turn out good?
It's more than who their father is, or the kind of life they lived.
Something happens in their lives that makes them cling to
habits or virtues most people give up on.
It comes down to choices, but in a world filled with evil, pain
and suffering, why do some men and women choose good?
That's the real question for our age.
How can I make the choice to choose good?

—SPOKEN BY TIBERIUS THE FIRST DURING HIS DEDICA-
TION SPEECH TO THE FIRST CLASS OF STUDENTS AT THE
UNIVERSITY OF GRANDFORD.

GUS STOPPED. "WE are here." He smiled at the bandits. They saw no house.
They saw a clear clearing.

Lor fumed. "This is it? A clearing?"

Tibs could see the house. Barely. The intertwined logs blended into
the forest camouflaging it perfectly in these woods. If the planks didn't
cover the door, he might not see it at all.

"The house is invisible," Tibs insisted confidently. "It's magic."

"That's not even a good lie. Who ever heard of an invisible house?" Lor sneered and the gang laughed too.

"No, no, the house is here," Tibs called out.

"Then how do we find it?" the Lor prodded.

"We step on the porch. Then you'll see it." Tibs pulled the ropes and strode what he hoped looked confidently toward the house.

Lor sneered. "Good plan. A good walk before your quick death."

"No, no, it's right there. You'll see it as soon as you step on the porch." Tibs had to brush sweat out of his eyes.

The picaroon stroked his mustache as he looked over the unwashed children. He cracked his knuckles, which seemed to signal some sort of change because the other rogues all relaxed. "All right, show me the house." He pointed at Toraline and Tibs and Fats waddled over and cut their ropes from the rest of the group. They were still tied together. "If you run away, I kill them all."

Toraline stumbled forward. Tibs took her arm and helped to steady her. She shook uncontrollably, afraid. They moved forward together. "Raise your foot," he instructed her. She lifted her foot, then put it on the porch, like they had done before.

Everyone gasped. They could see it now. Sy dropped to his knees.

"There it is!" Old Gus said. "Just like I remembered it."

Fats pointed his thumbs straight at each other and two fingers on each hand downward, shaking them, a superstitious reaction to ward away evil. Tibs almost laughed. As if a hand motion would protect them.

Lor plucked his goatee. He glided up to the house and stepped on the stairs and put his hand on the decaying banister. He floated up to the porch and then jumped up and down. Well built, the house didn't shake. He sidled toward the door.

"STOP!" Tibs cried out.

Lor stopped. "Why?" he demanded.

"If you touch the door, the house will move. That's not how you get in." Tibs remembered the house had disappeared on him twice. This time he would learn something new before it vanished.

The leader motioned for Rouge to bring the children closer.

"You sure dat's a good idée?" the Fats questioned.

Lor gushed, "Think of the money we can make with the stuff inside. Potions, talismans, strange ingredients. We're going to be sorry we didn't bring a dozen pack mules, it must be filled with all sorts of things we can sell, and we can get top price because no one will care we stole it." When all else fails, greed moves men to do risky things. They pulled the children right up to the porch.

"Well!" Tibs demanded.

The negligent never-do-well looked him straight in the eye. "Well, what?"

"Untie me." Tibs felt it must be obvious he'd need all of himself to open the house.

"Why, what are you going to do?" Lor poked him with his sword.

Tibs never blinked. "I'm going to get us inside." He didn't waver. He felt they could do it. He didn't know why; he just knew it. It was as if just standing on the porch his body filled with more and more confidence. They faced each other for a moment or two. Tibs began to feel taller.

Lor on the other hand blinked excessively. His lower lip twitched and he frowned. He made a motion and they untied Tibs.

Tibs rubbed his wrists.

Toraline tried to back off the porch, but Lor grabbed her rope and pulled her closer. "You like this one?" He found his smile again and turned toward Tibs, "I'm keeping her close, understand?"

Tibs nodded. Tibs had dreamed about this moment. Over and over, he had pictured himself on this porch and looking at the door. He knew he mustn't touch it. The house would move. There had to be some other way of opening the door. The words must mean something, but he couldn't make out what they meant.

"Sy! Come over here and tell me what you see!" Tibs motioned for the Cushite to be brought up onto the porch, maybe he could see something he didn't.

Lor looked uncomfortable. *Who's in charge here?*

"You want inside or not!" Tibs demanded.

Lor nodded, again frowning. They cut Sy from the group, keeping his hands tied.

Sy looked at the door. Three large planks covered most of it, but little ones were hammered over those, all of them covered with words and symbols. The large ones drew Tibs's interest and that's where Sy looked. "A riddle lock."

The bandits who at first were wary of a "magic" house, now drew closer. They pulled Gabe and Gus close. Magic, riddles, houses, they wanted in on what was happening. Lor said what they were all thinking, "A riddle lock?"

Sy stood up and looked the bandit square in the eyes. "Some powerful magicians don't use wood and metal to keep out thieves. They use magic. Some use magic in such a way so that those who can see and think can still go on. This is a riddle. All we have to do is answer the riddle, and we can get in."

"Riddle!" Gabe chimed, "I love riddles! Can I see it?"

Lor sighed. "Bring them all up here and be done with it." The porch became crowded. None of the kidnappers wanted to touch the boards, they knew evil magic when they saw it. They pushed and jostled on the porch finally leaving Gus on the ground. He had no interest in running away, so he stood smiling and rubbing his hands together. Sy and Tibs stood in front of the door with Gabe behind them, jumping up and down to see over Sy's shoulders. Toraline leaned back against the railing, and the pirates took up the flanks, ready for danger.

Lor lolled behind the boys, obviously become less sure by the minute. "What does it say!" He boomed.

"Oh!" Gus bellowed, pushing his bag of food into Gabe's hands and insisting that he be draped with the fur he took from Tibs' kitchen. "You're gonna need this, believe me." No one said anything about his eccentric behavior. They were used to it.

Gabe set the bag down on the ground, wrapping the rope that tied the top around his arm. He reached out to touch the door.

"DON'T TOUCH IT!" Tibs insisted loudly.

Gabe nodded. "Sorry, of course." He looked at the words. "This is Franish."

"You read Franish?" Sy said in astonishment.

"Gus taught me. He spent a lot time with the Frans." Gabe looked at the letters.

"Gus spent time with the Frans?" Sy stared at the man still standing on the ground, not believing what he just heard.

"He can hardly speak one language and you're telling me he speaks two?" Tibs questioned.

"They use the same letters, just give me a second." Gabe studied the letters very carefully. "I think I can translate it."

Lor poked the boy in the back. "Move aside," he said. "If anyone is going to open the door, it will be me."

Gabe picked up the bag and went to the far side of the porch.

"Tell me what it says." Lor twirled his mustache in excitement.

Gabe recited the riddle from memory. "My roots are deep, but I drink no water. My head is high, but I wear no crown, I have many a foot, but no feet."

Lor caressed his mustache back into shape. "That's it?"

"All you have to do is say the answer," Sy insisted.

"The answer? It could be a hundred things!" Lor ran his hands through his hair, wiping the grease on his pants.

"Such as?" Prompted Tibs.

"I don't know!" Lor pulled at his chin, looking at the letters as if they might reveal an answer he could understand. "A cloud?"

"Do clouds have roots?" Sy sneered.

"Little clouds? They have, ah, tendrils?" Lor clearly hated riddles. And knowledge. And learning. "A tree?"

"With feet?" Sy scoffed.

"There are no feet in this, a, a, riddle." Lor declared.

"Many a foot, but no feet, so you're saying trees have many a foot?" Tibs wanted to laugh, but dared not. Lor's nervousness grew. Sweat beaded on his forehead, and he fingered his sword far too often for his taste.

"If you know, if you, what, wh-wh-hat are you waiting for?" Lor yammered.

"You said you wanted to open it!" Toraline whittled her patience.

"Does everyone know the answer but me?" Lor screamed.

"I don't know it," Rouge confessed.

Tibs smiled. He looked over at Sy, who smiled back. Together they said, "I am a mountain." It was the first time they had every cooperated on anything.

In the next seconds, several things happened at once.

First, the door opened. The boards remained bound to the house. It resembled a sideways mouth with the planks as huge, menacing teeth. Second, the house lurched, it moved, tilting sideways slightly, enough to make everyone lose their footing. These two actions caused a cascading series of problems. Being the closest, the doors struck Lor square in the face, and he let loose a confetti of swear words. Light cracked the darkness in the house so severely that they could hear it. The weathered, dry, old floorboards just inside the house buckled in the sun. The darkness inched back in terror of the light. Then, the foul air in the room assaulted them with smells of death and decay. They could see cobwebs hanging everywhere.

This didn't seem as pressing as what happened outside. One moment they saw trees of the forest, the next a blizzard surrounded them. The light vanished, the sky turned grey and snow assaulted them. Cold clawed at them even as the house lurched. Gabe slipped sideways grabbing at the railing, but the bag of food pulled him into the snowbank. The house had moved, the cold air clawing at them. As the house lurched, Gabe fell off the porch. Still tied to Sy, they both grabbed the rope that joined them. Sy pulled, Gabe grasped in panic.

Thunder cracked. The house moved again.

Snow no longer swirled around them, flies did. Live flies. Live, biting winged avengers of the insect world. The cold air instantly changed to muggy, damp breath. They didn't notice the change in temperature, they noticed the evil denizens of the insect world trying to get at their blood. Sy held up the rope. The end burned, severed. Gabe was lost.

"Into the house!" Tibs ordered.

Toraline couldn't believe what he said, "It might be dangerous in there!"

"Like it's a picnic out here, get in the house!" Tibs roared.

Sy grabbed Toraline and threw her through. Tibs found himself dragged through the doorway. *Sy is strong*, Tibs thought. Sy dove in after them.

The kidnappers tried to follow. In the confusion, the door shut. Tibs looked up, himself, Sy and Toraline, plus three bandits. They could hear the fourth banging on the door outside. The house lurched again, obviously moving. They heard a scream, abruptly cut off. Would he rather be lost in the snow or the tsunami of flies? One pirate, one Gus, one Gabe, all gone.

The children sprawled out on the floor as the thieves attacked the door. It didn't budge when they pounded on it, or pulled on it.

"Do you really want to go back out there?" Tibs softly inquired, moving away from the door.

They paused for a moment, but Lor screamed, "Get us out of here!" Their fear renewed, they redoubled their efforts. They worked as individuals. They worked in unison, hammering the door with their fists as if they were part of a symphony. The door remained impassive. Lor produced a knife and stabbed the door, sparks filled the room, arching over the children, sending the leader to his knees, and setting his shirt sleeve on fire. Rouge jumped to his leader, putting out the fire. Lor didn't worry about the fire, he worried about breathing, gasping and clutching at his chest. The knife clattered helplessly to the floor.

No one saw Toraline quietly grabbing it.

"What's going on?" Lor screamed, pushing his comrades out of his way and bearing down on Tibs.

"How should we know!" Tibs cowered.

"I lost one of my men!" Lor's fingers curled into Tibs's shirt, choking the boy.

Sy pulled on Lor, "We lost two!"

Tibs choked out, "Gus stood on the ground when the house first moved. He's probably still at home. The others didn't die, they just aren't here, don't you think?"

Lor relaxed his grip. He looked suspiciously over his shoulder at his men. They stood watching him as if he were some sort of ghost.

"We don't know they're dead. Gabe fell into a snow bank and those bugs, it would take them some time to eat a whole person." Tibs poured out words like water on a fire. He felt Lor's hands shaking around his throat. "I just said I'd bring you to a magic house, I'd never been inside, how am I supposed to know?"

Things had gone so wrong. How could they be otherwise when everything began with kidnapping? What would his father say when he returned without Gabe? Or Old Gus? No treasure or mystery cleared would make up for that in his father's mind, Tibs knew that. *What if we can never return?* He thought to himself.

Lor looked at the blackened flesh of his hand, counting the red veins showing through his skin. Tibs knew that mark well, he'd seen on Nathan, twice. Magic. Magic permeated the door from both sides. Lor tore off his now-burned sleeve and wrapped up his hand.

"We get everything we find." Lor hissed into Tibs face. He tied the shirt tightly around the burns. If it hurt, it didn't show in his eyes. Lor took a deep breath with his eyes closed. He balled his hand and extended his fingers. He could use his hand. He pushed on Tibs and stood, turning back to the door. He brushed his hand against it, no mark on it at all.

"I wouldn't go that way," Sy warned.

"Then what way would you suggest!" Lor spat over his shoulder. He closed his eyes again and said, "Everything we find is ours. If we find enough we will let you go, if we don't, we will kill you for our trouble."

They looked around the room. Bare floor, bare walls, no furniture, no adornments, no trinkets or magic items at all. The large room had three doors along one wall. The doors stood opposite the door they came in. Two windows flanked the entrance door, the other walls were blank. Light seeped through the boarded-up windows. Whatever darkness encompassed the interior escaped when they came in. The dust looked like tendrils of yellow vines moving through the air, settling like a layer of volcanic ash and just as lovely on the lungs. Tibs felt the dust cling to this clothes as he slipped a few inches away from the adults. "Are you telling me I've lost a man for nothing?" Lor slavered.

"All I promised was an invisible house," Tibs stayed low in case Lor lost his temper again. "We've never been inside!"

Sy came up behind them, and apparently talking to Tibs, said, "Just so you know, if we live, I'm going to kill you."

"You'll have to get in line," Tibs managed to sputter, unable to turn away from the bandit.

"Where are all the magic items?" Lor spun around the room. "You said there were magic items!"

"There are still three doors to try," Tibs suggested.

Lor motioned, and Rouge went to the middle door. His hand stopped three inches from the doorknob. He pulled it back, quickly. "You want Me to touch this?" He pointed to himself.

"Rouge, don't question me!" Lor practiced his impatience.

Rouge Chemise's skinny fingers tipped with blackened fingernails reached for the doorknob. They shook.

"Grab it!" Lor shouted.

Rouge grasped the doorknob. It happened so fast that no one had a chance to scream. His whole body turned to smoke. His eyes disappeared last, filled with fear and pain. In a breath, he dissipated into the air.

Lor strode to the door. He waved around the air as if he'd be able to touch his lost compadre. Even the smoke vanished. He tapped himself on the forehead with a single finger. Lor spun around and hit Tibs across the face with the back of his hand. Tibs fell to the ground with his mouth bleeding. "This is your fault," the bandit captain said.

"He didn't know it was going to do that!" Toraline protested, getting to her knees and trying to help Tibs.

"We have to get out of here." The leader pointed at Toraline. "You, you go and touch another door."

Sy stepped between the bandit and the girl. "I'll do it."

The middle door meant certain death. Sy looked to the left and right.

Lor grabbed Sy by the collar. "Not you. You're worth money, if we ever escape." He threw the boy to the ground and motioned for Toraline to get to her feet. "You, girl, open that door." He pushed her to the left.

"Left it is." She brushed off her dress and touched the doorknob.

Nothing happened, that is, no sparks of lightning or fire or poison, the doorknob did rattle in the door. *Of course nothing happened, she suppresses magic,* Tibs thought. She pulled on the door. It didn't move.

Lor shook his hands trying to stop the shaking. "Does that mean this is the door we try to open or do we risk this last door?"

"Stop, stop, stop!" Tibs tried to stand up. "You've got to think your way through this. You have to think or everyone will die."

"That's not my fault, you little—" Lor stepped toward Tibs.

Tibs cut him off, "Did you think this was going to be easy? It's a magic house, any of these doors could still be a trap, if it were me, I'd trap all of them."

"Then why did you bring us here, you idiot!" Lor screamed.

"Because I wanted to live. What I'm not supposed to try and live?" Tibs scooted back to the wall of the house.

Lor's fury grew. "Where would you start, then?" He drew his sword and pointed it at Tibs's neck. It still shook. Lor held it with both hands and managed to steady the threatening blade. "Use those brains and think us out of this or you'll find yourself dead."

Tibs had to think fast. And he had to think right. His eyes darted up, left, right, down, there had to be something to get him out of this house. He pointed up.

The logs above their heads formed triangles with the point at the top and three straight beams across the room. At first glance the room had looked completely empty. But it wasn't. A large night colored black bird roosted in the rafters, all black except for a circle of white around its neck and a rectangle of white on its chest, like a necklace made of feathers. If it weren't for the fact that its eyes glowed red, he would not have been able to see it in the shadows.

The bird eyed them.

Lor looked down at Tibs. "Why didn't you tell me you saw a great big bird in the rafters!"

"I just noticed it."

Lor's sword drooped, he rubbed his nose as he said, "Oh, this will solve our problems, a bird in the rafters. He'll lead us out of this mess. He'll bring back my men. Of course if he doesn't, I will take all this rage in my heart out of your flesh, boy." He meant Tibs, of course.

"At least we'll have something to eat," Fats suggested eying the bird.

"You think there's any meat on that ragged thing?" Lor kicked at the air.

The bird moved its head, looking through its left eye at them. "Look at these, Ravensquick." The bird's alluring and luxurious voice caressed the group. "The children are smarter than the adults."

Lor's sword pointed it at the bird. "It speaks!"

"Will you throw the sword, oh man of action?" It laughed. "This one didn't answer the riddle." The bird looked at Toraline and Sy. "The children bear watching," The bird gave a second look to Sy. "You have magic." Sy took a step toward the bird, "And you have spirit, I can see it. You'll bear watching, if you live. Which I doubt you'll do for very long."

With that, the bird's eyes stopped glowing. The bird shook its head and chirped with a completely different voice, a squeak, and a cough. "I hate it when you do that!" The voice changed. When the eyes were red, it sounded seductive, and now it sounded raspy and thin. Then the bird looked at the people. "Visitors." The bird shifted nervously from one foot to another.

"Demon bird, tell us how to get out of this foul house," Lor screamed.

"Demon bird." The bird snorted and started cleaning his wing. "Really, that's too much. I'm going back to sleep."

The leader turned on Tibs. "If you don't tell me what's going on right now, I'm going to kill you."

"I think it's time we started working together, or we won't get out of this house. Threatening to kill me isn't going to help, people in village do that every day."

"He's right about that." Sy added helpfully.

Tibs stood up and brushed off his clothes.

Toraline stood up, too. "You have a plan?"

"I wonder what you eat, bird," Tibs said casually, hardly looking at the bird.

"I eat the flesh off of dead children," the bird said.

"How do you expect to kill us?" Sy put his hands on his hips, daring the bird to come down and attack.

"You'll die like all the others," the bird hissed.

"Talked to death?" Sy looked for something to throw at the bird, he found nothing.

"Starvation," the bird fluttered to another rafter.

"We'll dine on crow at least one night," Lor sheathed his sword.

"You'd have to kill me first, no one's been able to do that yet." He jumped to another rafter further away from Lor.

Tibs continued to study the bird. "How long has he been here, do you think?"

"There must be another way out." Sy went to the walls and started feeling them for a secret passage.

"The crow is not a familiar." Tibs had read that some magi had animal companions.

"I'm a raven, not a crow. RAVEN!" The bird flew in anger to another beam, and then snorted in disgust, "Familiar. Preposterous. POPPYCOCK."

Tibs examined the room at a deeper level. No furniture, no paint on the walls, not even dirt on the floor.

"Now that we can't run away, could you untie us?" Sy suggested harshly.

Lor looked from one boy to another and finally at Toraline.

"Why keep us tied up?" Toraline held out her hands.

Lor waved at Fats, who got busy cutting them loose. "If you don't get us out of here, I'll kill you all."

"What have we said about threats?" Sy reminded him. Lor pointed his sword at the blond boy. "Personally, I don't care, as long as long as you start with him." Sy indicated Tibs.

Toraline had finished her survey of the room. "What does the bird eat? I don't see any bones or seeds."

"No feadders." Fats put in. Lor shot him a look. "I'm just saying, don't birds, like shed? He must be enchanted."

"There's a big leap, thinkpots!" the bird derided. "The bird is enchanted! That's clever."

"Then he's a prisoner just like us." Tibs rapped on the walls. Mostly solid.

The bird made a sound like a horn.

"Be polite," Toraline chastised it.

"They left a bird to watch over what happens inside," Sy added.

Lor grew impatient. "Tell me, little scholar, why can't we use the other doors? One must be the way out."

"The doors are too obvious," Tibs pointed out.

"Ah, someone with a brain," the bird laughed. "You don't happen to have some food on you? I don't have to eat, but I miss it." He cocked his head expectantly.

Sy asked, "What do we do with the crow?"

"RAVEN!" The bird dived at Sy and pecked at his head.

"Ouch!" Sy rubbed his head. "I think you mean—dead raven."

"You can't kill me," the bird crowed.

"I can try." Sy made a jump for the ceiling, but missed, by quite a bit.

"What about names?" Toraline asked.

Lor hesitated. "He's Fats."

Fats shrugged. "A nickname, but I don't mind."

"You don't mind!" Lor snorted.

Fats scowled, smiled, and ended with a hurt pout on his face.

"What about you," Sy pointed at the bird. "Do you have a name?"

"Name? I did once. A long time ago." The bird sighed. It seemed to think for a moment, and then it shook its head. "I can't remember it anymore. How do you like that! That's the problem with having such as tiny head." The bird laughed for a moment, and then retreated to a corner of the rafters, into the darkness as the laughter turned to sobbing. The whole room went quiet.

The house suddenly felt very small.

"Test da doors," Fats insisted.

"No, Tibs is right," Sy reluctantly stated. "Enchant a house to move through space, to be invisible, leave a cursed bird here to do whatever he's supposed to do, and leave the way out through a door? Whoever did this would not make the escape a door. They're just temptation."

"I make it a practice to give in to temptation." Lor pondered.

"Obviously." Toraline chipped in.

"We have greatly underestimated the intelligence of the Cush, Toraline." Tibs surprised himself by saying that out loud.

"That's what made the tar and feathering so effective, you never expected us to use our brains." Toraline stifled a laugh. Tibs felt the heat coming from his heart to his head. His temper grew. He felt it.

"I did get out of chores for a few days. Some good came out of it." Tibs glanced at Toraline. She smiled. Tibs knew what his father would say. So Tibs did something he should have done weeks ago. He laughed. "That was rather brilliant. I just wished you used eagle feathers and not chicken. It's bad enough looking like a bird, but Nathan hadn't had lunch, and I thought he was going to tear off my leg for starters."

They laughed together for a moment.

"I have to ask, how did you get into the castle?" Sy asked.

"The castle?" Tibs looked at Toraline. They smiled at each other. "We can't tell you."

"You can't or won't," Sy pressed.

That's when Lor jumped between them, "The killing is about to commence." The children stopped talking.

Tibs examined the three doors. He put his hands close but did not touch. "Sy, can you feel this?" He felt a slight tingling. Sy came up to the left door and put his hand near Tibs's hand, right next to the doorknob without touching it.

Sy nodded. "Magic?"

"It must be," Tibs confirmed.

"Then why didn't it kill her?" Lor stamped the ground.

Of course Tibs couldn't tell Lor the answer to his question. "There are all sorts of reasons. Maybe it works when you open it, or when you close it, or when an old man touches it. All we know is that this is not the way out."

"There's no other way out!" Lor pointed all around them.

"Yes there is," Tibs insisted. It never occurred to him that it might be harder to get out than it was to get in. Getting in should have been the whole story. *Maybe not the whole story, it would have been nice to discover some great magic or adventure, but to get in and find nothing! That can't be it. If everyone who gets in dies, that explains why we couldn't find much written about the house. Still, there must be a way out or the person who built it wouldn't have left the bird, right?*

"Why would anyone go through so much trouble?" Toraline asked.

"Ask the crow," Sy sniped at the bird.

"Raven." The bird jumped up and down.

"Wanna make something of it?" Sy dared the bird to come after him.

The bird stopped jumping, thinking better of another attack.

"I swear, if you don't tell me how to get out in the next five seconds, I'm going to destroy you, boy!" Job requirements for thieves and kidnappers didn't include patience.

Tibs began, "Out? I know the way out. The question is whether the raven wants to leave or stay."

The bird jumped toward Tibs. He couldn't help it. "Leave?" He pecked at the underside of his wing. "Leave?" His head turned this way and that. "That's impossible."

"You only say that because no one's done it before," Tibs said confidently.

"You can't kill me, you know." The bird took another jump toward the boy. "That's part of the magic. I can't die. I've tried to die, a hundred times, I've begged soldiers and magicians who have come inside to kill me, but they've never been able to kill me, even when I try to help them. It won't work." He pecked at the rafters. "Still hurts, though."

"You can stay here if you want," Tibs added.

"Change me back? Is that what you're talking about? Changing me back?" The bird flapped his wings and actually flew down to the ground in front of the boy. "I'm the eyes of the Black Heart."

"All the same," Tibs said. "I'm your only hope." *The Black Heart? The children's tale? She wasn't real, was she?*

"She already knows you're here," The bird spat. "The others have all died anyway, trying the doors. Their bodies vanishing into the air, leaving nothing for me." The bird hopped toward Tibs to get a closer look. "You think you can get me out?"

"Why not me?"

"Forget about the bird, just get us out of here." Lor lunged at the raven who flew back up to the rafters.

"We may need him." Tibs kicked his left foot with his right.

"Are you going to do something?" Lor fumed.

The bird flew back up to the rafters. "You think I can just ride out on your arm?" The raven laughed. "I would have ridden the coach, hitched up the wagon, kicked the horse centuries ago if that would have worked. I can't leave this room."

"I think I can get you out, if you want to help us," Tibs said.

The bird shifted from foot to foot. He flapped his wings experimentally. "It won't work."

"You don't want to try?" Tibs tried to use his father's soothing voice.

"What makes you think, makes you think?" the bird cocked his head, staring at the ground.

"Stop it! I've had just about enough!" Lor stamped.

"Right, we don't go through the doors, we go through the floor." Tibs felt around the floor and found a seam. He tried to put his fingers in the cracks, but his fingers were too big.

Fats pulled out a knife put it between the cracks. It slid in perfectly. They thought it might be a floorboard, but as he pushed the knife down, a whole section lifted, a hidden trap door. They lifted it up and revealed a stairway leading into the earth.

"What do you know, you get to live," Lor stopped sheathed his sword and approached the opening. "Maybe, maybe...Fats try the steps."

"Me?" Fats looked hurt.

"Just take a one step down," Lor ordered.

Fats stepped down into the dimness first one, then two stairs.

Sy challenged Tibs, "How did you know about that door?"

Tibs said softly, so softly that only Sy could hear, "The bird's eyes. When I talked about leaving, it kept looking at the floor."

"It looked at the floor? With eyes on both sides of its head, how did you know it wasn't looking up?" Sylas hissed.

Tibs thought for a moment. "I didn't think about that."

Sy shook his head. "Yeah, I feel a lot safer."

Tibs stepped ahead of Toraline, giving her a look. She shrugged. "I always bet on you, most of the time I come out ahead." She smiled.

Tibs looked up into the rafters. "Coming?" he asked the raven.

"Coming?" The bird swooped down and landed on Tibs's shoulder. "I can't leave this room. Have you been listening? Magic barrier."

"Are you sure?" Tibs grinned at the bird.

"I'd crawl into your nose if I thought it would get me out of this room," the bird squawked.

Sy laughed from the middle of the stairs. "That I'd like to see. And I'll help."

The bird shifted nervously from one foot to another. Tibs reached out, grabbed Toraline, and pulled her close to him. He needed her if the bird could get out, or, rather, go down into the darkness. She suppressed magic, so the spell that kept the bird in the room should fail with her near the bird. He didn't want the bird on her in case people made the connection. He didn't want her dead.

They stepped down the stairs.

"I'm going down," the raven chirped. "You're not a boy, you're a demon, an imp, a wood sprite, a..."

"Don't swell his head. He's having a tough enough time getting down the stairs as it is," Toraline smirked.

It was true. Not the part about Tibs's head growing, but that they were going down the stairs. The bird's weight grew with every step they took down into the earth. By the time they got halfway down the stairs, Tibs shoulder hurt. He staggered to one side a few steps later under the weight of the bird. Without thinking, Toraline held out her arm, and the bird hopped on, jumping up to her shoulder. She grunted. The bird's weight didn't double, more like quadrupled or quintupled.

"What have you been eating?" She asked the bird.

The raven looked at her from one eye. "Eating? NOTHING! Haven't you been paying attention?" He didn't seem to understand he was changing. "I want food, but I don't need it." He almost sighed. Probably just as well he didn't understand. By the time he got to the bottom of the stairs, he would be unable to fly, but since he had nowhere to go, that didn't matter.

Almost as an afterthought, Lor came down the stairs last. "I don't like it."

He wanted to make sure they tripped any traps and died and he escaped. Years of experience with kidnappings and adventures and magic made him think that things were going to go wrong, very wrong.

CHAPTER 19

*Historians sometimes dwell on the kings and queens and roy-
alty who pit their lives against the backdrop of big events. The
royals seem to wield great power, moving people and armies like
pawns in a chess game. The reality, however, is stranger than
the rulers themselves.*

*What the kings and queens do is follow. They play out the will
of the people. They do nothing without the cooperation of the
general populace. The commoners are driven by fear, loyalty,
hunger, laziness, desire, but always they are driven. The leaders follow, and if they are good leaders, they appear to lead, a
delightful illusion—*

—FROM SENNACHERIB MACCAULEY'S *HISTORY OF THE 11
KINGDOMS*, 2ND EDITION, CHAPTER 2, "THE FORCES THAT
KEPT THE KINGDOMS FROM UNITING"

COBWEBS DRAPED THE rough-hewn stairway as it descended into an eerie light. It had been some time since anyone discovered the way down. The dim light didn't exactly dispel the dark, but they could see well enough. They couldn't determine from whence it came. Air hissed up the steps. Toraline couldn't get that sound out of her mind. She thought, *We should not be going down, we should be going out. We shouldn't have gone into the house at all, or set foot on the porch, this time or the time before. Tibs is such a, such a…*She couldn't finish the thought. She'd known him her whole life. Their parents expected them to be friends, though they were so different. She liked the difference, mostly. *The adventures we've had...* Then the sight of Gabe's face as the house spun out of existence. They left him in a snowstorm. Of course, he did have a great big bag of food and a heavy coat thanks to Gus. *How did he know? Who knows? Gabe might be better off than us. He might survive. Still, to die with friends is better than to die alone.*

She looked over the unraven-occupied shoulder, toward Lor. His left hand dragged down the carved wall, as if to slow him down. His right rested on the hilt of his sword, in readiness. His mustache twitched oddly making him looking more like a frightened rabbit than a criminal.

The raven ruffled his feathers nervously as they plodded down the stairs. Every step brought a chirp or caw, and even a few coughs. By the time he reached the bottom, his feathers flattened and his wings flapped in nervous joy.

"I'm at the bottom! I've never been at the bottom. Not since this was my wine cellar!" He spread his wings to fly when Tibs shouted.

"STOP!" Everyone stopped. Tibs scolded the bird. "Stay with Toraline," the boy commanded. "If you leave her shoulder, the magic that got you here will stop, and I don't know what will happen. Do you understand, bird?"

The bird turned his head quickly to the left and then the right, looking at the boy with each eye in turn. "I understand."

"Which way?" Sy asked the bird.

"Which way?" the bird laughed. "How should I know? There only used to be two doors, but now there are three."

Three doors greeted them at the bottom of the stairs; one to the left, the right and lastly one straight ahead. Tibs examined the doors at the bottom of the stairs. "You designed the house?"

The bird trilled. "It was a magnificent house. I could take it anywhere I wanted."

"You could take it anywhere? What kind of power did that take?" Sy asked.

"Power?" the bird laughed. "The house is a talisman. What good would a house be to a wizard if he or she couldn't take it with them?" He sighed. "I, I, must have drawn her attention somehow. She seeks us out, you know. She eats us whole, but she left me here." He stopped fidgeting and then put his head under his wing.

"What aren't you telling us?" Tibs insisted.

"Who are you talking about?" Sy asked.

"Who? The Black Heart, of course." The raven pulled his head out from under his wing and pecked at his feet nervously.

"The Black Heart is a myth," Lor snorted. He was at least five steps higher than anyone else, his feet fidgeting, as if he didn't know if he should go back or go forward. "Isn't she?"

"I wish," the raven whimpered. "She took my house, my body, my life. She chained me to that room to be her eyes and mouth whenever anyone made it into the house. For all I know, she's looking through my eyes now."

"Let's just get out of here." Toraline knocked on the right door.

Lor watched from higher up the stairs. "Which one, little parasite?" He looked at Tibs.

Tibs looked around the hall. "Why make the house move? Why make it invisible? What was the point?"

The bird laughed. "Point? Point? She doesn't need a point! She's cruel. Isn't that enough?"

"You made it jump from place to place," Toraline pointed out.

"And she made it jump from time to time," the bird stated.

"Wait, what is that?" Sy inquired.

"I've said too much." The bird hid his head again.

"Time, it jumps in time?" Sy asked.

"I thought you knew." The raven pulled his head out from under his wing. "You already knew a lot about it. I made it jump from place to place. She took it and found a way to make it jump from time to time as well as from place to place. She has a habit of building on the work of others."

"Why would she do that?!" Lor screamed sitting on the steps, "How are we supposed to get home, get out with the house moving all over everywhere?"

"To catch a few curious magi?" Tibs puzzled about the Black Heart. *The house must have a purpose to go through all this trouble. Could she be cruel for cruelty's sake?* "What is this Black Heart afraid of?"

"Afraid, she's afraid of nothing and everything. She has everything and nothing. She is darkness itself. She blots out the sun and the stars. The torch and the fire. The feeling heart and feet." The bird pecked his feet again. "The moon itself answers her call to rise and set."

"He's been a bird so long, it's gone to his head." Sy took a step or two down the hall.

Tibs turned to the bird. "How many have gotten this far, crow?" he demanded.

"None came back up," the raven mused. "None could take me down."

"How many!" Sy reiterated.

The bird jumped. "One, two, many..." That's as close as he could come. "I can't keep my own name in my head, how can I keep them?"

Tibs started to remember what his father had tried to teach him about war. "Sir Jesse used to talk about three kinds of traps," he began, "bear, lion and rabbit. Bears are trapped with cages that fall from above. Lions are trapped with pits from below. Rabbits were trapped with carrots under a box that falls on them. Some traps may be physical and some magical, but they can only come from above below or draw us right into them before they spring."

"Which do you think this Black Heart will think we are?" Sy asked.

"All three," Tibs said.

"You've forgotten the fox, you stupid, vacuous boy," Lor added. He drew his sword out of its sheath now, as if he was expecting big trouble. "The fox isn't fooled by any of these but relies on the fact that he can escape the cage, the pit, and the box by being clever. You need a dog to trap the fox, and if this is the black heart, which I doubt, she'll have plenty of dogs wherever we go."

"Dogs can be fooled." Toraline knew dogs, even of the human variety.

Lor sneered. "If it's really her, she will assume you're a fox. The bear is too stupid, led by his nose. The lion is too lazy; he doesn't look at the ground ahead of him. The rabbit is too greedy; he can't pass up a free lunch. But a fox, he's cunning, suspicious. He'll look up, he'll look below, and though he's greedy, he knows there no such thing as a free lunch."

The bird started hopping back and forth from shoulder to shoulder. "You should expect magic traps." He hopped even harder.

"Would you stop that!" Toraline protested. "You're getting heavier and heavier."

"Magic traps," Sy said. "Do you think there will be a lot of those?"

"We won't need to worry about those very much," Tibs interjected.

"You think you can 'scape magic, boy?" Fats chimed in. "Look at da bird! He's magicked, and now he's a bird."

"Bird changed soon!" The bird cackled.

"There is always someone more powerful," Fats reminded them.

"There's one more kind of trap." The bird became still. He closed his eyes. He concentrated. "People. People are a trap. People always trip you up." Silence. Three doors. No one looked at them. They all feared what lay beyond the portals.

Lor broke the silence. "Do we stay here forever, or do you make a choice?"

The bird said, "The right was the wine cellar, and to the left was the larder. The wine might still be good, but the food went bad ages ago. That's all I can tell you." He tucked his head under his wing. "And remember something else." His voice was muffled. "She is watching, she has eyes everywhere. Though this house was mine, it's now hers." The bird started what sounded like a cough, but became caws. He started to dig at his wings again. "You have no idea how much these feathers itch." With that his head disappeared again.

Tibs motioned for Sy to come closer to the where the hallway branched off. Three doors. Why were there always three doors?

He stood close to Sy. "Which way do you think?" Tibs asked Toraline quietly. Sy looked closely at the staircase, then reached for the door to the right: the wine cellar. As his hand approached the doorknob, Tibs noticed a shimmering. "Stop. See the doorknob?"

"Are you going to talk them to death?" Sy kicked Tibs's feet.

"We can't just touch the doorknobs. Look what happened upstairs." Toraline explained.

"She won't use the same spell twice, especially this close to the other one." Sy wanted to get moving.

"They're enchanted," Tibs explained.

"The doorknobs or the doors?" Sy challenged, "You almost make me think you know something about all this! But we've read the same scrolls, you don't know about this any more than I do, probably less. You're nothing more than the son of a minor knight from one of the smallest fiefdoms in all the eleven kingdoms. Brig'adel, please! You may as well live in the icy north." Sy reached for the doorknob on the left.

"Don't!" Tibs shouted.

Sy smirked, then moved his hands quick as lightning and turned the knob. "I'm leader by right, by gift. I'm older, stronger and a noble. And what have you got? Nothing!" The door opened easily. Sy smiled as he pushed it open. Then the door flung itself open, pulling Sy after it. He couldn't let go of the doorknob. It pulled him off his feet and flung him, not into a room exactly because the room contained a pit, no ground, no floor, only a deep, deep chasm. For a moment, Sy floated in the air. Toraline gasped. Then Sy fell. He flailed about for a moment and his hands connected with something hard. He grabbed instinctively.

His fingers dug into the side of the pit, leaving him looking up at the threshold of the door at Tibs, Fats, and Toraline. When Sy's body hit the hard stone that lined the pit, he lost his breath. He almost let go of the small ledge his fingers had managed to grab. He looked up and saw the door closing. He knew that when it closed, he would die.

Before he even knew what he was going to do, Tibs dove headfirst through the door.

The door couldn't close if his body blocked it. *I'll just slide in there and stop the door, and grab Sy's hands.* A worthy thought, but in practice it felt different. Tibs didn't prepare himself for the pain. The door didn't slow because a body happened to be in the way. It closed, hard, and Tibs felt a crunch. He imagined his father there in that instant. "Just a couple of ribs, don't worry about it."

Since he was there, he reached down to Sy.

Sy looked up at Tibs's face. Tibs smiled, "I know, you wish I was Toraline."

"For all sorts of reasons." Sy tried to return the smile.

Fats pushed his body against the door and managed to move it out a bit. He looked back at Lor. "You gonna help?" Lor moved higher up the steps further way from the doors and the danger. Toraline pushed against the door with the bandit.

Sy reached up to Tibs with this right hand. Sy noticed his hands bleed, the walls of the chasm were jagged. That's when his left hand slipped. "One less person to worry about." He tried to make a joke of it as he began to fall.

CHAPTER 20

The obvious things are not always seen first—

—FROM SENNACHERIB MACCAULEY'S *HISTORY OF THE UNIFICATION*

WITH TORALINE AND Fats both pushing on the door, it opened slightly. Tibs saw Sy beginning to fall. He pushed to his knees and dove down the shaft, headfirst.

"Tibs!" Toraline flung herself onto Tibs's legs, which began sliding over the threshold. The door shut on her body as she grabbed Tibs's pants.

"'Ere now!" Fats was alone at the door, but it wouldn't close because Toraline's body now barred it with the bird dancing on her back.

She could see down the shaft. The deeper it grew, the darker it became. She couldn't see the bottom. She felt blistering cold air coming from below, colder than anything she could remember feeling before. She started shaking. It might have been the fear as she looked down into that din of death, but she always maintained that the cold air made her shiver.

Tibs managed to grab Sy's wrists just as the boy began to slip further down the hole. Sy's head hit a stone.

Sy looked up at Tibs. "You can't possibly believe you can pull me out."

"No, but I might make a good rope," Tibs smiled.

Sy reached up and grabbed Tibs's sleeve. "You're a lousy rope." He reached up with his other hand and grabbed Tibs's shirt at the shoulder.

"But you'll do in a pinch." He found a place for his left foot and pushed himself up, grabbing Tibs's pants.

Clambering over Toraline, Sy found himself standing on the ledge.

Tibs looked down into the pit with Toraline holding onto his ankles. "It's a nice view, but I'd like to live please," he called back up.

Brushing the blood out of his eyes, Sy sniped, "It would be easier to drop him."

"What!" Tibs screeched, his voice echoing down.

Sy pulled Tibs out of the pit. Toraline crawled backward out of danger.

The door shut.

The children panted in fear.

Lor laughed. "Shall we say that's not the way out?"

"Shall we test the doors together?" Tibs suggested darkly.

"What do you mean?" Sy came closer to the door they just went through.

"Look." Tibs put his hand near the doorknob. Sy saw a glimmer there.

"Magic," Sy said.

They checked the other doors. Only one didn't have a shimmer, so at least they knew it didn't have a magic trap, or an obvious magic trap.

Locked, they knew they had to find a way to open it. Sy sighed. "How are we supposed to get through a locked door?"

Fats snorted, "Locked door, there's no such thing." He pulled out two long, thin sticks and stuck them in the lock. In a moment it popped open. "You think Lor keeps me around for my good looks?" he laughed.

"The only one with good looks is me." Lor added from the stairs.

The door swung open and stairs continued down. The air felt freezing.

"What do you think?" Sy asked Tibs.

Tibs smelled the air, it seemed clean, "More dangerous to stay still, I think."

Sy led the way down the stairs, followed by Fats and Toraline, who had the growing bird on her shoulder. Tibs came next and finally Lor lurked behind them. They could see that what had started as an engineering project had devolved into just some people carving a hole. At first supports held up the ceiling. The stairway changed from dirt, to mud to stone. And as it became stonier. It was less of a staircase and more a crude tunnel.

"How long do you suppose it took to do this?" Toraline asked as they made their way deeper.

A group of determined miners, working hard, together, would take years to build this kind of tunnel, though the disregard for any safety features made it clear that engineers had no part in it. Depressions in the stone gave clues as to who built it. Lor's eyes were only on the danger ahead instead of looking at the details. Perhaps he had learned to be short-sighted because he didn't expect to live very long.

As it was, only Tibs took note of the cave walls as they went down. Dark stone and layers of dirt lined the walls. He could see the tunnel wasn't carved, but torn. *Who could have done this kind of work?* Better eyes might have revealed handprints driven into the rock.

"I think—" Sy began.

"Shh!" Lor hissed.

"But—" Toraline tried to point out they had no idea where they were going.

"Shh!" Lor stamped his foot. "You want to be killed?"

The children and Fats shook their heads meekly.

"Then be quiet!" He adjusted his belt when he heard something again. "Who's making that noise!"

"It's water," Toraline said quietly. "Up ahead."

"Oh," Lor turned his head.

They could all hear it. Running water. But under the water, there were voices. Arguing, very far away.

"Look," Sy pointed at the raven.

The sound of voices came from the bird. His eyes burned red. Toraline gasped and flung the bird to the ground. He alighted gently as if he had done this all his life. He was definitely bigger. His mouth stood half open, sound pouring out of it as if five or six people were speaking from inside his head. Then the voices stopped.

"Still alive? How interesting." The bird's voice grew once again lilting and melodic. "Someone is smart." The bird looked at each one of them in turn, searching. He stopped on Sy. "You're the only one with magic." Now, Nathan knew Tibs had magic because he saw him stop the ax in the air. However, Tibs had no aura, so there was nothing for the bird to see. The only one in the group that had the telltale sign of magic was Sylas. The trained eye would never miss his unmistakable aura. Toraline had a gift too, but one couldn't see it with eyes, a wizard had to be next to her to feel her effects, so the bird stared at Sy. Sy's green aura flared under the gaze of the bird. Lor and Fats stepped back from the boy. The raven fixed his right eye on Sy. "You're the only one with magic, is it you? Must be. Do you have a name, boy?"

Toraline stepped in front of Sy. "Don't say anything."

The bird laughed. "No matter. I will send the house back to where you entered, or close enough. I'll know where you came from, and I'll know where to start looking, if any of you leave the house alive, which no one has ever done." The eyes faded and the laughter turned to squawks, and then the squawks turned to cries of pain.

Toraline couldn't bear to hear the cries and picked up the raven, cradling it. "Are you all right?" she asked.

The raven calmed in her arms, his shaking slowly stopping. "Out of your arms, I feel only pain." he said as he looked at Toraline with one eye.

Lor snorted, "Please, all this is an act." He then did something he hadn't done before. He strode down the passageway ahead of everyone else, expecting them to follow. "Look, nothing happens!"

Then the tunnel went dark.

The floor shifted, as if in an earthquake. Tibs didn't notice so much because he felt as if his body began to melt into the floor, and everything turned to sleep. He couldn't help it. He and Sy knew no more as they fell on the stones.

Tibs dreamed. Darkness swirled around him. His eyes wouldn't open, and he couldn't move his arms. Someone pulled on his body. Every fiber in his body felt drained of life, like someone squeezing it to get out all the water. He wanted to open his eyes, but he couldn't. It hurt. He wanted to scream, but he couldn't open his mouth. Even though his eyes were closed, he found that he could "hear" around himself. Other people were within the darkness. A great big mound of flesh to one side, other smaller mounds to another, thousands of tiny dots and dashes swirling around in the air. One close body, next to him glowed green. *Must be Sy*, Tibs thought. He couldn't see a face or a body, but he knew it was Sy. He'd felt that color before. Then he heard a voice. Over the hills, over the mountains, so far away. Then it chimed again closer. He couldn't make out what it said at first, but it became clearer and clearer as it moved toward him. He knew the voice.

"Tibs!"

Tibs opened his eyes. Toraline stared down at him. He lay on his back on the ground.

"What happened?" he asked.

"I don't know, exactly," Toraline said. "Everything went dark, and an earthquake hit. When the lights came back, you and Sy were on the ground."

"I hate to tell you, but I'm not liking your house so much," Sy complained to the raven.

"The neighborhood's changed." the raven shot back.

Tibs tried to sit up but couldn't. "What did Lor do!" Tibs cried out.

"Me!" Lor appeared over him. "I didn't do nothing."

"Didn't do nothing means you did do something," Sy corrected.

"You went down the hall and said—" Toraline began.

"I know what I did and said and I didn't do nothing!" Lor folded his arms on his chest, ready for a fight like a cornered dog. Then he noticed Fats sitting, leaning back against the wall as if he hadn't a want or care in the whole wide world. "What are you doing?"

"Noting." Fats smiled, "'Cepting waiting for orders."

"Get up and scout ahead," Lor commanded.

Fats laughed. "You're not in charge anymore."

Lor drew his sword and pointed it at the fat man. "I'll keep your cut."

"Cut? What cut? We haven't found anything. My cut will be living through dis."

"Could you look a bit ahead?" Toraline asked sweetly, batting her eyes a bit.

"Yeah, I could do dat." He stood, brushed his clothes, slipped past Lor's sword and walked down the tunnel a bit. "I'll get me a look ahead." Fats wandered down the tunnel. Stones blocked the passage about thirty feet ahead of them. He came back. "We're going to have to go back."

"We can't." Tibs sat up, but fell back, weak. He shook his head trying to clear it.

"Why not?" Toraline asked.

Tibs pointed back the way they had come. The ceiling had collapsed. "And that's not all." He pointed at the floor beside himself. A deep depression marred the floor. No one noticed it except him. He sat inside a footprint. A man type footprint almost as big as Tibs himself. It could only come from a giant.

"Have you seen these?" Sy asked Lor, but Lor only turned his back.

"And the walls." Tibs pointed at what they could now see as handprints. Huge fingers and strong palms had cleared the stone as if it was dirt. The stones were crushed and torn by something made to tame stone.

"Giant." Fats sighed. "I hate giants."

"How far away do you think it is?" Toraline stood and looked around her.

Tibs knew. He could feel the giant while passed out, just as he felt Sy. He didn't know what it was then, but he turned his head and looked ahead of them down the tunnel where Fats said there was a rock slide. Fats was wrong. The rocks piled from floor to ceiling had a strange look to them. Rocks shouldn't fall that way, one or two seemed suspended in the air defying gravity they way the tilted. Then the top rock moved.

The whole thing shifted and trumbled and stood up. The top rock again swiveled and the whole collection turned around. His nose looked broken and his brow shadowed his small blue eyes. His skin blended into the rock, having almost the same texture and color as the stones surrounding him.

"Who are you?" He swayed a bit on his feet, as if he wasn't sure of himself yet. He looked down at Lor.

Lor looked up at him.

He looked down at Lor and then at Lor's sword. He frowned.

Lor smiled weakly for a moment, then hacked at his leg with the sword. With a good, strong, expensive sword, Lor might have made some headway against the Giant's hide, but he didn't have a good, strong, expensive sword.

It took four or five whacks for the Giant to understand Lor was attacking him. He plucked the sword out of Lor's hand. "What's you chewing to do?" He brought the sword up to his nose and smelled it. "Iron, magnesium, oil. This sliver supposed to scare someone?" He sounded as if he had a cold. He his body took up the whole tunnel. One might have felt relief to know his feet were overly large, as were his hands, so his footprints didn't reflect his height. Still, he looked bigger than four men.

The giant stood up to his full height, hitting his head on the ceiling, a daily occurrence, if you must know—a hazard of being a giant. Dirt and rocks fell around the children and the two bandits.

"This way!" Tibs bobbed to his feet and started running at the giant. "It's our only way out."

Toraline picked up the raven, Sy grabbed Fats by the arm, and followed Tibs. If they knew his choice meant dashing between the legs of the giant, they might not have followed him, but as it was, their legs were moving and they had momentum, so they all threw themselves under the hulking monster and into the tunnel behind the behemoth.

Lor almost missed his chance as the stony troglodyte turned to see the party where it had been rather than where they moved.

"What? I never..." the giant said as they dashed by.

Tibs for a brief moment thought they might have lost the giant, the opening they dashed through wasn't large enough for him to follow. That wasn't a problem for the sub-titan, he made the tunnel bigger.

Stone and dirt showers followed the party as the giant shook the walls, ceiling and floor. They ran faster.

When they ran a hundred yards down the tunnel the giant spoke again. "Where's yous goin? Hey, you can't run!"

Not many people have been in the position of running in an underground tunnel away from a stone giant. Stone giants don't like people being in their tunnels. They aren't very sociable and have terrible manners. They walk where they like and normally don't mind if people are disturbed or put off. Those that object don't have an opportunity to object twice.

This is why people believe stone giants are poor neighbors.

At the very moment they might have slowed down, thinking they reached safety, they heard the giant begin his pursuit. The sound of his feet slapping the stone was so sharp and loud that they had to cover their ears. Pieces of rock fell on their heads, dust rose from the ground from the earth moving and their feet ran. Lor sprinted by everyone, followed closely by Fats.

For a moment Tibs tried to take into account the direction they were moving. A tunnel on the left, followed by two on the right, but soon gave up. They were lost, no doubt about that, but they were alive.

Behind them they could hear the giant trip and fall. He roared in anger. The party ran oblivious of which direction they took, but no matter the chaos, the monster followed. They might not have known about the giants acute hearing. Or the fact that they could feel vibrations through their hands and feet, though severely callused, and get a general idea where moving things moved. He could even tell Toraline's vibrations from Tibs' or Lor's.

Suddenly, to the right of Sy, the tunnel burst! The rock giant stuck his head through a new opening. He screamed at the group, "don't think I don't know what you're doing!"

Sy paused long enough to pull Tibs over the rocks as the giant reached for them.

"What now, Smartbrains!" Sy sneered at Tibs.

Tibs, always one for an answer, said, "Maybe if we take the smaller tunnels, it will be harder for him to follow."

"It couldn't hurt to try," Toraline chimed in.

"You mean, it couldn't hurt any more..." Sy pushed them down the hall after Fats and Lor. They could hardly hear the pair of bandits.

Again, suddenly, they sprinted down a promising tunnel when the giant burst out of a wall in front of them. "You won't lose me!"

"How many of them are you!" Sy screamed, turning around.

"Keep together," Toraline panted. If they lost each other now, it might take hours or days to find each other again, if they ever did. They dived left this time.

"Do any of these go up?" Tibs vented.

Sy stopped. They could hear the giant behind them, still pursuing, but he heard something else. "The water." He poked his head through a small opening to one side. He could see an underground river roaring past. He pulled at the stone, in a moment making it big enough for the children to pass through. "HERE!" he screamed and dove through.

Toraline slipped through the opening right behind him. What did she have to lose? Of course, the raven went along for the ride. What choice did he have?

Tibs swung his feet through the opening as someone grabbed his collar. His head jerked back and he looked into Lor's eyes.

"Trying to get away?" The bandit wouldn't let go.

"From the giant," Tibs said simply. "You were only a bonus."

Lor dragged the boy out and jumped through feet first. He stopped at the hips. Tibs scrambled to pull rocks away and to make the opening bigger. Lor's hips popped through, but now his arms and shoulders wouldn't pass. Tibs wasn't strong enough to make the opening any bigger.

"Stop, little bags of meat!" the giant roared.

They heard a shrill scream at the top of their hearing range. Fats. He had come back down the hall, looking for his leader and the children, when the giant burst into their part of the tunnel.

Lor panicked. "Get me through! I've got to get through!" He twisted and kicked and grunted.

The behemoth saw the pair trying to get through the hole into the river. He pounded the ground. "NO!" The ground and tunnels shook, and the tunnel around them began to collapse.

Many things happened at once.

One, a new opening to the river opened up, big enough for Tibs to slip through, which he did, going head first into the water.

Two, Lor's opening detached itself from the wall with Lor still trapped in it, something like a life preserver. A rock life preserver, which, if you know anything about water, would not actually preserve his life so much as end it very quickly. If the river had been deep, he'd be dead. He lived, swept down the river by the current, struggling to shed the rock ring around his waist.

Third, a large pile of rocks fell on Fats, trapping his legs. Fats tried to kick the rocks off his feet, and then use his hands to push them off his legs. "LOR!" he screamed for help.

Tibs looked back as he slid down the river channel. He saw Lor stop himself for a moment, looking back at Fats.

Fats implored for help from the giant. Fats cried out again. "LOR! Help me!" Fats frantically shifted rocks trying to free his legs.

Lor pushed the rock belt off and left his friend behind sliding down the river.

Fats screamed, "NOOOOO," the last sound Tibs heard from the thief.

CHAPTER 21

Death is really a mercy. If we didn't die when we do, all we'd have to look back upon was an accumulation of mistakes and bad choices, and that would kill us—

—FROM SENNACHERIB MACCAULEY'S *HISTORY OF THE UNIFICATION*

THEY WERE LOST in an underground maze of tunnels and channels. Tibs flew down the river, bobbing and twisting this way and that. Sometimes there was air, sometimes he flowed through a tight tunnel with only water around him. He pushed himself from this side to another, looking for a way out, gasping for air when he found a pocket. He tried to stop, but the smooth rocks left nothing to grab. One can't fight the swift and strong river. One has to ride it out.

It might have been minutes, or it might have been seconds, but Tibs found himself falling through the air. The waterfall cascaded triumphantly, pouring downward. Tibs slapped the water, his whole back stinging. Understandable when it's remembered that Tibs had little experience with falling from great heights. He didn't have time to wallow in the pain. When he came to the surface to take a big breath, Lor's boots came down on his head, with Lor still in them.

Tibs lost consciousness. Before, sleep overrode his mind, now, his brain ceased puzzling, pondering or worrying. He only knew darkness.

Then he saw a color. Green. Green overwhelmed him. It flowed into him, and then out of him. Everything felt green and he could feel it spread away from him. He hadn't the strength to open his eyes, but he felt a hand holding his right hand. The color came from his hand. Intense, like a thousand ants running through his veins, so much green he pushed it out of his other hand and it flowed into the ground beside him.

This gave way to pain.

Someone pulled his hand, "Let go, let go!" He could hear Toraline yelling, "Tibs, you have to let go."

Even though he felt pain, he did not want to let go. He felt a foot on his chest and he lost the hand. All the green stopped. That hurt worse. He sat up, coughed, and water spilled out of his lungs and his stomach. He took in a breath and coughed out more water. He opened his eyes and looked into Sy's disbelieving face. Tibs hadn't been able to see an aura before. Ever. When Nathan had asked, he guessed. But now Sy's face permeated green, a mist so thick it obscured his features. He could feel Sy's power. It flowed out of him. At their feet moss grew thick and green, spreading out from the pair like a pond.

A pair of hands pushed his shoulders. Sy yelled something, but Tibs couldn't see his face anymore. He couldn't hear anything. He could only feel the power. Things grew all around them, and life was connected to them. He fell backwards again, and someone pulled Sy away from him. The pain stopped. Mercifully, Tibs collapsed, closed his eyes and passed out again.

It felt like only a moment before someone shook him. He wanted more sleep. "We can't wait any longer." Sy's voice insisted. He seemed far away.

"You have to get up," Toraline shook him again.

Tibs opened his eyes. Sy stood about six feet away, his hands under his arms. He lay on a thick, soft patch of green moss, next to a lake, in a cave. The lake drew water from a waterfall that flowed from the ceiling and fell into what must be its center. He remembered falling. "Did we fall all that way?"

Toraline laughed. "You bet we did, and you fell with all the grace of a bag of rocks. We pulled you from the water. We thought you were dead. Can you get up?"

"Lor fell on top of me." He sat up, his head hurting. He touched his temple where a good-sized lump greeted him.

Tibs looked around the cave. The moss felt wonderful, thick and alive, the nicest bed Tibs had ever slept on. Sy impatiently tapped his feet, looking around at the four of them. Four? Yes, Lor lay on the beach, passed out next to the water.

"We should leave before he wakes up!" Sy hissed.

Tibs shook his head. "I gave my word."

"He wants to kill you." Sy's practicality smelled of good sense. The thief had done nothing to help them in their troubles. He was a burden, and because of him they lost Fats, who had at least tried to help them.

"I can't control what he does, I can only control what I do." Tibs said flatly.

"Was that your father I just heard?" Toraline asked shocked.

"I feel like something just went wrong in my brain," Tibs tried to stand. He legs buckled for a second, Toraline rushed to hold him up, but then they straightened and felt strong again.

"Your word." Sy put his hands on his hips. "My father said never argue with Sir Jesse, maybe the same goes for his dimwitted son."

Tibs took another few steps, almost fell over, but this time Sy and Toraline rushed to his right and left sides.

Tibs looked at Sy's hands. They were ripped and bleeding when they left the pit. He saw them break open and he still had the blood from Sy's hands on his clothes. But now. In the low light they looked perfect. "What happened to your hands?"

Sy looked at his own hand, his right hand, and touched it with his left. "I, I..." He turned them over as if he had just forgotten which side he destroyed. "When I dragged you out of the water, I held your hands, and you wouldn't let go."

"We couldn't get you to stop," Toraline explained.

"I felt power flow out of me." Sy gestured at the moss, "All these grew around us, it kept getting thicker and bigger."

"Till I tore your hand out of Sy's," Toraline took a deeper look at Sy's hands. "It must have happened then."

"Did you heal me?" Sy felt his palms, they were perfect.

"Or did you heal me?" Tibs questioned. "You pulled my body out of the water, he landed on me, all these grew. It must mean something."

"I can make a few flowers grow, but I've never done anything like this." Sy picked up some of the moss, it tore away easily.

"Don't look at me, plants die around me." Toraline had no explanation.

"I would have thought I could have broken the grip of a runt like you in a second, but you're stronger than you look." Sy rubbed his hand self-consciously.

"You both glowed green, and moss came from around your body and Sy's feet, spreading out, getting thicker and thicker. I thought you were both going to die, so I..." She indicated that she broke their hold. "There was a loud bang, and the two of you passed out. Sy woke up first."

"What about him?" Tibs asked about the bandit chief.

"He washed up after you and hasn't moved since. He's alive, that's all I know." They needed to do something, quickly, before the giant found them.

Tibs could see the raven picking around the rocks. "No longer in pain, raven?"

The bird cocked its head. "The farther from the house, the less the pain." He pecked between the rocks.

"At least we know how to get back to the house if we want to." Sy said.

"How?" Toraline pushed.

"Follow his pain." Sy smiled, which he did when he thought he had said something smart.

Tibs looked at the bird pecking around his feet. "Looking for something to eat? I thought you didn't get hungry." Tibs asked the fowl.

"I can't, can't help myself." The bird moved its wings as if to shrug.

Something moved on the shore. Tibs jumped to his feet, only to discover Lor sitting up. "How long have you been awake?"

Lor sneered. "Long enough." His wet and burned clothes hung loosely on his body, he clutched at them as if to take inventory. "Where's my cape, my sword, my knife?"

"You must have lost them in the fall." Toraline suggested.

"I've got to, I have, I mean..." He searched his pockets and then sighed delighted, pulling out a knife. "Oh, good. Good." He looked at the children staring at him. "I'm as good with this as I am with a sword."

"I'm not inspired," Sy mocked.

The bird chirped, prancing up. "Who knew all this was under my house?"

"Did we lose the giant?" Lor asked.

Tibs shrugged, "for the moment."

Sy took Tibs's cue. "Creatures like that are hard to shake when they get something in their minds."

"Met many giants, have we, boy?" Lor taunted Sy.

Sy tried to keep it all impersonal, "Giants built my father's castle. It must be a powerful bit of magic to keep him trapped here."

"Best be going," Tibs said.

Lor laughed. "Going?" He grabbed his shirt around his neck as if cold clawed his chest. "Is that a good idea?"

"We can't stay here." Sy began to wander the water's edge, looking at the walls for a way out other than up.

"Oh, so the noble knows about giants and caves and caverns, a perfect font of facts." Lor stood and staggered over to Tibs, "There are fish in the lake. We have light, water, there's no need to leave here till we gather some strength form a plan."

"You're welcome to stay." Toraline offered the thief a choice.

"I'm in charge." Lor turned to the lake and looked across it.

"A bird can stretch his wings in a place like this. And do you know that grubs are not that bad?" The raven stretched his wings and flapped them. "Can't seem to get the water out of my feathers. I can't fly."

Sy barked, "You can't fly because you're fat."

"Fat?" The bird looked inquisitive.

"No, no," Tibs added, shooting Sy a look. "You've grown since you left the room."

"The magic is wearing off," Toraline added.

Tibs knew it was something else. The farther the Raven traveled from his house, the more the enchantments on him weakened. Toraline's influence had yet to be turned on fully.

"Wearing off?" The bird positively danced. "You can change me back? You can change me back? You can change me back!"

"Stop it," Tibs ordered. Obediently, the bird went silent, waiting on Tibs's every word. "We have to get out of here first."

Tibs noticed something like coal on the ground and picked some up. "Grab some of this. To mark the caves we've been in," he suggested. The coal would leave a mark on the walls.

"And make it easy for the giant to find us?" Lor slapped the coal from Tibs's hand. "Figure out a way to make sacks from the moss so we can pack up supplies, or find wood to make a fire—that would be helpful."

"If we don't mark the caves, we could wander down here for months and never know how to get out."

"Out?" Lor chuckled. "There's no 'out' from this place. The bird, the giant, people come here and die."

"We wouldn't be in this cave if you hadn't tried to kidnap Sy!" Toraline challenged the bandit.

"Stop it. Fighting won't get us anywhere," Tibs interrupted.

"We have to pull together," Sy added.

Tibs and Toraline nodded.

Toraline kicked at the water. "Who knows what's in the lake? Monsters, killer fish, or more things that come down through the tunnels looking for water. Are giant spiders real?"

"Giant spiders? Spiders?" Lor paced along the beach, jumping when water touched his feet. "They don't kill you, they put you asleep, and monsters, there's, there's, I can't believe you even think about those things. Maybe we better leave." Lor stopped and looked toward the walls of the cavern. "No, no, we can't, we have to stay here." He turned and looked at the water again. "No, no, the tunnels. We have to take the tunnels."

"The tunnels then." Tibs started walking to the edge of the cavern.

"You try and leave, I'll kill you all, starting with the smallest and working my way up." Lor pointed the knife at the three children.

Somehow, they were no longer afraid of him. Something had changed. His hand shook as he pointed the knife and this time when he used his other hand to steady the first, they both shook. Seeing this, he put the knife behind his back.

The bird hopped. "I stay with the chicks, the lambs, the ah, childrens."

"You're afraid." Tibs almost had pity for the man.

"Only of open spaces. And enclosed places, and spiders and, and, oh it doesn't matter. You are staying with me." Lor laughed. "With you around I won't have to worry." He smiled at them.

The children exchanged glances and then began to walk toward the walls. The bird hopped behind them.

"Your brain getting better?" Tibs asked the bird, glancing down at the fowl, but really stealing a look behind at Lor. Lor stood at the lake side holding the knife in front of him as if to will his hands to stop shaking.

"How am I supposed to tell?" The bird squawked.

"You've been in that house a long time," Toraline led the way with Sy and Tibs following in case Lor tried something. Not that they could do any better than her, but they had it drummed in their heads heroes protected people.

"Long time." He snapped at the air. "Forever."

"Forever, I could use a piece of that," Sy tried to laugh.

Lor stopped his shaking and watched the children move away from him. Fear either left him or fear of being left behind filled him, because now he followed, but at a distance.

"You, you, you have no idea, idea, of what you're t-t-t-talking about," the bird managed to stammer. "To never die is to stop changing, to stop trying, to stop doing, to stop living." He scratched his wing with his beak. "A living death is not worth living. I don't know how long I've been in the house. I have no idea how old I am."

"The giant is under her spell then too?" Toraline asked.

"How am I to know?" the bird cawed. Then he stopped and looked over toward the water. "To be hungry again." He sounded wistful. "That would be something."

"Nathan says our thirst and hunger can only be quenched by what we're meant to do," Tibs added.

"What does that mean?" The bird prodded.

"I'm not sure I know." Tibs walked along the cavern wall, still listening for the bandit behind. They all had coal and could see an opening ahead.

The bird jumped up onto Toraline's shoulder, "Are you sure you haven't been eating?"

"Just a peck of pecks," he shook his body again, trying to get rid of the water.

"You're going to die in there," Lor yelled still trailing them.

Toraline ignored him and asked the raven, "What about sleep? Did you sleep?"

The bird scratched his head, thinking. "I can't remember. Must be the bird brain." He shook his head. "But I get tired."

The tunnel had the merit of being the first one they came across. It sloped upwards, so that was a plus. They all put a mark on the wall outside the door. They didn't even pause. They walked from the cavern to channel.

Behind them they could hear cursing. Lor stood outside the entrance kicking the ground and hitting his head. "You don't even know what you're going to find in there!"

"The worse that could happen is that we could die," Sy slung over his shoulder, "And since you were planning on killing us all, I don't see any reason to be upset."

Tibs laughed under his breath. "You think he'll follow us?"

The other two shrugged.

Toraline glanced behind. Lor stepped into the hole, testing the sides with his hands as if they would collapse onto him. They looked behind, and Lor followed, keeping a good distance between them and him. He crouched as if the cave had begun to close around him, but the eight foot ceiling posed no problem for any of them.

They walked for hours. Taking a left and a right, always looking for tunnels that sloped upwards. They looked for signs of the giant and found few that seemed fresh. Every once in a while he found a footprint. Others had been in the passage since the giant walked this way. They couldn't make out who made these other footprints. Sometimes they looked human, sometimes not. Could there be some other party that had made it below the house? The raven couldn't help them, he had no memory.

"A magus descends or dies," was all he could manage.

And then Toraline asked another good question: "Do you know why the Black Heart did all this?"

The bird squawked. "Why?"

"Yes, why?" The others chimed in.

The bird pecked at his feet, thinking. "Why?" He began to flex his wings. Then he continued, "I wasn't in her inner circle."

"But you knew her," Sy probed.

"Knew her?" the bird laughed. "To know her is to know fear and death. Yes, I knew her."

Tibs remembered what Nathan had said about auras. When one saw a black aura, one should run away. He wondered if the Black Heart had more than a black heart.

They had grown a little lax in watching where they were going. First, they went to the right, then they went to the left. They marked "x's" at the openings and at turn-offs just to know they had been there, but this long tunnel had no openings. It turned this way and that. Their first attempt brought them back to the cave of moss, as they decided to call it, and they backtracked to find a different turn.

Lor followed like an unwanted shadow. He lurked in the dark places and occasionally blasted them for their stupidity in trying to find a way out.

Most of the walls were carved by the giant. Some seemed more natural. They bent occasionally, and a few times became so narrow they didn't know if they should make the attempt. But looking back at Lor made them all feel the best plan pushed them forward.

They came to a pinch. Tibs went first, no trouble, Sy had a bit of trouble and they had to pull Toraline through. As she stumbled out of the fissure, they found themselves in another cavern. No waterfall. No lake. They had never been in this cave.

The floor grew stalactites. They could hear water drip from the ceiling. They looked up. They couldn't see the ceiling.

They took a moment to see what lay before them.

There, Tibs saw the last thing he expected. A city. And in the middle of the city, two giant women. They towered over the city. The children had no idea what to think or do.

CHAPTER 22

Streets of gold have rock foundations, or they wouldn't support
the weight of horses—

ANCIENT PROVERB

THEY WERE LOST in the underground tunnels below the raven's house. Darkness shrouded the ceiling of the cave into which they had just stepped. It hadn't occurred to Tibs to ask about the light and from where it came. It must be part of the magic. The darkness seemed natural and the light felt wrong, still he felt glad of it.

He turned to the city. It looked as though it stretched for miles. Towers and lights dotted the landscape, and colored lights floated between minarets. And he could hear music. Beautiful music. Hills of what looked like heather surrounded the city, blooming as if in the throes of spring. And again, he heard the music. Tibs knew he'd fall under its spell if he stood there another few minutes. And then he'd stand there forever wanting nothing but to hear it until he died.

Tibs raised his hand. His father would have done the same to bring his men to a halt. Sy and Toraline obeyed the gesture as if it came from a king.

"What do you think?" Tibs asked them.

"Another cave, there's got to be a way out of it." Sy surveyed his surroundings. "The fireflies shouldn't hurt us."

"Fireflies?" Tibs looked back at the city. He supposed someone could mistake them for that. "What about the city?"

"City?" Sy and Toraline said together, looking beyond the towers and houses.

"You don't see the city?" Tibs found this impossible.

"Glowing stalagmites and fireflies." Sy gestured ahead.

He looked back and understood. It didn't stretch for miles and miles. The two giants sitting in the midst of the light were regular sized old women, not giants and the city was small. Small because of magic, and the fireflies were not colored lights, but fairies flitting between buildings. Sy and Toraline couldn't see them because they were too old. He could because he'd always been able to see magic things. He remembered what Nathan told him about people who could see fairy folk. This couldn't be good.

"We've got to do something!" Tibs shook his head, clearing the music out of it. He turned to his friends and they stood there, jaws slack, heads cocked sideways, entranced in music they couldn't even hear. That was powerful magic.

"No, no, no!" Tibs pushed Sy and pulled Toraline.

"We just want to rest a bit, Tibs," Toraline protested.

"It couldn't hurt to have a rest." Sy hardly moved.

Listen to the music, listen to the music, Tibs could hear in his head. *What does the cave matter, really?* He thought to himself. *All we have to do is stand here and listen.*

He watched the fairies and it occurred to him in the recess of his mind he'd never seen fairies before. He'd seen imps, the pranksters of the magical world, and leprechauns, the fighters, but never the elusive fairies. Looking at the city and the clothes and hearing the music, Tibs thought the fairies must be the artists. Everything they made, touched, and did, translated into beauty. As far as he could tell, the fairies didn't walk; they danced and flew. They didn't speak; they sang.

How long they stood there changed in the telling. No one knew. All Tibs could tell you was it ended when he felt a great pain in the back of his head. He reached up and touched the back of his head and felt blood. He turned, furious and saw Lor through the fissure that led to this cave. At his feet a rock sat, obviously thrown by his would be captor.

"Are you going to stand there forever or find a way to get me through this crack!"

Tibs thought about a witty retort when he glanced at Sy and Toraline, still under the spell. He pushed them again, "Fairies! Don't listen to their music, fairies!" He yelled.

His bellowing attracted the attention of the fair folk. Sy seemed slow in shaking himself out of his trance, so he kicked him hard in the shin.

"What's the idea!" Sy jumped on one leg for two jumps and then fell over. "That hurt!"

"Fairies, their music entrances, pain keeps your head straight." Tibs explained.

Shaking her didn't break her reverie. She didn't want the spell to break. Sy smirked, "May I?"

"Oh, I insist." Tibs stepped back from the girl as Sy kicked her in the shin as hard as he could.

She didn't jump, she just punched him in the face, and he fell back to into the dirt.

She bent down to massage her leg, "There's a reason you did that?" She pressed.

Tibs gestured toward the city, "Fairies, their city, we've got to get out of here. Pain keeps your head clear."

"You'll have to kick harder next time," Toraline said, helping Sy stand.

"Not me, I try to make each mistake only once." His nose bled.

Now, it must be said that humans are as welcome in the fairy world as giants are in the human, and for the same reasons. Humans, in comparison to fairies, are clumsy creatures, destroying everything fairy-built.

The beautiful city light changed from a rainbow of beauty to a menacing red in a matter of seconds. The music changed too, from ethereal and beautiful, to menacing.

"I don't like the look of that," Sy pushed Toraline back toward the fissure.

"Sure, that you can see," Tibs complained.

Before they made three steps, a mass of fairies, or fireflies, had set upon them, pricking and buzzing. Tibs could see the fairies shooting tiny arrows and throwing tiny spears at him.

Toraline and Sy batted the air around them, "They're stinging me!" Sy protested.

"You can't see them," Tibs understood. Their magic made them think they saw insects and they swatted at these, but the bugs were just the arrows and spears, they couldn't fight while still under the influence of the magic.

Tibs put his back to a stalagmite. He concentrated on the fairies around him, not the delicious smell of the pool in the cave, nor the red city before him, just on the little things flying all around them pricking them with arrows and jeers. He didn't swat, though their little arrows hurt, he waited for his opportunity.

The arrows couldn't kill them, but if they stayed in one place very long they'd be hurting for weeks.

The fairies must have felt something was wrong with Tibs. He didn't move. Whoever directed their battle sent half their force to surround him and concentrate on making him move, making him feel pain. A group shot arrows at him, and he put up his arm to block the arrows.

"Stop it!" Tibs yelled. They didn't stop. More came at him than before. They started concentrating their might on Tibs, the smallest of the trio.

Sy and Toraline started retreating into crevice, Toraline's size made exiting problematic, and then Lor started yelling, "Get a move on, get back here! You're trying to kill us all!" He pulled her arm and she became stuck. Sy stood there taking the brunt of attack on the two of them.

"What kind of insects are these!" He complained.

Then Tibs saw his opening. His hand shot out and he grabbed a fairy. Quite a trick even when you can see them, he looked down into his hand and saw a beautiful girl with translucent wings, and delicate features pull out a knife and stab his hand. "Ouch!" He plucked the knife and it aside. "I almost thought you were beautiful!" He screamed at her.

A collective gasp came from the fairies "Jewel!" The battle stopped for a moment.

"We don't want to hurt anyone!" Tibs screamed at the fairies. "We're only looking for a way out!"

"Stop it!" a cracked, wizened voice sang out, dry as rice paper. The city disappeared, in the conventional way, by being hidden in the darkness, not in any magical way by vanishing into nothingness. The fairies themselves, that is the ones waging the war, remained. They still glowed red, including the one he held in his hand, and that one, a girl, struggled to escape. Sy and Toraline stood silent on hearing the voice, they hadn't noticed the old women till that moment.

The two old women came out of the darkness right up to Tibs. One looked him up and down.

"You're early." She said.

"You could have warned us about that," said the other to the first.

"Where would be fun then?" said the first and she laughed.

If their hair hadn't been different colors, they'd be impossible to tell apart. One had jet black hair piled high on her head like a disorganized bee's nest. The other had flaming red hair, arranged like a pile of straw. Their clothes appeared identical, worn in the same places, complete with matching rips and tears.

"Oh dear, they're children," the dark-haired one observed. "This is terrible, terrible. You'll be killed!" The two old women moaned quietly, looking Tibs up and down.

A fairy buzzed near the women. "I would swear this one can see us."

"And hear you." Tibs added.

The group arranged themselves around Tibs, hovering and glowing even brighter.

"We're just trying to get out," Tibs explained again.

"There's no way out," another fairy chimed.

"I got the bird out of the house." Tibs tilted his head back toward the entrance.

"The bird?" The old woman licked her lips. "Ravensquick! Is that you?"

The bird squawked. "Ravensquick!" He hopped out of the cave. "That's my name! Ravensquick!" He forgot all about the fairies as he continued toward the old women.

"Stop hopping, you idiot bird!" Tibs turned toward the raven and motioned for him to stop.

"She said my name. I remember it now, Ravensquick, it's Ravensquick." His excitement filled his chest and his wings shook in happiness that he remembered his name.

"They do not appear to like you much," Tibs said indicating the fairies.

"We don't like any of you." A warrior-type fairy came closer to Tibs, holding a bow and arrow right in his face.

"No one needs to get hurt." Tibs tried to reason with the fairy.

"The bird is loose!" a fairy pointed out what they all knew now.

"He's not going to eat anyone," Tibs assured them, turning toward the bird. "Are you?"

"I'm not hungry, but I wish I was…" The bird backed up a few hops.

"He's out of his house. How did he get you out?" demanded another fairy, and several echoed the same sentiment.

"He carried me out, he just carried me out of the house." Ravensquick tilted his head toward the boy.

This statement had a few consequences. The fairies color changed from red to an orange. They lowered their weapons, pointing at the ground and they all moved closer to Tibs to examine him.

"You're making me a little nervous," Tibs said.

"He's a boy!" one stammered.

"He's got no magic!" cried another. "See, no aura!"

"But he can see us!" A big debate started raging. Tibs didn't know what to do as the fairies argued among themselves.

"Silence!" A muscular fairy came to the old women, hovering right in front of her face. "Can you convince them to help us?"

"Help you?" *Why would they need help?*

"We're all trapped, deary," the red head claimed staring at Tibs. "Until you come, we'll all be trapped."

"But he is come," the other one reminded her.

"Then it's settled," The redhead turned around.

"Where are you going?" The black-haired one asked.

"We have to pack, if we're to leave," she said.

"Have we the time?" the other one asked.

"Uh..." The red head stopped to think a moment. Then she nodded "yes" while saying, "No, no, not now. We don't have time." She pointed to the ceiling of the cave.

"What is it sister?" the other asked.

"He's coming."

The fairies screamed and scattered. Tibs couldn't see what was going on.

"Will we die?" the one sister asked the other.

"We might yet," she replied.

And then it happened, just at the spot the redhead pointed. The ceiling collapsed into the cavern, and a rather large giant fell through the ceiling. Any other creature might have been impaled on the spires of stone below, but not a rock giant. It's not just that they have thick skins, but rocks really can't hurt them.

He stood up and roared.

The fairies fled. What else could they do? Magic though they were, they weren't even gnats compared to the giant.

The sisters started moving as fast as they could toward another cave mouth.

"My friends!" Tibs yelled at them.

"Have them come with us, by all means!" The women shouted over their shoulders. Tibs ran back to Sy and Toraline. "We're going with the old women."

"Can we trust them?" Sy interrogated.

"How should I know?" Tibs pulled Toraline's hands to get her out of the crack.

Then Lor came up and grabbed her other arm, pulling her into the tunnel. "No, she's coming with me."

"We've got to get out of here."

"I will not be left alone, I'm in charge." Lor's order seemed more like a plea.

Sy jerked Toraline's arm with all his strength and she popped out of Lor's hands and the cave's mouth. He didn't have to say anything.

"Look, the tunnel has to connect in that direction, go in that direction!" Tibs waved at Lor.

Lor whimpered as he looked down the tunnel away from the trio, but ran in that direction nonetheless.

Any vestiges of the fairy spell wore off when the giant fell through the ceiling. Tibs still gripped the fairy as he ran after the old women, but didn't notice her clawing at him or biting his hand. Truthfully, he'd forgotten she was there. The ceiling in the cave began to collapse all around them, and the giant threw huge rocks around the room, not really aiming at anything. He wondered what would be left of the city. In all their adventures underground the fairy city was the first thing shrouded in darkness. Everywhere they went had some low light from somewhere Tibs couldn't see, it must have been part of the magic. The giant stood in the middle of that darkness raging against everything.

Tibs, Toraline and Sy quickly caught up and passed the old women. "They're going to slow us down." Sy whispered to Tibs.

"Then go on without us." Toraline insisted.

"I'm just making an observation." Sy defended.

"They must know the cave network, don't they live here?" Tibs passed into the entrance of the tunnel and paused there looking back over the cavern. There'd be little left in a moment.

Then he felt Lor's hands on his neck.

"I could kill you for leaving me behind." Lor hissed into Tibs ear. He cut off the airflow and Tibs started choking. Sy came behind and pushed Lor backwards, off of Tibs. Tibs crumpled to the ground.

"He told you how to hook up with us, if you want to choke someone, try me, I wanted to leave you behind."

Lor sat there stunned for a moment. "You can't give me orders." He said momentarily.

"Orders?" Toraline laughed. "Come with us or not, we don't care."

Lor reached to his side for his sword and rediscovered his empty sheath. "If I had my sword," he gritted his teeth at them.

"I'd take it away and she'd break it," Sy picked up Tibs. "You okay?"

"I've been better." Tibs smiled.

The old women finally made it to the entrance.

"Who are they?" Lor protested.

"Our ticket out?" Tibs suggested.

Sy stood up to him and looked Lor in the eye. "If you want to do something useful, go out and kill that giant."

As if on cue, the giant appeared in the tunnel.

"YOU!" The giant came for them like a bear after honey.

"Now's your chance!" Sy spat as he ran, followed by everyone else. Lor froze in fear for a moment and then screamed.

Scrambling through the rough tunnel, Tibs found himself in the lead. The others had to leap and drag and fall through tight places and Tibs slid right through them. Of course the absence of mud didn't hurt his speed.

Toraline did double duty. She carried the bird, but also helped the women. Sy found himself trailing them, keeping an eye on Lor as they made their way up a tunnel to escape the rampaging giant.

Lor complained from the rear "Can't you move them along any faster?" He didn't want to lead, but he didn't like being last. And every time he tried to overtake Sy, the Cushite pushed him backwards.

The old women were the biggest puzzle. All this running seemed a joy-filled romp to them.

"Can't rush time," the red head explained.

"Or stop it," the black-haired one continued.

"Believe us, we've tried!" They both laughed at this, cackling like chickens for a moment before setting down and sighing in unison. The women seemed unaware of their danger.

"Forgive us," the black hair one panted. "We haven't had visitors in a long time."

"No, no, a long time," her sister said.

"We're not visiting!" Lor threw a rock at Sy, who easily dodged it.

The old women acted like their flight was merely an outing in the park. Tibs gave up marking the tunnels. The giant made new tunnels and collapsed old ones so fast, the marks meant nothing. They felt like a bunch of snails trying to run away from a hungry chef. But somehow they managed to stay ahead of the giant. The old ladies helped them the most remarkably. "No, go down this tunnel," they would hear one say, and off they would go. The giant could then be heard going a different direction. With their help, the party stayed ahead of the giant.

Then they came to another opening, another cave and the red-haired one said, "This is where we stop."

Tibs didn't want to stop. "What are you talking about?"

"Don't argue with my sister, she's always right about these things," the black-haired one explained.

"A giant is about to kill us!" Sy had a practical streak in him.

"He went after the fairies," the dark-haired one explained. "They've been at war for a long time. He finds them annoying, and they find him, well, I suppose they find him when they're not looking." She started laughing and sorting through her pockets. "I'm afraid we don't have any tea, but we have some biscuits!" The black-haired one pulled out five small cookies and gave one to each of the children and to Lor. Always a good host, she took one and broke it up for the bird.

Tibs looked at the cookie in his hand disbelievingly. "Have you any idea of the danger we're in?"

"Danger?" The black-haired one looked at the red-haired one.

"Yes, he's right, there's still danger ahead, but this is where we stop," the red-haired one explained.

The black-haired one introduced herself and her sister. "I am Tresta and this is Fresta," and as an afterthought introduced the fairy. "And that's Jewel."

"Do you think you could let me go?" the fairy asked.

Tibs looked in his hand. He'd forgotten he held her. He almost let her go in shock. Almost.

"We've been waiting for you," Fresta told Tibs.

"You could have told me," Tresta scolded.

"I thought I did," Fresta protested.

"If you remember it, then you haven't done it," Tresta explained.

"I forgot." Fresta giggled.

"Could you at least tell us if we get out?" Tresta asked.

"I'm afraid that's a little murky." Fresta looked sad.

"Oh." Tresta looked as sad.

"What are you two talking about?" Lor screamed.

"Don't you know?" Tresta asked. "We're part of the house." She said it as if that explained everything. "We're all part of the house, the fairy, the giant, even Ravensquick."

"Ravensquick?" The bird looked up from his crumbs. "That's my name! I remember my name. It's Ravensquick!"

"We know," Toraline explained.

"How are you part of the house?" Sy's confusion reigned over them all.

"It's the magic. When the spell was set, she used our magic, the giant's strength, the fairies' life force." The bird interrupted Tresta.

"And my house!" The bird went back to pecking the crumbs.

"The Black Heart has a talent for binding things together," Tresta finished.

"How do we get out?" Toraline asked.

"No one has gotten out in, in..." Fresta looked at her sister.

"Not in six hundred years," Tresta finished.

"Has it been that long?" Fresta asked.

"A bit longer," Tresta assured her sister.

Lor came up, finally interested, "You're six hundred years old?"

"A lady never tells her age," Fresta said.

"But then we're not ladies!" They both laughed.

"You live as long as you remain alive." Jewel tried to bite Tibs again.

"Ouch!" He still didn't let go. "If you do that again, you'll regret you can't die." Tibs promised. He wouldn't let her go because he couldn't be sure the fairies wouldn't fill him with tiny, annoying arrows if he did. His father taught him to keep as many options open as possible when facing a threat. Then Tibs had an impossible thought. *Impossible.*

"Were there three of you?" He asked.

"I was wondering when he was going to ask that." Fresta said.

Then they burst out laughing. "Look at us."

"Two silly old women."

"About to die!" Fresta laughed.

"What?" Tresta looked worried.

"Did I say that out loud?" Fresta laughed again, and her sister joined in. Then she stopped. "Why are we laughing?"

Toraline stepped close to the women. "You're Tresta, Fresta and Nesta."

"Nesta?" Said Fresta.

"You tell the past?" Toraline guessed.

"And my sister tells the future."

"If she can only remember the future, how can she have a conversation at all?" Tibs asked.

"Ah, a clever boy," Fresta said.

"Yes, we have to watch out for him, a clever boy." Tresta looked into Tibs's eyes. "It only appears that she's having a conversation with us. She almost always repeats whatever I say before I say it. Makes me bonkers. You see, she sees the future and tells us. When it is in her mind, it's the future, but as it comes out of her mouth, it becomes the past and she forgets it, because for her it hasn't happened. It makes her a better conversationalist than most of our family."

Fresta laughed. "All bores."

"Yes, all bores!" Tresta repeated.

Fresta gasped and then began to cry.

"What's wrong?" Toraline patted the woman on the back.

"She remembering what I'm about to tell you," Tresta said.

"Where's the other sister?" Toraline said.

"There's the question. The Black Heart killed our sister in front of us." Tresta wiped a tear from her own eye. "She thought we needed incentive to tell her future."

Fresta's tears cleared up as soon as Tresta finished talking. She actually smiled. "You're about to tell them about how she found us," Fresta said.

"I am not going to tell them that story." Tresta said.

"Yes, you will." Fresta ate some more bread.

"No, I will not." Tresta turned her back on her sister.

"Maybe not now, but you will," Fresta said.

"I won't," Tresta said meekly.

"If you say so," Fresta laughed.

"I hate you sometimes," Tresta said.

"How did you end up here?" Tibs asked, changing the subject.

Tresta said. "Fresta said some little thing about the house, and the Black Heart became obsessed." Tresta thought for a moment. "And then she blew it."

"I didn't." Fresta was emphatic.

"Oh, yes, that she remembers." Tresta turned her back on her sister.

"How?" Toraline asked.

"Sometimes it's impossible to know how things are actually going to play out in life. Some big things come out twice. She sees two futures, all the time. One will happen, the other may happen, but she can't tell them apart. She just told the wrong one." Tresta continued.

"I did not!"

"How can you even remember this conversation!" Tresta yelled.

"Because we have this argument again next week!" Fresta screamed.

"What future did she see?" Toraline asked.

Tresta thought a moment. "She said this:

Ravensquick's house spells your bane

If someone comes in and takes something away."

Sy pitched in, "That's why the Black Heart put a spell on the house."

"She took everything out of the house so nobody could take something away. The prophecy could never be fulfilled." Tresta dabbed her mouth gently with a napkin.

"You're going to tell them about the tunnels," Fresta said.

"At first we stayed in the two rooms at the bottom of the stairs, very cramped with the giant and the fairies. You see, the Black Heart made it so the basement moved with the house. The giant then made the tunnels, we thought we might escape, but they moved with the house too, and the magic wouldn't let us out." Tresta made it sound so ordinary.

"And you think you can get us out?" The fairy taunted Tibs, and emphasized it by stabbing him in the hand.

"I've kept us alive," Tibs said.

The fairy struggled again. "My kin will come for me, you know."

"I'm counting on that." Tibs scowled at the fairy.

"You're going to notice that he can see them," Fresta told her sister.

"What? Oh, he *can* see them!" Tresta pointed at Jewel.

"See who?" Toraline asked.

"The fairies." Tresta pointed at Tibs hand again.

"Fairies?" Toraline came closer. "It's a bug."

"Bugs don't make biscuits." Tresta smiled. "At least I've never seen them do it."

"It is a fairy?" Toraline looked closer at the bug in Tibs's hands, "Why can't I see it?"

"See *me*! You stupid girl," Jewel tried to scratch Toraline.

"It's trying to sting me!" Toraline protested.

Tibs sighed. "Let's see if I got this straight." Tibs turned toward the old women. "We're trapped in a magical house made by a powerful magician, captured and changed by an even more powerful magician. We're being chased by a homicidal giant and a murderous mob of fairies."

"Oh, you like how his mind works." Fresta smiled.

"I do like how your mind works, she's right." Tresta smiled too.

"I see death coming for us all." Fresta frowned for a moment, shook her head and then stood, brushing off her dress. "He's coming."

The fairy squirmed in Tibs's hand. "We'd be grateful for even death. We've been trapped down here a long time. I yearn to see a forest again."

"What are we going to do?" Sy sounded worried. They all looked at Tibs.

He had no time to answer. The giant smashed through another wall.
Lor screamed and ran down a tunnel.

"It's incredible how he can move so silently one moment and just fill the tunnel with smashing the next!" Tibs couldn't tell which sister said that.

All he could do is make everyone "RUN!"

They ducked down a tunnel. There must have been something in those cookies, because now the ladies ran faster than Toraline.

"Crusher!" Tresta cried out. "Do you have to make all that fuss?"

"Crusher crush!" the giant cried out. His fist came down on the floor and the whole tunnel shook.

"He's gotten so rude the last couple of hundred years," Tresta protested. They moved fast.

So fast they didn't notice that Lor had gone a different way. The giant went after them and for a moment the bandit laughed. "I'm safe now." He managed to wander down a tunnel. And then took a turn and another. He was free. He was alive. He sat. He was Lost. He began to cry.

The children dashed ahead of the giant, jumping over falling rocks, trying to keep sight of the path ahead, even as destruction came from behind. The giant gained for a moment, but they found a tunnel that required him to stoop, and that slowed him down.

At the fork Tibs had to pause, *Which direction?*

His decision came as the right fork filled with the fairy army. "BUGS!" Sy cried out, swerving left without even breaking stride.

Everyone followed Sy, the women, Tibs and Toraline, the giant and the fairy army.

They ran down the tunnel, which sloped slightly upward, making gains. Behind them they heard the sounds of the giant and fairies fighting, but they knew it would only be a matter of time before they both caught up with them.

And then they found the worst thing they could imagine. A dead end.

CHAPTER 23

*Times are shaped by how people live. When times are tough,
certain kinds of leaders find their way to the top. When
times are good, other kinds of leaders find a way to exert
their influence.
And when times are very bad, people seem to find heroes, and
pray that they lead them out of the bad times—*

—SPOKEN BY SENNACHERIB MacCAULEY WHILE DISCUSS-
ING THE DEVELOPMENT OF LEADERSHIP IN THE PRE UNIFI-
CATION PERIOD OF THE ELEVEN KINGDOMS

A DEAD END, with an army of fairies and a stone giant right behind them.

"Is this it? We're really going to die?" Sy asked. He turned to Tibs.
"Thanks for trying to save me, anyway." He stuck out his hand.

Tibs took the hand and felt it again. The green magic.

Above Sy's head something moved. "Snake!" He fell backward against
the wall.

Tibs laughed. "It's not a snake, it's a tree root." He grabbed it and
pulled it down. It ran up into the ceiling.

"Tree root?" Toraline came over and pulled on it too. "Doesn't that
mean...?"

"It's attached to a tree?" Tibs stood up. All three children took a hold
of the root. They couldn't tell what kind of tree produced it, but did it
matter?

Sy reasoned, "The root is here, the tree is outside."

"Does that mean we can get out?" Toraline asked.

"YES." Tibs dug around it.

"You can't dig your way out." Tresta came up behind the children. "If that were possible, Crusher would have escaped a long time ago."

Tibs took hold of the root again. "It takes more than strength."

"Magic?" Toraline didn't like suggesting that, but somehow she knew she had to.

Tibs turned to Sy. "Do you think you can make it grow?"

Sy took a hold of the root and closed his eyes for a moment. A few seconds passed. The root did nothing. He let go. "I need my wand."

"You don't need a wand." Tibs grabbed Sy's hand. Even before Sy picked it up again, the root grew. Sy's eyes went wide, and then he grabbed the root. Both boys closed their eyes. The green magic pushed upward. The roots scrambled through the earth in all directions. Both boys willed the roots to grow and followed them upward, in this direction and that. There came a point when they couldn't push.

Suddenly, Tibs felt more power flow into him. He opened his eyes. Jewel put her hands on his and closed her eyes, adding her power to Tibs and Sy. The trickle allowed them to push upward a little more. He felt he could almost feel the tree above the ground, but not quite.

Behind them they could hear rumbling. The fairies appeared in the recesses of the tunnel.

Jewel cried out, "He can get us out if we have more power!"

Tibs opened his eyes and looked at Toraline. "Grab the root!" She stepped up and took a hold of it. The magic that kept them inside the tunnel weakened. He could feel it.

Then a cloud of fairies overwhelmed the boys. They zipped past them and surrounded Tibs, alighting on every part of his and Sy's bodies. With each pair of feet and hands they felt more power enter their bodies and flow upward.

"The tree I can almost feel it!" Still, the tunnel stayed strong, keeping them in. "We need more power!"

That's when the giant stumbled upon them. "Crusher, crush!" He raised his fist to hit the ground.

"No, no." Fresta held up her hands and stood between the children and the giant.

Tresta stood next to her sister looking into the giant's face and pointing at Tibs, "He can get us out?"

"Out?" The giant blinked. "Crusher go home?"

The sisters nodded. "If they can get more power."

"Power?" Crusher looked at the two old women and smiled. "I am power."

He walked past Toraline and Ravensquick to the cloud of fairies and the boys. He reached through the cloud and touched Tibs on the back.

Tibs's concentration meant he didn't see or hear the giant. When the giant made contact, power exploded through Tibs.

Sy and Tibs felt the tree. Outside. The tree reveled in the night drinking in the oxygen in the absence of daylight. It rained. "Make the roots grow!" Tibs urged Sy.

Sy willed the roots downward from the surface, a mass of tendrils pushing, pushing, and pushing. The root in his hand began to move and squirm like worm trying to escape. The Magic that held them prisoner began to break.

Dirt showered everyone, no one dare move. "Push!" Tibs said. Now all the fairies and Crusher started to concentrate on pushing. The power flowed through the boys, upward, downward, sideways. They willed the roots to grow deeper and wider and deeper.

Crusher could sense the surface first. Rock giants have many talents. They can make wondrous sculptures. Potatoes are magnificent things in all their recipes. And they know how far the surface is above them at all times. Only the magic kept Crusher in the tunnel. Crusher stood up, still touching Tibs. As he did so, his head merged with the ceiling and the rocks and dirt fell around them all. He shook his head and laughed. Roots grew everywhere around them.

Crusher made a fist with his free hand. He pulled it back and smashed the ceiling. They were showered in dirt, cascading roots and then water.

They looked up. Clouds, in the night sky. It rained above them.

CHAPTER 24

The difference between a leader and a follower is often one thing; a willingness to try—

—FROM SENNACHERIB MACCAULEY'S *HISTORY OF THE UNIFICATION*

WATER POURED DOWN on Tibs and Sy's faces. The fairies speed out into the night. Sy started jumping up and down! "We did it, we did it!" He kept saying it over and over. Tibs would have joined him, but Crusher had picked him and he too jumped like Sy.

"Crusher, Crusher! Human being dying, ah! Ack!"

Crusher looked down and apologized. "Putting you down, little man. You saved Crusher. Crusher never forget." He didn't so much as put Tibs down as drop him from ten feet in the air into a pile of soft dirt. Toraline and Sy pulled him to his feet. The three of them stood together looking up into the night. It rained, not too hard, not too soft. The water drizzled over their bodies deliciously, but that wasn't as nice as the air. They breathed deep.

Something changed, and they didn't even see it yet. They had gone into the house as enemies. Coming out alive changed everything for them. No armistice to sign, no peace treaty to ratify. They were friends.

Sy looked up at the giant. "Do you think you could give us a hand getting out?" he asked.

The stone giant looked down on the little boy and smiled. "Crusher help."

Toraline came over with the raven still on her shoulder. "I've never met a stone giant before!"

The two old women gasped.

Crusher spun on the girl, anger pouring out of his pores. "Not giant! TITAN!" Crusher hit the wall beside him, hard. Rubble fell from the ceiling, and the wall and the tunnel became about three feet wider.

"He doesn't like to be called a, ah, what you said," Tresta tittered.

"And I still haven't met a stone giant, I've met a titan, of course..." Toraline thoughts moved at lightning speed.

Crusher's scowl instantly turned to a small smile. "That's right. ME TITAN!" he bellowed. The walls shook almost as bad as when he hit them. "Me son of sky and land, hold up the world!" He rubbed his arm across his nose. "Me not no trouble giant. Giants small. Me big!" He looked menacingly down at Toraline. She smiled weakly.

Crusher ignored her and bent over, picking up the old ladies. "Friends first." The giant carefully put them all out.

"Friends?" Tibs questioned.

"Well, the war between Crusher and the fairies really only happened because we were all so bored," the sisters explained.

They stood in the rain, and it felt cold, but good. Then Crusher followed, pulling on the dirt, making the hole huge so he could just walk to the surface. Why climb when one could walk?

The rain changed from drizzling to pelting. "Where are we?" Toraline's hair fell into her face.

"Didn't I hear something about sending us home?" Tibs said, trying to get his bearings.

"That's right," Sy chimed in, "but this doesn't look like Brig'adel."

"Looks are deceiving," Toraline reminded them all.

A group of fairies appeared before Tibs. They still had spears, and their skin glowed orange. The woman in the middle pointed with her spear at Tibs hand. He looked down and saw Jewel. She waved at him and then scratched good naturedly at his hand, with a polite smile, of course.

"I'm sorry, I forgot." He let go. She floated into the air, spinning and stretching her wings. Immediately the fairies changed colors, from the orange to pink, green, blue and brown, all wonderfully glowing.

"We'd never have got out if I wasn't holding you." Tibs said. "Please forgive me, I only wanted to be friends."

The fairies saluted Tibs. "We are indebted to you," Jewel said and then groped for something.

One of the male fairies came up behind her. "We don't forget. We always pay our debts."

"I'd rather be friends," Tibs offered.

Jewel and the male looked at each other. "You're so big," she said, "but we will consider it."

Fresta came up behind Tibs and put her hands on his shoulders, "She's waiting for your name. You know hers. She wants yours."

He smiled. "Tibs."

Fresta shook him, "No, no, you're going to say Tiberius."

"Tiberius?" Sy looked over at the boy. "That's your real name?"

"I didn't pick it," Tibs deflected.

Fresta glanced at Sy. "Oh, I picked the wrong boy to say the name."

Jewel smiled at Tibs. "We are indebted to you, Tiberius." The fairies sped off into the night.

Crusher sat in the grass, breathing deeply. He laughed. "Air! I like rock, but this good too." He smiled at the little group below him. "Now what?" He was now one of the group, from rampaging enemy to friend in a few short miles.

Ravensquick jumped over to Tibs. "Me, it's my turn, my turn."

Tibs looked down at the bird. He had gotten him this far. Could he actually change him back? He pondered how they had all worked together to get out of the tunnel. He wished the fairies hadn't left; he could have used their magic. But then again, maybe magic was the problem.

The bird seemed even bigger, like a small goose. If he grew any bigger, he might consider having the children for lunch, in same way we have bacon.

Ravensquick looked at Tibs with one eye and then the other. "My turn."

"Toraline." She stood behind him. He motioned for her to grab the wings of the bird, which she did.

"Oh, ow!" The bird started crying out. "Not good, not good!"

Tibs grabbed the bird's head and pulled with his magic. It was like pushing with the tree roots but reversed somehow. Instead of pushing the magic into the tree, he was trying to pull the magic out of the bird.

Immediately, the bird's eyes turned red. The Black Heart returned.

The bird's eyes glowed, "You survived?" Her voice no longer melodious, became shrill. "You escaped?"

"Hold the bird still!" Tibs yelled.

"You shall not live!" The bird's voice became shrill, menacing. "I will come for you!"

The bird hopped, struggled, and they all fell to the ground. He could feel something happening, although he didn't know quite what. "Don't let go!" Tibs yelled again.

The bird turned his head toward Sy, eyes still red and menacing. "You, you're the one with magic, but it's only green! How can you be the threat?"

That's when Tibs saw it: the pattern of white feathers around the bird's neck weren't feathers at all. He saw a talisman. In the house, in the presence of strong magic, it might have been all feathers, but out here, with Toraline suppressing it, it became a vial attached to a white rope.

Tibs reached out and plucked it from the bird's neck.

Ravensquick screamed and his eyes turned white, throwing all the children off of him. "NOOOOO!" The bird stood on his legs, shaking, growing, the feathers growing longer. His head shrank, his legs grew, feathers covered everything. Then there were no feet, no beak, no wings, just a pile of feathers that grew longer and straighter. Ravensquick jerked to the right, and then the left. Two hands appeared, and they reached out and started pulling feathers this way and that, pulling, and throwing handfuls of feathers aside.

Tibs rushed up and started pulling off feathers, followed by the Sy and Toraline and then the old ladies.

The pile grew taller. The hands flung feathers everywhere. Two legs appeared. The beak changed into a nose, which was actually longer than the beak.

In another minute they had pulled off all his feathers. And there stood the man, Ravensquick.

"Good heavens, am I naked?" he asked the group. He was. Politely, the children said nothing. The old ladies started laughing, and this time Fresta knew why she laughed.

CHAPTER 25

I've heard that philosophers say that a journey ends in a single step. I've always thought that those philosophers don't carry any bags with them, because my journeys never end until I've put away all the clothes

—FROM SENNACHERIB MACCAULEY'S *BATTLE TACTICS OF THE ELEVEN KINGDOMS*

"WE'VE GOT TO get out of the rain," Toraline urged them. Practicality is a virtue in Toraline.

Fresta reached under her skirt. "I did remember that you would need this." She gave Ravensquick a long cloak. He didn't really look much different as a person than he had as a raven. His black hair, slicked back against his head, looked like feathers. His long and pointy nose offset his lack of a chin and gave him a birdlike look. True, he did have arms and legs, but they were so skinny they didn't hardly show from under the black cloak. The spell only brought out the bird in Ravensquick.

They looked up. Crusher towered over them, watching the scene. At least he blocked the wind. As he smiled down at them, they could hardly remember why he had made them frightened. He said, "I titan," and then he smiled, his missing teeth and crooked chin make him seem normal and not lopsided. They offset each other in a strange way. However, his ears weren't even, and he kept one eye closed all the time, so he had an unfinished look.

Tresta stepped up and grabbed Crusher's hand.

The giant smiled back. "Titan," he said softly.

"Oh, he's in a good mood now, aren't you, Crusher?" She laughed.

Toraline reminded them, "The rain?"

Tibs laughed and started walking through the trees.

"Where are you going?" Sy cried out as everyone else started following the small boy. "Do you have any idea of where you are?"

"Any idea?" Tibs laughed. "These are my woods!" In seven steps they came out of the forbidden forest a few feet from where they started this adventure.

They came to the main road and started walking toward the castle of Brig'adel when they heard voices cry out, "The children!"

By the time they came to the fortress, tired, hungry, and dirty, the whole town walked with them. The townsfolk didn't come too close. Strangers like the two old women would have been welcomed, but the giant, pardon, the titan, caused feelings of trepidation, fear and terror.

Saunders and Zips guarded the gate. The rain stopped and the stars peaked out of the disappearing clouds. Saunders looked up at Crusher. Crusher smiled.

Zips asked, "Where will he sleep?"

Sy laughed. "Where ever he wants." And they walked inside.

The giant stooped to get in the large double doors into the castle itself, and once inside the courtyard, which doubled as the marketplace, he just sat down, leaned against a wall, closed his eyes, and snored like a forest fire.

From behind them they heard hoof beats. The children turned and saw a group of horses roaring down the street toward the courtyard. The crowd parted, letting the men ride into the castle. Tibs supposed they had been gone a few hours at the most. *It can't be after midnight, too many people awake.* He started to wonder how badly he would be punished.

Three horses rode into the castle, Fibber led with Sir Jesse in full mail armor upon the warhorse. Lord Telford rode second, easily recognized by his girth, he too in full armor. Tibs didn't' recognize the man in the middle. His shield bore the double panthers of the Cush. He had long blond hair and a perfectly trimmed beard. Later Tibs would see that his eyes were steel blue. His cape flew behind him, a deep purple, his riding boots perfectly polished, glinting in the torchlight. Toraline actually sighed looking at him. Tibs punched her in the arm for it. She punched him back. He rubbed his arm *better rethink punching Toraline.*

Everyone stood back from the figure in awe, except one person. That one person sprinted toward the figure. Who could be so bold? How could anyone feel anything but awe and respect in the presence of this man?

"Father!" Sy cried out.

Father? The lord leapt from his horse and swept his son into his arms. "Sylas! Oh, Sy! Where have you been?"

"Been? We were only gone a couple of hours!" Sy laughed. "No one told me you were coming to visit!" Somehow the whole kidnapping that had started this adventure faded from their minds.

The man's face turned serious. "You've been gone three weeks."

Lord Telford and Tibs's father dismounted. Sir Jesse picked up Tibs and hugged him so tight he thought he might not be able to breathe again. "What does he mean, three weeks?" he tried to say, but what came out was "Whaaa doooaa haaa maaa threaaa waahh."

Toraline, the swiftest, outran her father, "We've only been gone a few hours! Stop embarrassing me!"

"You went missing three weeks ago," Lord Telford explained. "I can see you're a little worse for the wear. Who are your cohorts?"

The children made the introductions, explaining that without the help of the sisters and Crusher, they might not have escaped.

"Why are we standing around here?" Telford proclaimed. "Tomorrow we will have a feast to celebrate that what was lost has now been found! Everyone in the village is to come!"

Cheering commenced! The crowd knew the time had come for them to go home, but they left now with the expectation that tomorrow with the food would come the story. The parents herded the children and the sisters into the great room of the castle.

"Are you sure you're all right?" Sy's father kept asking his son. He put his hands on Sy's shoulders and looked him over, as if he was sick and just needed someone to find the place disease came into his body.

"I don't understand, three weeks?" Toraline pushed her father back.

Lord Telford sat them in the kitchen and ordered food be brought and the adults forced the children to tell their story. Toraline fell asleep first, followed quickly by the little old ladies. As the fire burned down, Sy, Tibs, their parents, and Lord Telford anxiously went over the details of the story.

Tibs turned toward the adults. "I'm sorry, I did my best." His eyes teared up.

The adults looked confused. Sy's father turned to Tibs, putting his heavy hand on the boy's shoulder, "My boy, I'm sure you have nothing to be sorry about. I'm indebted to you. You saved my son."

"If I had—" Tibs began, but Sy's father cut him off.

"Don't second-guess yourself. They would have killed you and Toraline, asked for the ransom, and killed Sylas." The lord stared at Tibs reassuringly. "You could have run away, but you stood your ground. You are a credit to your father." He smiled.

"But Gabe is dead," Tibs explained. "He's not the kind of friend you forget, even if you wanted to. He always had a kind word, never lost his sense of humor, and of all the people in town who should have been angry all the time, Gabe had the right. It isn't fair. It should have been me."

From out of the shadows Old Gus appeared. "I'm not dead, Tibs, I'm fine." He smiled.

"I'm talking about Gabe," Tibs protested.

"It's me." Gus smiled.

"What?" Tibs was confused.

"I am Gabriel." Tibs looked at Gus, the old man who plagued them with idiocy. His face had changed. He stood straighter. His eyes were clear and confident. "When I was a boy I went with you to the house. I flew off the porch and found myself in winter in the mountains of Svalvard. I found a village. They raised me, and in time I came back here to find you."

"That made sense..." Tibs was shocked he could understand everything the old man had said.

"When I got back to Brig'adel, I'd already been born. My mind went a little strange, because I was so close to myself." Old Gus, no Gabe, laughed, "We're not meant to be that close to ourselves."

"One soul, two bodies," Fresta prompted her sister.

"Yes, one soul, two bodies, a contradiction in time. They either fight and die," Tresta said.

"Or one steps aside and lets the other live." Gabe smiled.

"How can you even talk to me after what I've done to you?" Tibs said.

"First of all, it was a long time ago!" Gabe laughed. "Almost thirty years ago for me. How strange to live the same moments twice, watching myself chop the wood, walking through town. I knew it would all work out, because here I am." He held out his hand.

That wasn't good enough for Tibs. He flung himself into the old man's arms and they hugged.

They continued to talk, but Tibs stopped listening. He wanted to listen, but weariness stole over him like fog in the morning and soon he slept. When he opened his eyes, the sun hung high in the sky. Tibs staggered outside. The town's feast had begun and when they saw him they cheered. They would have cheered for anyone who gave them meat or a reason to have meat.

Noon slipped to one, to three and about four Lord Telford gathered the group to come to the feasting hall. Sir Jesse and Sy's father and a few of the other fighting men were there. "I'm calling for my knights to be prepared."

"We have to send out a general alarm," one of the captain's suggested.

"I don't understand," Tibs looked to his father for an answer.

Sir Jesse stepped over to his son and children. "Your story presents some difficulties."

"It's the truth," Toraline protested.

Sir Jesse shook his head. "Not those kind of difficulties." He gathered all the children. "Where is Ravensquick?"

They looked around.

Lord Telford chimed in, "We've gone to where you came out of the ground, and where you said the house sat, and it's gone."

"Ravensquick must have taken his house away."

"The problem is that the Black Heart spoke through him, saw through his eyes, that kind of intimacy is hard to discard, even when a person has been used, like this Ravensquick. And then there's what she said to you." Lord Telford pointed out.

"But, but, but—" Tresta protested, "no one carried anything out of that room, there was nothing to carry out!"

Sir Jesse corrected her, "The bird."

Sy tried to remember, "Toraline carried Ravensquick out on her shoulder."

Toraline stood up, "no, Tibs carried him down the steps. I carried him through the tunnels."

Sy's father stood up and spoke to all the assembled men and women. "The Black Heart will look to destroy all of you just in case."

"You're saying she's going to come for us?" Toraline couldn't see why she would do that.

"It took all three of you to break the enchantment. She doesn't understand how Sy can be a threat, but then it doesn't pay to let your enemies grow into men and women sometimes."

Did Sy's father have experience with that? Tibs thought.

"She will try to kill all three of you."

"That doesn't make sense?" Sy complained.

"You don't live to be one hundred and ten by being stupid," Lord Telford chuckled.

"One hundred and ten?" Toraline disbelieved.

"The eleven kingdoms have remained beneath the Black Heart's notice for years. I had hoped that would stay true for my lifetime, but she has told you she is coming. The good news is that she finally has something to fear." Sy's father sounded confident.

"It's not like that!" Tibs corrected, "They don't see the future, they see some futures and see other futures and who knows what's going to be true."

"She believes it, Tibs." Sir Jesse stood. The conversation ended with that.

Tibs thought no one would ever be able to be as kingly as Sy's father. For years the eleven kingdoms had talked about a single king to lead them all. Could this be the man? Who would not want to follow him? *But he is Cush! But then, so is Sy, and isn't he a friend now?* Tibs buried his confusion, *I'll sort it out later.*

Sy's father took Tibs by the chin and looked him in the eyes. "You have delivered my son safely to me. As you are not my servant, I have no means to reward you…" He paused, looking at Sir Jesse and winked. "Or punish you, but I am in your debt."

"And that's saying something," Sy added, slapping Tibs on the back, much too hard for the boy.

Lord Telford then turned to the children with a very serious expression. "We would like to know—where is Nathan?"

"Nathan?" They exchanged looks. They didn't know.

"We thought he went with you." Sir Jesse suggested.

"Have you looked in his house?" Tibs replied.

"He disappeared, his cottage and everything, the same day you did," Sir Jesse looked worried.

"He wasn't with us," Tibs knew Nathan had been experimenting, and something could have gone wrong.

A lot could still go wrong. They would begin to prepare for war and look for a man to lead them against the threat from the continent. The Black Heart knew who they were, and where they were. But for today, they would finish the feast and prepare for the harvest.

Made in the USA
Middletown, DE
07 February 2017